PENGUIN  CLASSICS

FATHERS AND SONS

IVAN SERGEYEVICH TURGENEV was born in 1818 in the province of Oryol, and suffered during childhood from his tyrannical mother. After the family had moved to Moscow in 1827 he entered St Petersburg University, where he studied philosophy. When he was nineteen he published his first poems and, convinced that Europe contained the source of real knowledge, went to the University of Berlin. After two years he returned to Russia and took his degree at the University of Moscow. In 1843 he fell in love with Pauline Garcia-Viardot, a young Spanish singer, who was to influence the rest of his life. He followed her on singing tours in Europe and spent long periods in the French house of herself and her husband, both of whom accepted him as a family friend. He sent his daughter by a sempstress to be brought up among the Viardot children. After 1856 he lived mostly abroad, and became the first Russian writer to gain a wide literary reputation in Europe; he was a well-known figure in Parisian literary circles, where his friends included Flaubert and the Goncourt brothers, and an honorary degree was conferred on him at Oxford. His series of six novels, which reflects a period of Russian life from the 1830s to the 1870s, are *Rudin* (1856), *Home of the Gentry* (1859), *On the Eve* (1860), *Fathers and Sons* (1862), *Smoke* (1867) and *Virgin Soil* (1877); and he wrote a further novel, *Spring Torrents* (1872). He also wrote plays, including the comedy *A Month in the Country*, short stories and *Sketches from a Hunter's Album* (1852), as well as literary essays and memoirs. He died in Paris in 1883 after being ill for a year and was buried in Russia.

PETER CARSON learnt Russian during National Service in the Navy at the Joint Services School for Linguists, Crail and London, and at home – his mother's family left Russia after the Bolshevik Revolution. His working life has been spent on the editorial side of London publishing. He has translated Chekhov's plays for Penguin Classics.

ROSAMUND BARTLETT has a doctorate from Oxford University. She is the author and editor of many books, among them *Wagner and Russia, Shostakovich in Context* and *Chekhov: Scenes from a Life*. Her Penguin Classics anthology, *Chekhov: A Life in Letters*, is the first uncensored edition of the writer's correspondence in any language.

IVAN TURGENEV

Fathers and Sons

Translated by PETER CARSON,
with an Introduction by ROSAMUND BARTLETT

PENGUIN BOOKS

PENGUIN CLASSICS

Published by the Penguin Group
Penguin Books Ltd, 80 Strand, London WC2R ORL, England
Penguin Group (USA) Inc., 375 Hudson Street, New York, New York 10014, USA
Penguin Group (Canada), 90 Eglinton Avenue East, Suite 700, Toronto, Ontario, Canada M4P 2Y3
(a division of Pearson Penguin Canada Inc.)
Penguin Ireland, 25 St Stephen's Green, Dublin 2, Ireland (a division of Penguin Books Ltd)
Penguin Group (Australia), 250 Camberwell Road, Camberwell, Victoria 3124, Australia
(a division of Pearson Australia Group Pty Ltd)
Penguin Books India Pvt Ltd, 11 Community Centre, Panchsheel Park, New Delhi – 110 017, India
Penguin Group (NZ), 67 Apollo Drive, Rosedale, Auckland 0632, New Zealand
(a division of Pearson New Zealand Ltd)
Penguin Books (South Africa) (Pty) Ltd, 24 Sturdee Avenue, Rosebank, Johannesburg 2196, South Africa

Penguin Books Ltd, Registered Offices: 80 Strand, London WC2R ORL, England

www.penguin.com

First published 1862
This translation first published in Penguin Classics 2009

027

Translation, Chronology, Further Reading and Notes copyright © Peter Carson, 2009
Introduction copyright © Rosamund Bartlett, 2009
All rights reserved

The moral right of the translator and editors has been asserted

Set in 10.25/12.25pt Postscript Adobe Sabon
Typeset by Palimpsest Book Production Limited,
Falkirk, Stirlingshire

Printed and bound in Great Britain by Clays Ltd, Elcograf S.p.A.

ISBN: 978-0-141-44133-7

www.greenpenguin.co.uk

Penguin Books is committed to a sustainable
future for our business, our readers and our planet.
This book is made from Forest Stewardship
Council™ certified paper.

Contents

Chronology

(Unattributed works are Turgenev's own.)

1818 28 October (O.S.) Ivan Sergeyevich Turgenev born in Oryol, the second son of Colonel Sergey Nikolayevich Turgenev and Varvara Petrovna Lutovinova

1825 Alexander I dies and is succeeded as Tsar by his younger brother as Nicholas I; 14 December (O.S.): Decembrist uprising

1825–31 Publication of Pushkin's verse novel *Eugene Onegin*

1834ff. At Universities of Moscow and St Petersburg

1836 *Sovremennik* (*The Contemporary*) journal founded by Pushkin

1837 Death of Pushkin

1838 At University of Berlin, where he studies philosophy; friendships with many Russian radical intellectuals, notably Bakunin

1839–41 Travels in Europe

1842 Birth of illegitimate daughter Pelageya (Paulinette) by a serf girl
Gogol's *Dead Souls* (Part I)

1843 Meets the singer Pauline Garcia-Viardot (1821–1910), the central relationship of his life; friendship with the critic Belinsky

1843–5 Brief career as a civil servant in the Ministry of the Interior

1847–50 Abroad, mainly in France, often with the Viardots, to whom he entrusts his daughter's education; friendship with Herzen

1850 His best-known play, *A Month in the Country*, completed; death of autocratic mother; inherits family estate of Spasskoye

1852 *Sketches from a Hunter's Album* and obituary of Gogol lead to a short prison sentence and exile to Spasskoye for almost two years

1852–6 Tolstoy's autobiographical novels *Childhood*, *Boyhood* and *Youth*.

1853–6 Crimean War between Russia and an alliance of Great Britain, France, Sardinia and the Ottoman Empire

1855 Nicholas I dies and is succeeded by his son, Alexander II

1856 *Rudin*
Flaubert's *Madame Bovary*

1856–61 Travels in Germany, England, France, Italy, Austria

1857–67 Herzen's journal *Kolokol* (*The Bell*) published from London

1859 *Home of the Gentry*
Goncharov's *Oblomov*; Wagner's *Tristan und Isolde*.

1860 *On the Eve*; the novella *First Love*; maps out characters of *Fathers and Sons* while staying on the Isle of Wight
George Eliot's *Mill on the Floss*

1860–61 Dickens's *Great Expectations*

1861 Quarrel between Turgenev and Tolstoy
Emancipation of the Serfs

1861–5 American Civil War

1862 *Fathers and Sons*
Dostoyevsky's *The House of the Dead*; Verdi's *La Forza del Destino* launched in St Petersburg

1863 Viardots settle in Baden-Baden; Turgenev follows them and eventually builds a house there (1868)
Chernyshevsky's *What Is to Be Done?*

1865 Leskov's *Lady Macbeth of Mtsensk*

1867 *Smoke*; quarrel with Dostoyevsky
Zola's *Thérèse Raquin*

1868 Saltykov-Shchedrin's *Golovlyov Family*

1869 Tolstoy's *War and Peace*

1870–71 Franco-Prussian War; the Viardots and Turgenev leave Baden-Baden for London

1871–83 The Viardots and Turgenev return to France, living in Paris and Bougival; friendships with Flaubert, George Sand, Zola

1877 *Virgin Soil*

1878 Reconciliation with Tolstoy

1879 Oxford honorary degree, the first ever conferred on a novelist; passionate friendship with the actress Maria Savina Tchaikovsky's opera *Eugene Onegin*

1880 Dostoyevsky's famous speech in Turgenev's presence about the universality of Pushkin's poetry reconciles him with Turgenev

1881 Last visit to Russia and Spasskoye

1883 3 September: dies aged sixty-five from cancer, at Bougival, near Paris, and later buried in the Volkovo cemetery, St Petersburg

Introduction

'Never was a writer so profoundly, so whole-souledly national'
Joseph Conrad

Turgenev was forty-four years old when he published *Fathers and Sons*. He had already penned three slim novels and would write two more over the next two decades, but from the moment *Fathers and Sons* appeared in 1862, this was the work with which his name was primarily and irrevocably associated. The sensation it caused was unprecedented in the history of Russian letters, both in terms of the intensity of the reactions it provoked and the longevity of the ensuing arguments. Certainly no other Russian novel in the nineteenth century was surrounded by greater controversy. All this is somewhat ironic given how shy and retiring Turgenev was in his private life, as recorded in numerous affectionate memoirs written by contemporaries such as Guy de Maupassant, for whom the writer's imposing physical stature was utterly at odds with his gentle nature. But however self-effacing Turgenev was, he was also a brave man who did not shrink from setting his fiction in present-day Russia and creating characters who responded to and reflected its rapidly changing social and political reality. What is more, Turgenev had the courage to acknowledge that his own generation was essentially a spent force. In a country whose rulers had invested so much for so long in preserving a barbaric social system which depended on the connivance of the gentry, sympathizing intellectually with those members of Russia's younger generation whose very existence posed a threat to the survival of his own unfairly privileged class was a noble – and foolhardy – undertaking. Combining an interest in the contemporary political scene with an essentially poetic vision almost guaranteed that Turgenev's work would be criticized and misunderstood. *Fathers and Sons* contains a remarkably balanced treatment of topical themes, but it is first and foremost a work of art. Turgenev's unshakeable artistic integrity obliged him to obey laws of nature and thus remain open to unpredictable narrative outcomes – but it also produced fiction of the highest order.

Turgenev had been in the public eye ever since making his literary debut with the self-financed publication of a narrative poem called *Parasha* in 1843. As the populist critic Nikolay Mikhailovsky (1828–1905) was later to comment, the 'unforgettable' decade of the 1840s was a dark and difficult time in which to begin a literary career in Russia.[1] Born in 1818, Turgenev grew up during the oppressive, militaristic regime of Nicholas I, which was characterized by police surveillance, censorship, a vast centralized bureaucracy and a policy of nationalism predicated on the glorification of Russian autocracy, personified by the Tsar himself. Having had to contend with the Decembrist uprising immediately upon assuming the throne in 1825, Nicholas was determined to stamp out all forms of subversive activity, and his repressive measures only intensified as a wave of revolutions spread across Europe in 1848. It was just at this time that Turgenev began publicly to nail his political colours to the mast, having published the previous year 'Khor and Kalinych', which would later become the first of twenty-five *Sketches from a Hunter's Album* (as the pithy title *Zapiski okhotnika* ('Notes of a Hunter') is often translated into English). His transition from poetry to prose indicates the shift taking place at this time in Russian literature from Romanticism to realism, but for all the verisimilitude of his descriptions, this did not mean his writing became any less poetic. It was these richly detailed, and often intensely lyrical, sketches of Russian rural life which made Turgenev's reputation.

Turgenev himself was an avid huntsman (of mostly woodcock, quail and partridge, but occasionally bears) and was fortunate enough to come from a wealthy noble background which enabled him to indulge in such pursuits. His position also gave him the opportunity to travel. He spent his early childhood on his family's spacious country estate, located several hundred miles south-west of Moscow, near the town of Mtsensk, but he had lived for six months in Paris even before he was five years old and for the rest of his life he was something of a nomad. First he moved with his family to Moscow for his education; then he took a degree at the University of St Petersburg, after which he spent three years studying at the University of Berlin. In 1856, he decided to base himself in Western Europe, not least because he wanted to be near Pauline Viardot, the celebrated but married opera singer with whom he had fallen hopelessly in love in 1843. From now on his habit was to come back regularly to Russia in the summer months. He would probably have moved abroad earlier but for the fact he was exiled to his estate for a year and a half in 1852 – nominally for his obituary of Gogol, but in reality for the implicit social criticism contained in his *Sketches from a Hunter's Album*, first published in book form just at that time.

A key role in Turgenev's intellectual evolution at this stage in his career was played by Vissarion Belinsky (1811–48), who was Russia's first professional critic and his close friend. Belinsky was the guiding spirit behind *Sketches from a Hunter's Album*, and Turgenev's dedication of *Fathers and Sons* to his friend's memory says a lot about his importance to the novel's conception. It was an unlikely friendship, as the urbane, cosmopolitan and aristocratic Turgenev and the plebeian, radical and ascetic Belinsky had vastly different backgrounds and temperaments, but, as committed 'Westernizers', they were united by their opposition to the Slavophile thinkers whose rejection of the Europeanist reforms of Peter the Great had steadily been gaining currency in certain intelligentsia circles of Moscow and St Petersburg. And their friendship certainly ran more smoothly than Turgenev's close but fraught relationship with his neighbour and literary rival Count Tolstoy, which almost degenerated into a duel during the writing of *Fathers and Sons*. Belinsky was more than just a literary critic to his contemporaries, most of whom revered him regardless of their political views. In Isaiah Berlin's words he was one of the 'greatest of heroes of the heroic 1840s, when the organised struggle for full social as well as political freedom, economic as well as civic equality, was held to have begun in the

Russian Empire'.[2] Perhaps in another age Belinsky would have been less uncompromising, but, as he saw it, as long as the horror of serfdom existed in Russia, the first duty of writers was to expose it. Thus he had little time for art which was not politically engaged – and none at all for art that was politically engaged in the wrong direction. Turgenev never abandoned the pursuit of artistic goals in his writing, as is particularly apparent in the short stories and novellas he continued to write, but he was also a writer with a strong social conscience and love of his country, who devoted himself to finding ways in his longer fictional works to express and understand the turbulent times in which he lived. *Fathers and Sons*, his best novel, represents the culmination of a journey he embarked on some twenty years earlier under the tutelage of Belinsky, who had clearly endorsed it.

Turgenev came into Belinsky's orbit in 1843 (the momentous year of Pauline Viardot's debut on the Petersburg stage, and his own literary debut), when the latter published several of his poems and an early drama as chief critic of the influential journal *Notes of the Fatherland (Otechestvennye zapiski)*. Belinsky then joined the staff of *The Contemporary (Sovremennik)* under the new editorship of Nikolay Nekrasov, and it was on the pages of this journal, which immediately became Russia's leading progressive periodical, that Turgenev's 'Khor and Kalinych' appeared in 1847. In his survey of Russian literature for that year, Belinsky praised Turgenev for having approached the people in a way no one had ever approached them. Turgenev, indeed, for the first time in Russian literature had provided realistic portraits of peasants, about whose lives next to nothing was really known (Nicholas I was so squeamish about Russian society being placed under the microscope that he even censored statistical research). Perhaps more importantly, Turgenev also treated the peasants in his fiction as dignified human beings, equal to their masters. Turgenev's hatred of serfdom had originated with his tyrannical mother, whose despotic treatment of her serfs instilled in him a deep hatred of violence and social injustice. He justified living abroad, where he wrote most of his sketches and much of his subsequent fiction, by reasoning that he could attack his great 'enemy' (the institution of serfdom) more effectively at a distance.

By the time he came of age, the 'landowning and serf-owning stratum of society' to which he belonged by birth aroused in him feelings of such 'embarrassment and indignation, and finally disgust' that he simply could no longer 'breathe the same air' as those who stood for the things he hated so much, as he later explained in the preface to his memoirs (by the end of Nicholas I's reign in 1855 the atmosphere in Russia was so suffocating that barely anyone could breathe).[3]

Since he was abroad, Turgenev was one of the first to be able to read the incendiary letter Belinsky addressed to Gogol in the last months of his life, castigating him for his reactionary views in defence of serfdom and the autocracy. Written in 1847 in Germany, where Belinsky had gone in a futile atttempt to improve his failing health (he was dying of tuberculosis), the letter circulated widely in *samizdat* in Russia via handwritten copies, but there was no question of the censor passing it for publication. Belinsky's untimely death a few months later was a huge blow to Turgenev, and also a setback to the Russian government, who had been hoping to arrest him. The Tsarist authorities were more successful with Turgenev a few years later, using the publication of his obituary of Gogol as a convenient pretext to arrest him in March 1852. It was no coincidence, however, that *Sketches from a Hunter's Album* had just been approved for publication in book form by the censor (who was subsequently sacked). Turgenev was released from exile on his estate at the end of 1853 through the intercession of Crown Prince Alexander, upon whom *Sketches from a Hunter's Album* had made a deep impression. That Alexander's resolve to abolish serfdom was hardened after reading these stories was a matter of great pride to Turgenev, and it is telling that it was soon after Nicholas I died that he began his first novel, *Rudin*. He now began to cast his gaze more widely over contemporary Russian society. Alexander II's accession, and the end of the Crimean War, were greeted with relief and a feeling of optimism about the future. The immediate liberalization of Russian society was reflected in the relaxation in censorship and the arrival in St Petersburg of Johann Strauss, Jr, whose waltzes brought some much-needed *joie de vivre* to Russian life. Dostoyevsky was finally allowed to return from exile (having been arrested and almost executed in 1849 for reading an illicit copy of Belinsky's letter to Gogol), and the Tsar's liberal-minded younger brother, Grand Duke Konstantin, was now able to send a group of young writers on a remarkable expedition down the Volga to study the lives of those involved in its navigation. A direct result was Ostrovsky's play *The Storm*, first performed in 1859 and perceived by radical critics to be a thrilling allegory of social protest that could never have been allowed under Nicholas I. It was also in 1859 that Turgenev began work on his third novel, the title of which, *On the Eve*, is emblematic of the state of anticipation Russia found itself in before Alexander II launched the 'Great Reforms' of the 1860s. But it was his fourth novel, *Fathers and Sons*, begun in the months leading up to the Emancipation of the Serfs and completed in its immediate aftermath, that caught the *Zeitgeist* more than any other artistic work of the period.

Turgenev began *Fathers and Sons* in a spell of bad weather during a stay in Ventnor on the Isle of Wight in August 1860. He did not find it an easy novel to write and was apparently evicted by his first landlady for smoking too much. Nevertheless, perhaps with the help of the sea view from his new lodgings on the Esplanade, he made progress. When he left three weeks later, he had made notes on his central protagonists, including physical characteristics and precise ages, and resolved that the action would take place in 1859. This was how his novels always began in his creative imagination: character before plot. Back in Paris that autumn, he sketched out the complete storyline. Then began the task of fleshing it out, which took place in fits and starts, between games of chess at the Café de la Regence. It is understandable why Turgenev should have only completed the first half before he left for Russia in April 1861. All that spring Turgenev and other liberals among the expatriates had been anxiously awaiting the long-expected Emancipation of the Serfs to be made official, and in his distracted state it must have been hard sometimes to concentrate on fiction. As soon as the Manifesto was published, Turgenev and others organized a service of thanksgiving in the Embassy church in Paris, and he wrote to friends that he had been reduced to tears by the 'very clever and moving' address given by the priest.[4] Once back at his estate in Russia in May, Turgenev was able to focus again, and the first draft of *Fathers and Sons* was complete by the end of the summer. Next came the process of making revisions to the manuscript, on the recommendations of close friends like Pavel Annenkov and, more controversially, the editor of the journal where it would first appear – which was not *The Contemporary*.

The Russian literary scene had changed significantly since Alexander II had become Tsar. As a result of the general loosening up of Russian intellectual life, Nekrasov had been able to appoint the radical critic Nikolay Chernyshevsky (1828–89) to the editorial board of *The Contemporary*. Both he and Alexander Dobrolyubov (1836–61), who joined the journal the following year, came from the same stock as Belinsky: they were *raznochintsy*, that is to say, educated members of the intelligentsia who came from non-noble stock, often being children of clergy (as in their case) or, like Belinsky, of doctors, who also occupied a low position in Russian society. They were much more extreme and dogmatic about the need for art to serve a political purpose, however. As 'men of the sixties' ('*shestidesyatniki*'), as they came to be referred to, they were people who had come into the public arena with an expectation of being able to act. Thus they came from a new and very different generation from that of the liberal Turgenev and his contemporaries, whom they associated with the stagnant 1840s and aristocratic values, and dismissed as ineffectual idealists. The clash between these two generations is essentially the theme of *Fathers and Sons* and is most graphically represented in the relationship between Pavel Kirsanov and Bazarov. As a result of Nekrasov's support of his radical younger colleagues, the left-wing political agenda of *The Contemporary* was now placed to the fore, at the expense of artistic criteria, and in 1858 the journal lost writers such as Turgenev, Tolstoy, Goncharov and Ostrovsky to the Moscow-based and still mildly liberal *Russian Messenger* (*Russky vestnik*). It was thus to its editor Mikhail Katkov that Turgenev submitted *Fathers and Sons* for its first publication in journal form, as he had already done with his most recent novel, *On the Eve*. When *Fathers and Sons* was finally published in early 1862 it filled pages 473 to 663 –

Russian literary periodicals were not called 'fat journals' for nothing – of the February issue of *Russian Messenger*. Criticism from those who espoused the ideology of *The Contemporary* was an inevitability, but Turgenev had no idea quite how vicious it would be.

From the beginning, Turgenev had conceived a novel which would be about modern Russia – not just about people from his own patrician milieu living in present-day Russia, as in his previous novels, but about the single-minded new social types now able to thrive in the new Russia of Alexander II. In his young country doctor Bazarov, on whom all the post-publication controversy centred, Turgenev created the first fictional *raznochinets*. Bazarov is typical of his class in finding the old nobility irrelevant, and has no compunction about showing his lack of respect for those senior to him. Breathing life into a character whose beliefs (about the value of art, for example) were sometimes antithetical to his own was a courageous endeavour on Turgenev's part. It is striking, for example, that the *raznochintsy* were of no artistic interest to the aristocratic and egocentric Tolstoy, who had entered the literary arena some ten years earlier, nearly a decade after Turgenev, and who continued to focus on gentry and peasants in his fiction. The barriers between social classes in Russia's highly segregated society were now beginning to break down, but Turgenev was in the vanguard where the depiction of this process in literature was concerned. Even more courageous was his desire to turn Bazarov into a real hero, which went against the grain of the profiles of the flawed male protagonists of previous Russian novels (such as Pushkin's *Eugene Onegin*, Lermontov's *A Hero of Our Time* and Goncharov's *Oblomov*). With a nod to the ironic title of Lermontov's earlier masterpiece, Turgenev declared Bazarov to be truly 'a hero of our time', behind whom it is hard not to see the shadow of the inspirational Belinsky (who was, of course, also a humble doctor's son). But creating his character proved fiendishly difficult, and involved keeping a diary in his name and imagining his reactions to various contemporary issues. The 'men of the 1860s' would in time become instantly recognizable, but at the beginning of the decade it is understandable that Turgenev could only intuitively feel the contours of this new personality. With hindsight it is difficult to appreciate the challenge he faced in creating a three-dimensional character proud to call himself a 'nihilist': Bazarov, after all, is still really only a prototype. As Turgenev wrote to the poet Sluchevsky in April 1862, while the furore about the novel was at its height, 'I dreamed of a tall, dark, wild figure, half grown out of the ground, who was strong, angry, and honest, but still doomed to perish because of standing only on the threshold of the future'. It is not surprising that Turgenev should mention in the same breath that he imagined Bazarov as a 'strange offshoot of Pugachev', the leader of the Cossack uprising against Catherine the Great, for, as he explains earlier in the letter, 'if he is called a nihilist, you should read that as revolutionary'.[5] This is certainly how the great anarchist Mikhail Bakunin (a friend to Turgenev during his milder student days in Berlin) understood Bazarov, exhorting Alexander Herzen in 1866 to appreciate the energy and strong will of the radical Russian youth. As a pronounced Anglomane, Turgenev's editor Mikhail Katkov may well have bridled at the portrayal of Bazarov's foppish opponent Pavel Kirsanov but he was truly shocked by Bazarov's 'force, power, superiority over the crowd'.[6] Katkov's relations with Chernyshevsky and the editorial team at *The Contemporary* had become increasingly antagonistic since the late 1850s, and now here was Turgenev seemingly wanting to celebrate the enemy! 'Even if Bazarov has not been raised to an apotheosis,' Katkov wrote to Turgenev, 'you have to admit, he has somehow managed to end up on a very high pedestal. He really does crush everything around him. Every thing before him is either worn out rags, or feeble and green.'[7] Katkov insisted Turgenev introduce revisions to the novel's manuscript to render Bazarov's portrait less positive, but in so doing probably only fomented the critical storm which greeted the novel upon its publication.

The terms of the Emancipation Act the previous year had dissatisfied all sections of Russian society, leading to a wave of demonstrations and arrests. Simultaneously, the introduction of ill-conceived university reforms prompted widespread student protests in October 1861, particularly among those *raznochintsy* who could not afford to pay the new obligatory fees and objected to compulsory attendance at lectures. The twenty-four-year-old Dobrolyubov had entitled his review of *On the Eve* for *The Contemporary* the previous year 'When Will the Real Day Come?', and there were huge expectations among the revolutionary youth that Turgenev's new novel would finally deliver an unequivocal positive hero on whom they could project their hopes and dreams. By March 1862, when the novel was published, Dobrolyubov was no longer around to express their sense of betrayal at Bazarov dying, since he himself had died of tuberculosis a few months earlier. (Interestingly, Turgenev's character notes from the Isle of Wight reveal that Bazarov was in fact partly modelled on Dobrolyubov, whom he respected.) In his stead, another critic wrote a withering review, claiming that Turgenev had ridiculed Russian youth through his character of Bazarov. The young generation certainly felt that the portrait of Bazarov was, in Turgenev's words, 'an insulting caricature, a slanderous lampoon'.[8] Chernyshevsky, meanwhile, had been put under police surveillance for writing illegal anti-government tracts and inciting the peasants to revolt. In July 1862, a few weeks after the government had succeeded in shutting down *The Contemporary*, he was arrested and imprisoned in the St Peter and Paul Fortress. Instead of reviewing *Fathers and Sons*, he wrote an inflammatory riposte in the form of his revolutionary novel *What Is to Be Done?*, which was smuggled out of prison and published in 1863.

The American scholar and diplomat Eugene Schuyler, who produced the first English translation of *Fathers and Sons* in 1867 (and met Turgenev later that year en route to become US consul in Moscow), summarized well the general reaction to the novel in his foreword:

A tempest was raised in Russia by its appearance; passionate criticisms, calumnies, and virulent attacks abounded . . . Each generation found the picture of the other very life-like, but their own very badly drawn. The fathers protested, and the sons were enraged to see themselves personified in the positive Bazarof . . . Of course the more the book was abused, the more it was read. Its success has been greater than that of any other Russian book.[9]

The publication of *Fathers and Sons* was indeed a sensation, and not just in the Russian literary world. The novel was discussed all over the country, and according to one of Turgenev's contemporaries even caused a stir in sleepy provincial towns like Lenin's home town of Simbirsk, where no book had apparently ever made any kind of impact. As Avdotya Panayeva records in her memoirs, it was read even by those who had not picked up a book since leaving school. Daughters threatened their parents they would become nihilists if they were not bought new frocks and taken to balls, while the government condemned the doctrine of 'nihilism' as seditious. It was recommended that young men should be forbidden from appearing in public with long hair and dark-blue spectacles, while young women should be prohibited from appearing in public with short hair, and without chignons and crinolines.

In his 1917 study of Turgenev, Edward Garnett describes the novelist's many critics as a 'crowd of critical gnats dancing airily around the great master and eagerly driving their little stings into his flesh'.[10] Turgenev definitely was stung by the vehemence of the attacks, so much so that when *Fathers and Sons* came to be published as a separate book (by an old-believer merchant and philanthropist who had set up his own company in Moscow, every other publisher having shied away), he thought at first he should add a foreword to try and explain what he had set out do. In the end he explained in his brief introduction that he had resolved the novel should speak for itself and declared that he had not changed his views. As he wrote to Sluchevsky in April 1862, 'My entire tale is directed against the nobility as the leading class.'[11] Thus he could in 'clear conscience' place on the title page the name of his 'unforgettable' friend Belinsky. Towards the end of the 1860s, however, Turgenev wrote a short essay on his novel as part of his *Literary Reminiscences*, in which he recounted the experience of being attacked on all sides – and was criticized on all sides for that too.

In truth, because Turgenev was an artist and not a pamphleteer, Bazarov emerges as a contradictory and ambivalent figure, but this is of course precisely why he succeeds as a literary character, and why his creator exhorted readers to love him despite his 'coarseness, heartlessness, pitiless dryness and sharpness'.[12] As Turgenev later conceded in a letter to Annenkov, it was likely 'no author really understands what he is doing. There is a sort of contradiction here, which you *yourself* can never resolve, however you approach it.'[13]

Rosamund Bartlett

NOTES

1. Nikolay Mikhailovsky, 'Iz "Pisem postoronnyago" (stat'ya po povodu smerti Turgeneva)', in P. Pertsov, ed., *O Turgeneve: russkaya i inostrannaya kritika 1818–1918* (Moscow: Kooperativnoe izdatel'stvo, 1918), p. 61.

2. Isaiah Berlin, 'Vissarion Belinsky', *Russian Thinkers* (Harmondsworth: Penguin, 1979), p. 152.

3. Ivan Turgenev, 'Instead of an Introduction', *Turgenev's Literary Reminiscences and Autobiographical Fragments*, tr. David Magarshack, with an essay by Edmund Wilson (London: Faber and Faber, 1984), pp. 92–3.

4. Letter to Pavel Annenkov, 22 March (3 April) 1861, I. S. Turgenev, *Polnoye sobraniye sochineniyi i pisem v tridsati tomakh. Pis'ma v vosemnadtsati tomakh*, 2nd revised edition, vol. 4, ed. I. A. Bityugova and S. A. Reiser (Moscow: Nauka, 1987), p. 309.

5. Letter to Konstantin Sluchevsky, 14 (26) April 1862, cited in *Roman I. S. Turgeneva 'Ottsy i deti' v russkoy kritike*, ed. I. I. Sukhikh (Leningrad: izdatel'stvo Leningradskogo universiteta, 1986), p. 29.

6. Description of Katkov's response in letter from Pavel Annenkov to Turgenev, 26 September 1861, cited in V. Y. Troitsky, *Kniga pokoleniy: o romane I. S Turgeneva 'Ottsy i deti'* (Moscow: Kniga, 1979), p. 21.

7. Ivan Turgenev, 'Po povodu "Otysov i detey"', *Roman I. S. Turgeneva 'Ottsy i deti' v russkoy kritike*, p. 37

8. Letter to Ludwig Pietsch, 22 May (3 June) 1869, *Polnoye sobraniye sochineniy i pisem v tridsati tomakh Pis'ma v vosemnadtsati*

tomakh, vol. 9, ed. N. S. Nikitina and G. V. Stepanova (Moscow: Nauka, 1995), p. 223.

9.   Eugene Schuyler, 'Preface' to Ivan Turgenef, *Fathers and Sons*, tr. Eugene Schuyler (New York: Leypoldt and Holt, 1867), p. vii.

10.   Edward Garnett, *Turgenev* (London: Collins, 1917), p. 20.

11.   *Roman I. S. Turgeneva 'Ottsy i deti' v russkoy kritike*, p. 27.

12.   Ibid., p. 28.

13.   Letter to Pavel Annenkov, 1 January 1870 (20 December 1869), *Polnoye sobraniye sochineniy i pisem v tridsati tomakh. Pis'ma v vosemnadtsati tomakh*, vol. 10, ed. L. N. Nazarova and G. A. Time (Moscow: Nauka, 1994), p. 102.

Further Reading

The standard edition of Turgenev's Russian text is the Soviet Academy of Sciences Complete Collected Works, I. S. Turgenev, *Polnoye sobraniye sochineniy, Sochineniya*, vol. 8 (Moscow and Leningrad, 1960–68; 2nd complete revised edition, *Sochineniya*, vol. 7, Moscow, 1981). In *Turgenev's Literary Reminiscences and Autobiographical Fragments* (tr. David Magarshack, London, 1959) he expounds his literary credo; this translation has the bonus of an introductory essay by Edmund Wilson. Ivan Turgenev, *Letters* (ed. A. V. Knowles, London, 1983) is a useful selection. Alexander Herzen, *My Past and Thoughts* (tr. Constance Garnett, rev. Humphrey Higgens, introduced by Isaiah Berlin, London, 1968) presents Turgenev's intellectual context. Franco Venturi, *Roots of Revolution* (tr. Francis Haskell, London, 1960) explores the radical political ideas of the time. The Norton Critical Edition of *Fathers and Sons* by Michael R. Katz (New York, 1995) adds a selection of Turgenev's own comments on the novel and of contemporary and more recent criticism, including Isaiah Berlin's stimulating Romanes Lecture of 1970, '*Fathers and Children*: Turgenev and the Liberal Predicament'. The best biography of Turgenev is Leonard Schapiro's *Turgenev: His Life and Times* (Oxford, 1978). April FitzLyon's *The Price of Genius* (London, 1964), a biography of the singer Pauline Viardot, the love of Turgenev's life, is also interesting. Among works of criticism see V. S. Pritchett's *The Gentle Barbarian: The Life and Work of Turgenev* (London, 1977); also Richard Freeborn, *Turgenev: The Novelist's Novelist* (Oxford, 1960) and Frank F. Seeley, *Turgenev: A Reading of His Fiction* (Cambridge, 1991).

Translator's Note

The Russian title of Turgenev's novel, *Ottsy i deti*, means 'Fathers and Children'. But the large majority of its translations in all languages have been titled *Fathers and Sons* or its equivalent from the start, often with Turgenev's knowledge and presumably approval. It is reasonable to assume his children were male. Moreover the Russian of 'Fathers and Sons' sounds awkward. But it should be noted that Isaiah Berlin referred to the novel as *Fathers and Children*.

A couple of things about my translation: I have by and large adhered to Turgenev's paragraph structure but have sometimes broken up long ones. Turgenev more often refers to Odintsova, thus, by her surname alone; occasionally as Anna Sergeyevna. I have done the reverse. While Russians do make more use of women's surnames alone, it seems more comfortable not to (except for operatic divas). I don't understand the nuances of Turgenev's usage if there are any. Tolstoy certainly does not refer to Karenina.

I have used the text of the Soviet Academy of Sciences edition: I.S. Turgenev, *Polnoye sobraniye sochineniy, Sochineniya*, vol. 8 (Moscow and Leningrad, 1964).

I owe thanks to Simon Dixon and David Moon for some most useful information on the contemporary value of the rouble; and to Eleo for a final encouraging and valuable reading of my text.

Through the accident of a holiday home near by I completed this translation only a few miles from the esplanade at Ventnor where Turgenev first worked out the characters of his novel and their relationships in the late summer of 1860.

Seaview, Isle of Wight, 2008

FATHERS AND SONS

Dedicated to the memory of
Vissarion Grigoryevich BELINSKY[1]

I

'Well, Pyotr, can you see anything yet?' It was 20 May 1859.[1] The speaker was a gentleman a little over forty years old, wearing a dusty coat and checked trousers, who had gone out without his hat on to the low porch of an inn on the *** Highway. He was asking his manservant, a round-faced young fellow with fair down on his chin and small, colourless eyes.

Everything about Pyotr – his turquoise earring, dyed and pomaded hair and deferential body movements – in short, everything – declared him to be a man of the modern, educated generation. He gave a supercilious glance down the road and answered, 'Nothing, sir, I can't see anything at all.'

'Can't you see them?' the gentleman repeated.

'No, nothing,' the servant answered a second time.

The gentleman sighed and sat down on a bench. Let us acquaint the reader with him while he is sitting with his feet tucked in beneath him and looking thoughtfully around.

His name is Nikolay Petrovich Kirsanov. Ten miles from that little inn he has a decent property of 200 souls,[2] or, as he now puts it since he settled the boundaries with the peasants and started a modern 'farm', of 5,000 acres of land. His father, a general and a veteran of the War of 1812,[3] a semi-literate Russian type, coarse-grained but decent, had served in the army all his life. He commanded first a brigade, then a division, and had always lived in the provinces, where by virtue of his rank he played a fairly important role. Nikolay Petrovich was born in the south of Russia, like his elder brother Pavel, of whom we shall speak later, and till the age of fourteen he was educated at home, surrounded by ill-paid tutors, easy-going but obsequious adjutants and other regimental and staff personnel.

His mother, *née* Kolyazin, as a girl had been known as Agathe[4] but when she became the general's lady, as Agafokleya Kuzminishna Kirsanova. She could be classed as a 'barracks matriarch'. She wore splendid caps and rustling silk gowns; in church she was first to go up and kiss the cross; she spoke loudly and a great deal, in the mornings she gave her children her hand to kiss, and at night she blessed them – in short, she did exactly as she pleased.

As a general's son Nikolay Petrovich was destined for the army, like his brother Pavel – although not only was he far from being a hero, he even had the reputation of being 'a bit of a softy'. But he broke his leg on the very day the news of his commission arrived. He spent two months lying in bed and for the rest of his life he had a 'bad leg'. His father gave up on him and let him follow a civilian career. He took him to St Petersburg as soon as he was eighteen and enrolled him in the university. At the same time his brother happened to get his commission in a Guards regiment. The young men began sharing an apartment, under the distant supervision of a cousin on their mother's side, Ilya Kolyazin, a senior civil servant. Their father returned to his army division and his spouse, and only occasionally sent his sons large sheets of grey paper scrawled in his bold clerk's hand, the last sheet graced by the words 'Piotr Kirsanov, Major-General', laboriously surrounded by flourishes.

In 1835 Nikolay Petrovich left university with a degree, and in the same year General Kirsanov, who had been forced into retirement after a poor performance by his troops on review, came with his wife to live in St Petersburg. He intended to rent a house near the Tauride Garden and had put his name down for the English Club, but he suddenly died of a stroke. Agafokleya Kuzminishna soon followed him. She could not get used to an obscure life in the capital. The boredom of a pensioned existence consumed her.

Meanwhile Nikolay Petrovich, while his parents were still alive and to their considerable chagrin, had managed to fall in love with the daughter of Prepolovensky, a minor civil servant who was his former landlord. She was a pretty young lady, and a 'cultured' one too: meaning that she read the serious articles in the 'Science' section of the reviews. He married her as soon as the period of mourning for his parents was over. He left the Ministry of Crown Lands – where his father had got him a position through connections – and led a life of bliss with his

Masha, first in a dacha[5] near the Forestry Institute, then in the city, in a small and attractive apartment with clean stairs and a chilly drawing room, and eventually in the country, where he finally settled, and where after a short time he had a son, Arkady. The couple lived very happily and quietly: they were almost never parted, they read together, sang and played duets on the piano. She planted flowers and looked after the poultry yard, he occasionally went shooting and looked after the estate, and Arkady grew and grew – also happily and quietly.

Ten years passed like a dream. In 1847 Kirsanov's wife died. He was hardly able to bear that blow, and his hair went grey in a few weeks. He was planning to go abroad for a little distraction . . . but then came 1848.[6] He had no choice but to go back to the country and after a rather long period of doing nothing he occupied himself with introducing changes on his estate. In 1855 he took his son to university and spent three winters with him in St Petersburg, hardly ever going out and trying to get to know Arkady's young classmates. The final winter he couldn't go to Petersburg – and so we see him now in May 1859, completely grey-haired, a little plump and slightly bent: he is waiting for his son, who has just got his master's degree as he had once done himself.

The manservant, out of a feeling of propriety but maybe also not wishing to remain under his master's eye, went out through the gates and lit a pipe. Nikolay Petrovich bent his head and began to study the dilapidated steps of the porch. A sturdy speckled hen sedately walked up and down the steps, firmly tapping with its big yellow feet, and a dirty cat posed curled up on the rail and gave it hostile looks. The sun was baking. A smell of warm rye bread came from the half-lit entrance of the little inn. Our Nikolay Petrovich fell into a reverie. 'My son . . . a graduate . . . Arkasha . . .' were the thoughts that went through his head. He tried to think of something else, and the same thoughts came back. He remembered his dead wife . . . 'She didn't live long enough!' he whispered sadly . . . A fat grey pigeon alighted on the road and hurriedly went to drink from a puddle by the well. Nikolay Petrovich started to watch it, but his ear now caught the rattle of approaching wheels . . .

'This time they're coming, sir,' his servant reported, dashing in from outside the gates.

Nikolay Petrovich jumped up and directed his eyes along the road. A *tarantas* appeared, harnessed to a trio of carriage horses.[7] In it he caught a glimpse of the peak of a student's cap, and the familiar outline of a beloved face . . .

'Arkasha! Arkasha!' Kirsanov shouted; and he ran out waving his arms . . . A few moments later his lips were touching the beardless, dusty and sunburnt cheek of the young graduate.

II

'Papa, let me just give myself a shake,' said Arkady cheerfully responding to his father's embrace in his resonant young man's voice, a bit hoarse from the journey, 'otherwise I'm going to make you dirty.'

'It doesn't matter, it doesn't matter,' Nikolay Petrovich said over and over with a tender smile, giving his son's greatcoat collar and his own coat a couple of brushes with his hand. 'Let's have a look at you, let's have a look,' he added standing back. He then moved quickly off towards the inn, giving orders: 'Out here, out here, hurry up and bring the horses.'

Nikolay Petrovich seemed much more nervous than his son. He seemed confused and awkward. Arkady stopped him.

'Papa,' he said, 'let me introduce you to my good friend Bazarov whom I've written to you about so often. He's been kind enough to agree to come and stay with us.'

Nikolay Petrovich quickly turned round. He went up to a tall man in a long tasselled cloak who had just got out of the carriage and firmly grasped the red and gloveless hand which Bazarov at first didn't offer him.

'I'm really delighted,' he began, 'and thank you for deciding to visit us. I hope . . . may I ask your name and your father's?'

'Yevgeny Vasilyev,'[1] Bazarov answered in a slow, manly

voice. He opened the collar of his cloak, and Nikolay Petrovich saw his full face – long and thin, a broad forehead, a nose flat on top and quite pointed at the end, big greenish eyes and drooping sandy side whiskers. His face, lit up by a calm smile, radiated confidence and intellect.

'I hope you won't get bored with us, my dear Yevgeny Vasilyevich,' Nikolay Petrovich went on.

Bazarov moved his thin lips a fraction but didn't reply and only raised his cap. His light-brown hair was long and thick, but didn't hide the massive contours of his large skull.

'So, Arkady,' Nikolay Petrovich began again, turning to his son, 'shall they harness the horses right away? Or do you want to rest?'

'We'll rest at home, Papa. Tell them to harness the horses.'

'Right away, right away,' his father agreed. 'Hey, Pyotr, do you hear? Get them going, lad, and be quick about it.'

Pyotr – who as a modern servant hadn't come up to kiss the young master's hand but only bowed to him from a distance – disappeared again through the gates.

'I've got the carriage here, and there are three horses too for your *tarantas*,' Nikolay Petrovich said fussily. Meanwhile Arkady was drinking water from an iron cup the hostess of the inn had brought him, and Bazarov lit his pipe and went up to the driver, who was unharnessing the horses. 'Only the carriage is for two, and I don't know if your friend . . .'

'He'll go in the *tarantas*,' Arkady interrupted in a low voice. 'Please don't stand on any ceremony with him. He's a marvellous fellow, so straightforward – you'll see.'

Nikolay Petrovich's coachman led out the horses.

'Well, get a move on, Big Beard!' Bazarov said to the driver.

'Did you hear what the gentleman called you, Mityukha?' said another driver, standing by with his hands stuck in the back slits of his sheepskin coat. 'Big Beard is what you are.'

Mityukha just gave his cap a twitch and pulled the reins from the sweat-covered shaft-horse.[2]

'Hurry up, hurry up, lads, lend a hand,' exclaimed Nikolay Petrovich, 'you'll get something for a drink!'

In a few minutes the horses were harnessed. Father and son

got in the carriage, and Pyotr climbed up on to the box. Bazarov jumped into the *tarantas* and leant his head against a leather pillow – and both carriages moved off.

III

'So here we are, at last you've finished university and come home,' said Nikolay Petrovich, patting Arkady's shoulder and knee. 'At last!'

'And how is Uncle? Is he well?' asked Arkady, who for all the genuine, almost childish joy he felt wanted to move the conversation as quickly as possible from high emotion to the commonplace.

'He is. He thought of driving with me to meet you but for some reason he changed his mind.'

'And were you waiting for me long?' asked Arkady.

'About five hours.'

'You're so good to me, Papa!'

Arkady quickly turned to his father and gave his cheek a smacking kiss. Nikolay Petrovich laughed quietly.

'I've got a wonderful horse for you!' he began. 'You'll see. And your room has been papered.'

'And is there a room for Bazarov?'

'We'll find one for him.'

'Please be nice to him, Papa. I can't tell you how much I value him as a friend.'

'Did you meet him quite recently?'

'Yes.'

'I thought I didn't see him last winter. What's he studying?'

'His main subject is natural science, but he knows everything. Next year he aims to qualify as a doctor.'

'Ah! He's a medic,' Nikolay Petrovich remarked and fell silent for a moment. 'Pyotr,' he added pointing. 'Aren't those our peasants?'

Pyotr looked where his master was pointing. Several carts drawn by horses with no bridles were clattering along a narrow track. Each held one or at most two peasants, in open sheep-skin coats.

'Indeed they are, sir,' pronounced Pyotr.

'Where are they going, to the town?'

'One must assume so. To the tavern,' he added scornfully, inclining slightly towards the driver as if asking for his opinion. But the driver didn't stir. He was a fellow of the old school and didn't hold with new-fangled views.

'I'm having a lot of trouble with the peasants this year,' Nikolay Petrovich went on, turning to his son. 'They aren't paying their quit-rent.[1] What can we do?'

'And are you happy with the hired labourers?'

'Yes,' Nikolay Petrovich said in a low voice. 'The trouble is that people are getting at them. And there is still no real will to work. They are ruining the harnesses. But their ploughing hasn't been too bad. It'll all come right in the end. So are you becoming interested in farming?'

'It's such a pity you've no shade at home,' Arkady remarked, not answering the last question.

'I've put up a big awning above the balcony on the north side,' said Nikolay Petrovich. 'Now we can have dinner outside.'

'It'll look pretty suburban . . . but none of that matters. The air is so good here! It smells so wonderful! I really think there's nowhere in the world where the air smells as good as in this bit of country! And the sky . . .'

Arkady suddenly stopped speaking, looked surreptitiously behind him out of the corner of his eye and fell silent.

'Of course,' remarked Nikolay Petrovich, 'you were born here, so everything here must seem special to you . . .'

'But, Papa, it makes no difference where a man is born.'

'Still . . .'

'No, it makes absolutely no difference.'

Nikolay Petrovich looked sideways at his son and the carriage went another quarter of a mile before their conversation resumed.

'I can't remember if I wrote to tell you,' Nikolay Petrovich began, 'your old nanny Yegorovna died.'

'Did she? Poor old woman! And is Prokofyich still alive?'

'He is and he hasn't changed a bit. He's just as grumpy. Generally speaking you won't find big changes at Marino.'

'Do you still have the same bailiff?'[2]

'I've changed my bailiff. I decided I wouldn't any longer employ old house serfs[3] who'd been freed, or at any rate I wouldn't give them jobs involving responsibility.' (Arkady looked meaningfully at Pyotr.) *'Il est libre, en effet,'*[4] Nikolay Petrovich said in a low voice, 'but he's just a valet. My new bailiff's a townsman.[5] He seems a sensible fellow. I'm giving him 250 roubles a year.[6] By the way,' added Nikolay Petrovich, rubbing his forehead and eyebrows with his hand, which with him was always a sign of embarrassment, 'I told you just now you wouldn't find any changes at Marino . . . That's not quite true. I feel I ought to warn you, although . . .'

He faltered for a moment and went on, now speaking in French.

'A strict moralist would find my frankness inappropriate, but firstly this is something which can't be concealed, and secondly you know I've always had definite principles about the relationship of father and son. Of course you are quite entitled to condemn me. At my age . . . In a word, the . . . the girl, of whom you've probably already heard . . .'

'You mean Fenechka?' Arkady asked, casually.

Nikolay Petrovich went red.

'Please don't say her name so loudly . . . Well, yes . . . she's now living with me. I've put her in the main house . . . there were two small rooms free. But all that can be changed.'

'For goodness' sake, Papa, why?'

'Your friend will be staying with us . . . it's awkward . . .'

'Please don't worry about Bazarov. He's above that kind of thing.'

'And then there's you,' said Nikolay Petrovich. 'The trouble is the rooms in the wing are so bad.'

'For goodness' sake, Papa,' Arkady went on, 'you seem to be apologizing. You ought to be ashamed of yourself.'

'Of course, I ought to be ashamed of myself,' answered Nikolay Petrovich, getting redder and redder.

'Stop it, Papa, do me a favour and just stop it!' Arkady gave him a tender smile. 'Why's he apologizing?' he thought to himself, overcome by indulgent tenderness towards his kind, softhearted father, which was mixed with the sense of a sort of secret superiority. 'Stop it, please,' he said again, involuntarily enjoying the consciousness of his own maturity and freedom.

Nikolay Petrovich looked at him through the fingers of the hand with which he was continuing to rub his forehead. Something stabbed his heart. But here he blamed himself.

'These are our fields now,' he said after a long silence.

'And aren't those our woods ahead?' Arkady asked.

'Yes, they are. Only I've sold them. They're going to be felling them this year.'

'Why did you sell them?'

'I needed the money. And also this land is going to the peasants.'

'Who aren't paying you rent?'

'That's their business. But they will one day.'

'I'm sorry about the woods,' said Arkady and began to look around.

The country through which they were driving could hardly be called picturesque. Fields, nothing but fields, rolled gently up and down, stretching to the horizon. Here and there they could see small woods and winding gullies, covered with sparse, low-growing bushes, which looked just the way they are shown on old maps from the time of Catherine the Great.[7] They passed streams with crumbling banks and tiny ponds with broken dams. There were little villages of low huts beneath dark roofs, with thatch often half gone, and crooked threshing barns with walls of woven wattle and gaping doors, next to empty threshing floors. There were churches, brick ones with plaster peeling here and there, wooden ones with crosses askew and ruined cemeteries.

Arkady's heart slowly sank. As if it had been planned, all the peasants they passed were dressed in rags and riding wretched little horses. The willows by the road stood like tattered beggars, with torn bark and broken branches. Emaciated, rough-skinned cows, all bone, hungrily munched the grass in the ditches; they looked as if they'd just been torn from the murderous claws of some awesome beast. And on that beautiful spring day the pitiful sight of these exhausted animals called up the spectre of unending, cheerless winter with its blizzards and frosts and snow . . .

'No,' thought Arkady, 'this country is poor, it doesn't have either prosperity or industry. It mustn't, mustn't remain like this, changes are essential . . . but how are we to achieve them, where do we begin? . . .'

Those were Arkady's reflections . . . and while he was thinking, spring was coming into its own. Everything around was green and gold, everything gently and lavishly rippled and glistened in the quiet breath of a warm breeze, every single plant – trees, bushes and grass. Everywhere larks burst into an endless flow of song. Lapwings cried circling above the low-lying fields or silently ran through the tussocky grass. The cranes made beautiful specks of black as they walked through the tender green of the young spring corn. They disappeared in the rye, now just brushed with white, and from time to time only their heads showed above its rippling haze. Arkady looked and looked, and his thoughts gradually became feeble and vanished . . . He threw off his overcoat and looked at his father so cheerfully, so much like a little boy that Nikolay Petrovich again gave him a hug.

'It's not far now,' said Nikolay Petrovich. 'We just have to climb this little hill and we'll be able to see the house. We're going to have a wonderful life together, Arkasha. You'll help me with the farming, if you don't get bored with it. You and I must now become really close and get to know each other properly, mustn't we?'

'Of course we must,' said Arkady, 'but what a beautiful day it is!'

'To welcome you, Arkady dear. Yes, spring is here in all its glory. But I must say I agree with Pushkin – do you remember in *Eugene Onegin*: [8]

'Spring, spring – season of love and passion,
Your coming fills my heart with gloom,
Your . . .'

'Arkady!' Bazarov's voice rang out from the *tarantas*. 'Pass me over a match, I haven't got anything to light my pipe.'

Nikolay Petrovich fell silent, and Arkady, who had been beginning to listen to him with some amazement, though not without sympathy, quickly took a silver match box from his pocket and sent it over to Bazarov with Pyotr.

'Would you like a cigar?' Bazarov shouted again.

'Yes, please,' answered Arkady.

Pyotr came back to the carriage and handed him the box and a fat black cigar, which Arkady at once lit. It gave off such a strong and acrid smell of rank tobacco that Nikolay Petrovich, who had never smoked in his life, had to turn away his nose, but unobtrusively so as not to hurt his son's feelings. A quarter of an hour later both carriages stopped in front of the steps of a new wooden house, painted grey and with a red iron roof. This was Marino, also known as New Town, or, as the peasants called it, Poor Man's Farm.

IV

No crowd of house serfs spilled out on to the steps to greet the gentlemen: a single twelve-year-old girl appeared. She was followed out of the house by a young fellow who looked very like Pyotr, in a grey livery jacket with white crested buttons. This was Pavel Petrovich Kirsanov's manservant. He silently opened the carriage door and unfastened the leather apron of the *tarantas*. Nikolay Petrovich, his son and Bazarov went through a dark, almost empty hall – through a doorway there was a glimpse of a young woman's face – into a drawing room furnished in the latest fashion.

'We're home,' said Nikolay Petrovich, taking off his cap and running his fingers through his hair. 'The main thing now is to have some supper and rest.'

'It'd be no bad thing to have a bite to eat,' said Bazarov, stretching, and he sank down on to a sofa.

'Yes, yes, let's have supper, let's have it right away.' Nikolay

Petrovich for no obvious reason stamped his feet. 'And here's Prokofyich.'

A white-haired man entered: about sixty, thin and swarthy, wearing a brown tail coat with copper buttons and a pink kerchief round his neck. He gave a grin, kissed Arkady's hand and, bowing to the guest, went over to the door and put his hands behind his back.

'So, Prokofyich,' began Nikolay Petrovich, 'he's come home to us at last . . . So? How do you think he looks?'

'Very well, sir,' the old man said and grinned again, but then quickly brought his thick eyebrows together in a frown. 'Would you like me to serve?' he said solemnly.

'Yes, yes, please. But won't you first go to your room, Yevgeny Vasilyich?'

'No thanks, no need. Just tell them to stick my case in there and this old thing too,' he added, taking off his cloak.

'Certainly. Prokofyich, take the gentleman's coat.' (Prokofyich, looking puzzled, took Bazarov's 'old thing' in both hands and went off on tiptoe, holding it high above his head.) 'And, Arkady, don't you want to go to your room for a minute?'

'Yes, I must clean myself up,' Arkady answered and moved towards the door. But at that moment a man came into the drawing room. He was of medium height and wore a dark English suit, a fashionable low-cut cravat and patent leather boots. It was Pavel Petrovich Kirsanov. He looked about forty-five. His short-cut grey hair shone with the dark sheen of new silver.[1] His features, while revealing irritability, were unlined; they were exceptionally regular and clean-cut, as if chiselled with delicate, light strokes, and showed the remains of remarkable good looks. His brilliant, dark, elongated eyes were particularly fine. Arkady's uncle's whole way of holding himself displayed elegance and breeding; he had kept a young man's grace and that upright carriage, standing very straight, which usually disappears after thirty.

Pavel Petrovich took his shapely hand, with its long pink polished nails, out of his trouser pocket – a hand whose looks were set off by the snowy whiteness of a cuff fastened by a link set with a single big opal – and offered it to his nephew. Having first given him a European *'shake hands'*[2] he then kissed him three times in the Russian way, that is, he three times brushed Arkady's cheek with his scented moustache and said, 'Welcome.'

Nikolay Petrovich introduced his brother to Bazarov. Pavel Petrovich gave a slight inclination of his graceful torso and a half smile, but he didn't offer his hand and even put it back in his pocket.

'I was beginning to think you wouldn't come today,' he began in a pleasant voice, amiably rocking back and forth, shifting his shoulders and displaying fine white teeth. 'Did something happen on the way?'

'Nothing happened,' answered Arkady, 'we just got held up a bit. But we're now hungry as wolves. Papa, make Prokofyich hurry up, and I'll be right back.'

'Wait, I'll come with you,' exclaimed Bazarov, suddenly getting up from the sofa. Both young men went out.

'Who is that person?' asked Pavel Petrovich.

'A friend of Arkasha's; he says he's a very clever man.'

'Is he going to be staying with us?'

'Yes.'

'That hairy creature?'

'Well yes.'

Pavel Petrovich drummed his nails on the table.

'I find Arkady *s'est dégourdi*,'[3] he commented. 'I'm glad he's back.'

There wasn't much conversation during supper. Bazarov in particular said almost nothing but ate a great deal. Nikolay Petrovich told various stories out of what he called his 'farmer's life' and talked of forthcoming government initiatives, of committees and delegates, of the need to introduce machinery and so forth. Pavel Petrovich slowly paced up and down the dining room – he never ate supper – occasionally sipping from a glass filled with red wine and even more occasionally making remarks or rather exclamations like 'ah!', 'eh!', 'hm!' Arkady gave them some Petersburg news but he felt a slight awkwardness, the awkwardness which tends to come over a young man who has just left boyhood and come back to a place where people have

been used to seeing and thinking of him as a boy. He talked at
too great length, he avoided the word 'Papa' and even once said
'Father' instead, even if in a very low voice. With too liberal a
hand he poured much more wine in his glass than he wanted
and drank it all. Prokofyich didn't take his eyes from him and
just chewed his lips. After supper they all went to their rooms.

'Your uncle's a strange creature,' said Bazarov to Arkady,
sitting by his bed and sucking on a small pipe. 'Such exquisite
clothes out here in the sticks, imagine! And his nails – you could
send them to an exhibition!'

'But there's something you don't know,' Arkady answered.
'He was a real social lion in his day. Some time I'll tell you his
story. He was extremely good-looking and turned women's
heads.'

'So that's why! It's all for old times' sake. It's a pity there are
no hearts to conquer here. I kept looking at him. His astonish-
ing collar, like a piece of sculpture, and that beautifully shaven
chin. Arkady Nikolaich, isn't he ridiculous?'

'I suppose he is. But, you know, he's a good man.'

'An archaic phenomenon! But your father's a decent fellow.
His quoting poetry isn't up to much and he doesn't understand
a great deal about estate management but he's a good sort.'

'My father's pure gold.'

'Have you noticed how shy he is?'

Arkady shook his head, as if he weren't shy himself.

'These antique romantics are amazing,' Bazarov went on,
'they work up their nerves till they get irritable . . . then their
equilibrium's all gone. Anyway, goodnight! My room has an
English wash-stand but the door won't shut. Still we must be
encouraging . . . English wash-stands are progress!'

Bazarov went out, and Arkady was overcome by a feeling of
happiness. It was so good to sleep in his own home, in a familiar bed, under a blanket worked by beloved hands, maybe his
nanny's, tender, kind, untiring hands. Arkady thought of
Yegorovna and gave a sigh and said a prayer for her to enter the
kingdom of heaven . . . He didn't pray for himself.

Both he and Bazarov were soon asleep, but others in the
house were awake for a long time. Nikolay Petrovich was dis-

turbed by his son's return. He got into bed but didn't put out the candle and, leaning his head on his hand, he was lost in his thoughts. His brother sat up well after midnight in his study in his Gambs[4] easy chair, before the feebly burning coals of a fire. Pavel Petrovich didn't undress, only replaced his patent leather boots with backless red Chinese slippers. He held the latest issue of *Galignani*[5] but he didn't read. He gazed fixedly into the fire, where a bluish flame trembled, dying down, then flaring up . . . God knows where his thoughts wandered but they weren't only in the past. His expression was set and grim, not like that of a man just thinking of his memories.

And in a small back room a young woman sat on a big trunk, wearing a blue jacket with a white kerchief covering her dark hair. Fenechka listened and dozed and watched the open door, through which she could see a cot and hear the regular breathing of a sleeping baby.

V

Next morning Bazarov was the first to wake and went out of the house. 'Oh ho!' he thought, looking around him. 'This place isn't much to look at.' When Nikolay Petrovich had settled boundaries[1] with his peasants, he had to make his new house and grounds out of ten acres of completely flat, bare land. He built a house, service buildings and farmhouse, laid out a garden, dug a lake and two wells; but the young trees didn't take well, the lake held little water and the wells had a brackish taste. Only an arbour of lilac and acacia thrived, where they sometimes had tea or dinner. In a few minutes Bazarov had been round all the paths of the garden, visited cattle yard and stable and come across two farm boys with whom he quickly made friends. He went off frog-hunting with them to a small swamp half a mile or so from the house.

'What d'you need the frogs for, sir?' one of the boys asked him.

'This is why,' Bazarov answered him. He had a special ability to inspire in himself the trust of the humblest people, although he never pandered to them and was quite offhand with them. 'I cut up a frog and have a look at what's going on inside it, and as you and I are just like frogs, except that we walk on two legs, I'll then know what goes on inside us.'

'Why d'you want to?'

'So as not to make a mistake if you become ill and I have to look after you.'

'Are you are a *dokhtoor* then?'

'Yes.'

'Vaska, do you hear that, the gentleman says you and me are just like frogs. That's funny!'

'I'm scared of frogs,' commented Vaska, a boy of about seven with hair white as flax, barefoot and wearing a grey smock with a standing-up collar.

'What's there to be scared of? They don't bite.'

'Come on, philosophers, get in the water,' said Bazarov.

Meanwhile Nikolay Petrovich too had woken and went in to Arkady, whom he found dressed. Father and son went out on to the terrace covered by an awning. The samovar was already going, set on a table by the balustrade, between big bouquets of lilac. A small girl appeared, the same one who had been the first to greet the arrivals on the porch, and announced in a little voice:

'Fedosya Nikolayevna isn't feeling very well and can't come to the table. She's told me to ask you, will you pour the tea yourselves or shall she send Dunyasha?'

'I'll do it, I'll pour myself,' Nikolay Petrovich said hurriedly. 'Arkady, how do you take your tea, with cream or with lemon?'

'With cream,' Arkady replied and after a short silence said in an inquiring tone, 'Papa?'

Nikolay Petrovich looked embarrassedly at his son.

'What is it?' he said.

Arkady lowered his eyes.

'Papa,' he began, 'I'm sorry if you find my question out of place, but with your own frankness yesterday you yourself prompt me to be frank . . . you're not cross? . . .'

'Go on.'

'You give me the courage to ask you . . . Isn't Fen . . . isn't my being here the reason for her not coming to pour the tea?'

Nikolay Petrovich turned away a little.

'Maybe,' he said eventually, 'she supposes . . . she feels ashamed . . .'

Arkady quickly looked at his father.

'She's wrong to feel ashamed. Firstly, you know my way of thinking,' (it gave Arkady great pleasure to utter these words) 'and secondly, why would I want to constrain your life and habits one jot? Furthermore, I am certain you couldn't make a bad choice. If you've let her live with you under one roof, she must deserve it. Anyway, a son doesn't sit in judgement on his father, particularly a father like you who has never constrained my freedom in any way.'

At first Arkady's voice had trembled: he felt himself being magnanimous, yet at the same time he realized he was more or less giving his father a lecture. But a man is strongly affected by the sound of his own speeches, and Arkady spoke these words firmly, even dramatically.

'Thank you, Arkasha,' said Nikolay Petrovich in an indistinct voice, and his fingers again went to his eyebrows and forehead. 'Your assumptions are quite correct. Of course if the girl didn't deserve . . . It's not a passing fancy. I feel awkward talking to you about it. But you understand that it was difficult for her to come in when you're here, especially on the first day of your visit.'

'In that case I'll go and see her myself,' exclaimed Arkady with a new onrush of generous feelings and jumped up from his chair. 'I'll explain to her that she has no reason to be ashamed in front of me.'

Nikolay Petrovich also got up.

'Arkady,' he began, 'please . . . how can you . . . there . . . I didn't warn you . . .'

But Arkady no longer heard him and ran from the terrace. Nikolay Petrovich looked after him and sank into his chair embarrassed. His heart began to beat faster . . . Did he see at that moment the inevitable strangeness of future relations between him and his son, did he recognize that his son might have shown him more respect if he had completely avoided the subject, did he blame himself for being weak – it's difficult to say. He had all these feelings – but they were just sensations, and muddled ones. He continued to blush, and his heart was beating.

There was the sound of hurried steps, and Arkady came on to the terrace.

'We've introduced ourselves, Father!' he exclaimed with an expression on his face of affectionate and good-natured triumph. 'Fedosya Nikolayevna is really not feeling very well, and she'll come a little later. But why didn't you tell me I have a brother? Yesterday I would have covered him with kisses as I did just now.'

Nikolay Petrovich wanted to say something, he wanted to get up and open his arms and hug Arkady . . . Arkady flung his arms round his neck.

'What's this? Embracing again?' Pavel Petrovich's voice came from behind them.

Father and son were both equally pleased at his appearing at that moment. There are emotional situations which one wants to escape as quickly as possible.

'Why are you surprised?' Nikolay Petrovich said merrily. 'I've been waiting for Arkasha for such an age . . . I haven't yet looked enough at him since yesterday.'

'I'm not surprised at all,' said Pavel Petrovich, 'I'm not even against embracing him myself.'

Arkady went to his uncle and again felt on his cheeks the brush of his scented moustache. Pavel Petrovich sat down at the table. He was wearing an elegant morning suit, in the English taste; his head was decked with a little fez. The fez and his carelessly knotted necktie alluded to the freedom of country life, but the tight collar of his shirt – not a white one, it's true, but multicoloured, as befits a morning toilette – held in his well-shaven chin, relentless as ever.

'Where's your new friend?' he asked Arkady.

'He's not in the house. He usually gets up early and goes off somewhere. The main thing is, you mustn't pay him any attention: he doesn't like ceremony.'

'Yes, one can see that.' Pavel Petrovich began unhurriedly to spread butter on his bread. 'Will he be staying with us long?'

'It depends. He's stopped here on his way to his father's.'

'And where does his father live?'

'In our province, fifty miles from here. He has a little estate there. He used to be a regimental doctor.'

'Yes, yes, yes . . . I've been wondering, where have I heard that name, Bazarov? . . . Nikolay, do you remember, wasn't there a Doctor Bazarov in Papa's army division?

'I think there was.'

'Precisely. So that doctor is his father. Hm!' Pavel Petrovich twitched his moustache. 'Well, and what exactly is Mr Bazarov?' he asked in a deliberate tone.

'What is Bazarov?' Arkady grinned. 'Uncle dear, do you want me to tell you what he really is?'

'Please, dear nephew.'

'He's a nihilist.'

'What?' asked Nikolay Petrovich while Pavel Petrovich raised his knife with a bit of butter on the end of the blade and didn't move.

'He's a nihilist,' repeated Arkady.

'A nihilist,' pronounced Nikolay Petrovich. 'That comes from the Latin *nihil*, nothing, in so far as I can make out. So the word must mean a man who . . . who acknowledges nothing, mustn't it?'

'Say rather, a man who respects nothing,' interrupted Pavel Petrovich and returned to the butter.

'Who approaches everything from a critical point of view,' commented Arkady.

'But isn't that just the same?' asked Pavel Petrovich.

'No, it isn't just the same. The nihilist is a man who bows down to no authority, who takes no single principle on trust, however much respect be attached to that principle.'

'And so, is that a good thing?' interrupted Pavel Petrovich.

'It depends from whose point of view, Uncle. For some it's good, for others very bad.'

'Really. Well, I can see it's not for us. We, the older generation, think that without principles,' (Pavel Petrovich pronounced the

word *princípes*, in the soft French way, while Arkady on the
contrary pronounced it 'príntsiple', stressing the first syllable)
'without *principes*, taken on trust, as you say, we can't move one
step forward or breathe. *Vous avez changé tout cela*,[2] God grant
you good health and a general's rank,[3] and we will just gaze at
you, gentlemen . . . what do you call yourselves?'

'Nihilists,' Arkady said very clearly.

'Yes. Once there were Hegelists[4] and now there are nihilists.
We'll see how you'll manage to exist in a void, in space without
air. And now, brother Nikolay Petrovich, please ring, it's time
for me to have my cocoa.'

Nikolay Petrovich rang and called 'Dunyasha!' But instead
of Dunyasha Fenechka herself came out on the terrace. She was
a young woman of about twenty-three, all white and soft, with
dark hair and dark eyes, with red, full lips like a child's and
delicate hands. She wore a neat cotton printed dress and a new
pale blue scarf lay on her rounded shoulders. She carried a big
cup of cocoa and as she put it in front of Pavel Petrovich, she
was overcome with confusion; a hot red flush came up underneath the tender skin of her pretty face. She lowered her eyes
and stopped at the table, just leaning on the very tips of her
fingers. It was as if she was ashamed of having come but also as
if she felt she had the right to come.

Pavel Petrovich frowned sternly, and Nikolay Petrovich was
embarrassed.

'Good morning, Fenechka,' he muttered.

'Good morning,' she answered in a low but audible voice
and with a sideways look at Arkady, who gave her a friendly
smile, she quietly left. She swayed a little as she walked, but it
suited her.

Silence reigned on the terrace for a few minutes. Pavel Petrovich sipped his cocoa and suddenly raised his head.

'Here's Mr Nihilist coming to join us,' he said in an under-
tone.

Indeed Bazarov was coming through the garden, stepping
over the flowerbeds. His canvas coat and trousers were spat-
tered with mud. There was a clinging marsh plant round the
crown of his old round hat. In his right hand he held a small

bag, and in the bag something live was moving. He quickly came up to the terrace and said with a nod of his head:

'Good morning, gentlemen. I'm sorry I'm late for tea, I'll be back in a minute. I've got to find a place for my prisoners.'

'What have you got there, leeches?' asked Pavel Petrovich.

'No, frogs.'

'Do you eat them or breed them?'

'They're for experiments,' Bazarov said calmly and went into the house.

'He's going to dissect them,' commented Pavel Petrovich. 'He doesn't believe in principles but he does believe in frogs.'

Arkady gave his uncle a pitying look, and Nikolay Petrovich furtively shrugged a shoulder. Pavel Petrovich himself sensed his joke had fallen flat and began to talk of farming and the new bailiff who had come to him the day before to complain of Foma, one of the workmen, for his 'deboshery' and impossible behaviour. 'He's such an old Aesop,'[5] he'd said among other things, 'going around everywhere proclaiming his wickedness. He'll live a fool and die a fool.'

VI

Bazarov came back, sat down at the table and quickly began to drink his tea. Both brothers watched him in silence while Arkady stealthily glanced at his father and his uncle.

'Did you walk a long way from here?' Nikolay Petrovich eventually asked.

'You've got a little swamp here, by the aspen copse. I put up five or six snipe there. You can go and kill them, Arkady.'

'Don't you shoot?'

'No.'

'Are you actually studying physics?' asked Pavel Petrovich in his turn.

'Yes, physics. And the natural sciences in general.'

'People say the Teutons have recently had a lot of success in that field.'

'Yes, the Germans are our teachers there,' Bazarov said casually.

Pavel Petrovich used the word Teutons instead of Germans ironically, but nobody noticed.

'Do you have such a high opinion of the Germans?' Pavel Petrovich said with extreme politeness. He was beginning to feel a secret irritation. His aristocratic nature was offended by Bazarov's complete relaxedness. This doctor's son not only displayed no shyness, he even answered curtly and unwillingly, and there was something coarse, almost impertinent, in the tone of his voice.

'The scientists over there are a clever lot.'

'Really, really. Well, you probably don't have such a favourable opinion of Russian scientists, do you?'

'I suppose not.'

'That is very laudable self-denial,' said Pavel Petrovich, straightening his posture and putting his head back. 'But how is it that Arkady Nikolaich was telling us just now that you don't recognize any authorities? Don't you believe in them?'

'Why should I start recognizing them? And what should I believe in? If people talk sense to me, I agree with them, that's all there is to it.'

'And do Germans always talk sense?' said Pavel Petrovich, and his face took on a detached and distant expression as if he had gone off to some empyrean height.

'Not all of them,' said Bazarov with a small yawn; he clearly did not want to continue the conversation.

Pavel Petrovich gave Arkady a look, as if wanting to say to him: 'Your friend's polite, you must admit.'

'As far as I'm concerned,' he began again, not without some effort, 'I for my sins am not too keen on the Germans. I'm not talking now of the Russian Germans: we know what kind of beast they are. But I don't care for the German Germans. In the past they weren't so bad; they then had – well, Schiller, or Goethe . . . My brother here is particularly fond of him . . . But they're now nothing but chemists and materialists . . .'

'A decent chemist is worth twenty times any poet,' interrupted Bazarov.

'Really,' said Pavel Petrovich and slightly raised his eyebrows as if he felt sleepy. 'So you don't acknowledge art?'

'The art of making money or getting rid of piles?' exclaimed Bazarov with a scornful smile.

'Well, well. That's your little joke. So you must reject everything? Let's assume that. That means, you only believe in science?'

'I've already told you I don't believe in anything. And what is science – science in general? There are sciences, as there are trades and professions; but science in general terms doesn't exist at all.'

'Very good. And do you have such a negative attitude to the other rules accepted in human society?'

'What is this, a cross-examination?' asked Bazarov.

Pavel Petrovich went slightly pale . . . Nikolay Petrovich thought he should enter the conversation.

'One day we'll talk to you about this in a bit more detail, dear Yevgeny Vasilyich. We'll learn what you think and tell you what we think. For my part I'm very pleased you're studying the natural sciences. I've heard Liebig[1] has made amazing discoveries about the fertilizing of fields. You can help me in my agricultural work: you can give me some useful advice.'

'I'm at your service, Nikolay Petrovich. But we've a long way to get to Liebig! We need first to learn the alphabet and then tackle a book. But we haven't yet got to A.'

'Yes, I see you really are a nihilist,' thought Nikolay Petrovich. 'All the same, do let me come to you if I need to,' he added aloud. 'But now, Brother, I think it's time for us to go and talk to the bailiff.'

Pavel Petrovich got up from his chair.

'Yes,' he said, not looking at anyone, 'it's a pity to have been living like this for five years in the country, far away from great minds! You just become an utter fool. You try not to forget what you've been taught, and then – whoosh! – it turns out that it's all nonsense and you're told that sensible people don't bother any more with such rubbish and that you're just a backward idiot. What can one do! The young are clearly cleverer than we are.'

Pavel Petrovich slowly turned on his heels and slowly went away. Nikolay Petrovich went off after him.

'Is he always like that?' Bazarov coolly asked Arkady as soon as the door had closed behind the two brothers.

'Look, Yevgeny, you really were too rough with him,' said Arkady. 'You insulted him.'

'So, why should I indulge these provincial aristocrats! It's all just vanity, dandyism, the little ways of a society lion. Well, he should have continued his service career in Petersburg, if that's what he wanted . . . Anyway, let's not bother with him! Do you know, I've discovered a quite rare specimen of water beetle, *Dytiscus marginatus*. I'll show it to you.'

'I promised I'd tell you his story,' Arkady began.

'The story of the beetle?'

'Stop it, Yevgeny. My uncle's story. You'll see he's not the man you think him. He deserves sympathy rather than ridicule.'

'I'm sure he does. But why are you going on about him?'

'One ought to be fair, Yevgeny.'

'How does that follow?'

'No, listen . . .'

And Arkady told him his uncle's story. The reader will find it in the next chapter.

VII

Pavel Petrovich Kirsanov was educated first at home, like his younger brother Nikolay, then at the Corps des Pages.[1] Since childhood he had been exceptionally good-looking; furthermore he had self-confidence, and a slightly mocking and sardonic wit – he couldn't fail to please. He began to be seen everywhere as soon as he was commissioned an officer. He was made a fuss of and he indulged himself, he even played the fool and put on airs; but that too suited him. Women went mad over him, men called him a fop and secretly envied him. As has been said, he shared an apartment with his brother, whom he loved sincerely, although they were quite different. Nikolay Petrovich had a slight limp, small features, attractive but slightly sad, small, black eyes and soft, fine hair. He was happy doing nothing but he was also happy reading, and he was frightened of society. Pavel Petrovich never spent an evening at home, he was known for his courage and agility (he started to create a vogue for gymnastics among young men of fashion) and had read only five or six French books. At the age of twenty-eight he was already a captain. A glittering career awaited him. Suddenly everything changed.

At that time there occasionally used to appear in Petersburg society a woman who is remembered to this day, Princess R. She had a husband, well educated and respectable if a bit of a fool; they had no children. She would suddenly go off abroad and as suddenly come back to Russia; she generally led an odd life. She had the reputation of being a giddy flirt, gave herself enthusiastically to all kinds of pleasures, danced till she dropped, laughed and joked with the young men to whom she was at home before dinner in the dim light of her drawing room. But at night she would weep and pray – she could find no peace anywhere and often used to walk up and down her room till morning, wringing her hands in misery, or she would sit, all pale and chilled, over her prayer book. Day broke, and again she was transformed into the society lady, again she would go out, laugh, chatter and virtually throw herself at anything that could afford her the slightest distraction. Her body was amazing; her plait of hair, golden in colour and heavy as gold, fell below her knees; but no one would call her a beauty; her face's only good feature was her eyes, and not really her actual eyes – which were small and grey – but their gaze, swift and deep, carefree to foolhardiness and pensive to desperation, their enigmatic gaze. Something unusual shone there even when her tongue was babbling the most vacuous of speeches. She dressed exquisitely.

Pavel Petrovich met her at a ball, danced with her the whole mazurka, during which she uttered not a single word of sense, and fell passionately in love with her. Accustomed to conquests, here too he quickly achieved his goal; but the ease of his triumph did not cool his ardour. On the contrary: he became ever more painfully, ever more strongly attracted to this woman, who, even at the moment when she irrevocably surrendered herself, kept secret and inaccessible a place where none could penetrate. What lay enshrined in that soul – God knows! She seemed at the mercy of some secret powers, powers she herself was unaware of; they played with her as they chose; her small mind could not cope with their whims. Her whole behaviour displayed a series of contradictions; the only letters which could have aroused her husband's justifiable suspicion she wrote to a man who was practically a stranger, and her love showed itself as melancholy; she didn't really laugh and joke with the man she had chosen, whom she would listen to and watch with bewilderment. Sometimes, usually quite suddenly, that bewilderment became cold terror; her face assumed a deathly, wild expression; she would lock herself in her bedroom, and her maid, putting her ear to the keyhole, could hear her muffled sobs. Several times, returning home after a lovers' meeting, Kirsanov felt in his heart that shattering and bitter disappointment that rises in the heart after a decisive failure. 'What more do I want?' he asked himself, but his heart went on aching. Once he gave her a ring with a sphinx engraved on its stone.

'What is it?' she asked. 'A sphinx?'

'Yes,' he answered, 'and that sphinx is you.'

'Is it really me?' she asked and slowly raised her enigmatic gaze towards him. 'Do you know, that's very flattering?' she added with a slight smile, but her eyes still had that strange look.

It was painful for Pavel Petrovich even while Princess R. loved him; but when she became indifferent to him, and that happened quite soon, he nearly went mad. He was racked with jealousy; he gave her no peace and trailed everywhere after her; his persistent pursuit of her got on her nerves and she went abroad. He resigned his commission, in spite of the pleas of his friends and the exhortations of his superiors, and went off after the princess. He spent four years in foreign climes, sometimes pursuing her, sometimes deliberately losing sight of her. He was ashamed of himself, he was angry at his cowardice . . . but nothing helped. Her image, that mysterious, almost meaningless but spell-binding image, had entered too deep into his soul.

Once in Baden[2] they renewed their former relationship; it seemed she had never loved him so passionately . . . but in a month it was all over: the flame flared up for the last time and was extinguished for ever. Foreseeing the inevitable parting, he wanted at least to remain friends with her, as if friendship with such a woman was possible . . . She quietly left Baden and thenceforth consistently avoided Kirsanov. He returned to Russia and tried to live the life he had before, but he couldn't settle into his old routine. Like a man with poison in him, he roamed from place to place; he still went out, he kept all the habits of a man of the world; he could boast of two or three new conquests; but he no longer expected anything very much either of himself or of others, and he undertook nothing new. He aged and went grey; evenings in his club, a sardonic ennui, dispassionate arguments in male society became necessities for him – a bad sign, as we know. Of course he didn't even consider marriage. He spent ten years in this way, sterile, dull years which went by quickly, terrifyingly quickly. Nowhere does time fly as in Russia; they say, it goes quicker in prison. One day at dinner in his club Pavel Petrovich learnt of the death of Princess R. She had died in Paris in a state very close to insanity. He got up from the table and for a long time walked through the rooms of the club, standing by the card players as if rooted to the ground, but he didn't go back home any earlier than usual. In a short while he received a parcel addressed to him; it contained the ring he had given the princess. She had drawn a cross on the sphinx and sent him a message that the cross was the solution to the riddle.

This happened in 1848, at the very time when Nikolay Petrovich, having lost his wife, was coming to St Petersburg. Pavel Petrovich had hardly seen his brother since he'd been living in the country: Nikolay Petrovich's marriage coincided with the very first days of Pavel Petrovich's relationship with the princess. When he came back from abroad, Pavel Petrovich went to his brother's with the intention of staying with him a couple of months, to enjoy his happiness, but he only lasted a week with him. The difference in the two brothers' situation was too great. In 1848 this difference became less: Nikolay Petrovich had lost his wife, Pavel Petrovich had lost his memories; after the princess's death he tried not to think of her. But Nikolay had the consciousness of a well-spent life, he could watch his son growing up. Pavel on the other hand was a lonely bachelor and was coming to that troubled twilight time, a time of regrets that resemble hopes, of hopes that resemble regrets, when youth is past but old age has not yet come.

This time was even more difficult for Pavel Petrovich than for others: in losing his past, he had lost everything.

'I am not asking you now to Marino,' Nikolay Petrovich once said to him (he had called his property by that name in honour of his wife),[3] 'even when my wife was alive you were bored there, and now I think you'd die there of boredom.'

'I was still foolish then, and restless,' answered Pavel Petrovich, 'I've settled down since then even if I haven't grown wiser. But now, if you'll let me, I'm ready to come and live with you for good.'

Instead of answering, Nikolay Petrovich embraced him; but more than six months went by after this conversation before Pavel Petrovich decided to make good his intention. However, once having settled in the country, he didn't again leave it, not even in those three winters which Nikolay Petrovich spent in Petersburg with his son. He began to read, mostly in English; generally speaking, he organized his whole life in the English manner; he saw little of the neighbours and only went out to attend the elections, during which he usually said nothing, just occasionally scaring landowners of the old sort with his liberal sallies, without getting closer to the representatives of the new generation. Both parties found him arrogant; and both respected him for his fine aristocratic manners and for his rumoured conquests; they respected him because he dressed beautifully and always stayed in the best room of the best hotel; because he generally dined well and had even once dined with Wellington at the table of King Louis-Philippe;[4] because he always travelled with a sterling silver dressing-case and a portable campaign bath; because he always smelt of an unusual, strikingly 'noble' scent; because he played a masterly game of whist and always lost; finally they respected him too for his irreproachable honesty. The ladies found him a charming melancholic, but he had nothing to do with the ladies . . .

'So you see, Yevgeny,' said Arkady, finishing his story, 'your view of my uncle is quite unfair! I'm not mentioning that he has several times got my father out of difficulties and given him all his money – perhaps you don't know, their estate isn't divided[5] – but he is ready to help anyone, and by the way he always speaks up for the peasants; it's true, when he talks to them he wrinkles his nose and sniffs eau-de-cologne . . .'

'It's quite obvious: a case of nerves,' Bazarov interrupted.

'Maybe, only he has a very kind heart. And he's far from stupid. He has given me really useful advice . . . especially . . . especially about relationships with women.'

'Aha! He's burnt himself on hot milk and now blows on other people's water. An old story.'

'Well, in a word,' Arkady went on, 'he is deeply unhappy, believe me; it's wrong to despise him.'

'Who is despising him?' Bazarov countered. 'But I'll still say that an individual who has staked his whole life on the card of a woman's love, who, when he's lost that card, collapses and lets himself go so he's no good for anything, isn't a man, isn't a male. You say he's unhappy: you know best; but all the nonsense hasn't been knocked out of him. I am certain he seriously imagines himself to be an intelligent man because he reads old Galignani[6] and once a month gets a peasant off a flogging.'

'And remember his education, and the period when he lived,' Arkady commented.

'His education?' Bazarov continued. 'Every man should educate himself – like me, for example . . . And the period – why should I depend on a period? It can depend on me. No, my friend, it's nothing but decadence and frivolity! And what of those mysterious relations between man and woman? We physiologists know all about those relations. Just go and study the anatomy of the eye: where does that enigmatic gaze you're talking about come from? It's all romanticism, nonsense, decay, artist's trickery. Better come and look at a beetle.'

And the two friends went off to Bazarov's room, which had

already developed a kind of surgical smell, mixed with that of
cheap tobacco.

VIII

Pavel Petrovich didn't stay very long during his brother's conversation with the bailiff. The bailiff, a tall, thin man with a
saccharine, feeble voice and dishonest eyes, answered all
Nikolay Petrovich's remarks with 'Most certainly, sir, that's no
news to me, sir,' and tried to cast the peasants as drunkards and
thieves. The estate, which had recently been put on the new
basis, squeaked liked a wheel that hadn't been oiled, cracked
like home-made furniture made of unseasoned wood. Nikolay
Petrovich didn't lose heart but quite often would sigh and get
abstracted in thought: he felt that things wouldn't work without money, but he had almost run out of funds. Arkady had
been telling the truth: Pavel Petrovich had more than once
helped his brother; more than once, seeing how he was strug-
gling and racking his brain for a way out, Pavel Petrovich
slowly went up to a window and, putting his hands in his pockets, muttered through his teeth: '*Mais je puis te donner de
l'argent*'[1] – and gave money to him; but on this particular day
he himself didn't have any and he thought it better to remove
himself. Domestic unpleasantness made him feel depressed; he
also very often thought that Nikolay Petrovich, for all his keenness and diligence, didn't have the right approach to things,
though he couldn't have pointed out where Nikolay Petrovich
was making mistakes. 'My brother isn't practical enough,' he
used to say to himself, 'people cheat him.' On the other hand
Nikolay Petrovich had a high opinion of Pavel Petrovich's practical sense and always asked his advice. 'I am soft and weak,
I've lived all my life in the sticks,' he used to say, 'but you've
lived a lot among people, and it shows, you know them well:
you have an eagle's gaze.' In response to these words Pavel
Petrovich only turned away, but he didn't disabuse his brother.
  He left Nikolay Petrovich in his study and walked along the

corridor which divided the front part of the house from the back. When he got to a low door he hesitated and stopped, tugged his moustache and knocked.

'Who is that? Come in.' It was Fenechka's voice.

'It's me,' said Pavel Petrovich and opened the door.

Fenechka jumped quickly off the chair on which she had been sitting with the baby and, handing him to a girl, who at once carried him out of the room, she hastily adjusted her kerchief.

'I'm sorry if I disturbed you,' Pavel Petrovich began, not looking at her. 'I just wanted to ask you . . . I think they're sending to town today . . . Could you ask them to buy me some green tea?'

'Of course,' answered Fenechka. 'How much do you want?'

'I suppose half a pound will be enough. But I see you've had changes here,' he added, with a quick look round the room, which also took in Fenechka's face. 'These curtains,' he said, seeing she didn't understand him.

'Yes, the curtains. Nikolay Petrovich gave them to us. They've been up a while.'

'But it's a long time since I've been in your room. It's very nice here now.'

'Thanks to Nikolay Petrovich,' Fenechka whispered.

'Are you more comfortable here than in the wing where you were?' asked Pavel Petrovich politely, but without a trace of a smile.

'Of course we're more comfortable.'

'Who's been put there now instead of you?'

'The laundrywomen are there now.'

'Ah!'

Pavel Petrovich fell silent. 'Now he'll go away,' thought Fenechka, but he didn't, and she stood stock-still in front of him, slightly moving her fingers.

'Why did you have your little boy taken out?' Pavel Petrovich said eventually. 'I love children. Do show him to me.'

Fenechka blushed with embarrassment and pleasure. She was frightened of Pavel Petrovich: he hardly ever spoke to her.

'Dunyasha,' she called, 'please bring Mitya in.' (Fenechka

used the polite form of address[2] to everyone in the house.) 'But no, wait. We must put some clothes on him.'

Fenechka moved to the door.

'It doesn't matter,' said Pavel Petrovich.

'It won't take me a minute,' answered Fenechka and rushed out.

Pavel Petrovich was alone and this time he looked round with particular attention. The small, low-ceilinged room in which he was standing was very clean and comfortable. It smelt of new varnish on the floor, of camomile and lemon balm. Chairs with lyre-shaped backs stood along the walls; they had been bought by the late general in Poland, during the campaign against Napoleon. In one corner rose a bed under a muslin curtain, next to an iron-bound trunk with a domed lid. In the opposite corner a lamp was burning in front of a big dark icon of St Nicholas the Thaumaturge;[3] a tiny china egg hung on the saint's breast, attached to his halo by a red ribbon. On the window-sills stood glass jars of last year's jam, green and translucent, and carefully sealed; Fenechka herself had written 'goozberry' in big letters on their paper covers; it was Nikolay Petrovich's favourite jam. A cage with a short-tailed siskin hung from the ceiling; the bird never stopped hopping and twittering, and the cage never stopped shaking and trembling; seeds of hemp pattered on the floor. Between the windows, above a small chest of drawers, hung some rather poor photographic portraits of Nikolay Petrovich in various poses, taken by an itinerant photographer; there too hung a photograph of Fenechka herself, which was extremely unsuccessful: a face with no eyes giving a strained smile in a dark frame – that was all one could make out. Above Fenechka, Yermolov[4] in a Circassian cloak was frowning menacingly at the distant mountains of the Caucasus, glaring from under a silk pin-holder that had slipped right down his forehead.

Five minutes went by. There was rustling and whispering from the next room. Pavel Petrovich picked up a well-thumbed book from the chest of drawers, an odd volume of Masalsky's *Streltsy*,[5] and turned over a few pages . . . The door opened, and Fenechka came in with Mitya in her arms. She had put on him a little red shirt with braid on the collar, had brushed his hair and wiped his face. He was breathing noisily, jerking his whole body about and moving his little hands to and fro as all healthy babies do. But his smart shirt clearly had had an effect on him: his whole plump little face radiated pleasure. Fenechka had tidied her own hair and put on a better kerchief, but she could have stayed as she was. And indeed is there anything in the world more delightful than a beautiful young mother with a healthy baby in her arms?

'Big boy,' Pavel Petrovich said condescendingly and tickled Mitya's double chin with the tip of the long nail of his index finger; the baby stared at the bird and laughed.

'That's Uncle,' said Fenechka, bending her head towards him and rocking him a little while Dunyasha surreptitiously put a lit scented candle on the window-sill and stood it on a coin.

'How old is he, then?' asked Pavel Petrovich.

'Six months. Seven very soon, on the eleventh.'

'Won't it be eight, Fedosya Nikolayevna?' Dunyasha shyly ventured.

'No, of course it's seven!' The baby laughed again, stared at the trunk and suddenly grabbed at his mother's nose and lips with his whole hand. 'Naughty boy,' said Fenechka, without moving her face away from his grasp.

'He looks like my brother,' Pavel Petrovich observed.

'Who else could he look like?' thought Fenechka.

'Yes,' Pavel Petrovich went on as if talking to himself, 'a definite likeness.' He looked at Fenechka attentively, almost sadly.

'That's Uncle,' she repeated, now in a whisper.

'Ah! Pavel! That's where you are!' There suddenly came the voice of Nikolay Petrovich.

Pavel Petrovich hastily turned round and frowned; but his brother gave him a look of such joy and gratitude that he could only respond with a smile.

'You've a splendid little chap,' he said and looked at his watch. 'I came in here about my tea . . .'

And resuming his expression of indifference, Pavel Petrovich now left the room.

'Did he come in just like that?' Nikolay Petrovich asked Fenechka.

'Yes, just like that. He knocked and came in.'

'Hm. And has Arkasha been to see you again?'

'No, he hasn't. Nikolay Petrovich, shouldn't I move into the wing?'

'Why should you?'

'I wonder if it wouldn't be better for a while.'

'N . . . no,' Nikolay Petrovich stuttered and rubbed his forehead. 'It's too late . . . Good morning, baby,' he said with sudden animation and he went up to the little boy and kissed him on the cheek. Then he bowed slightly and put his lips to Fenechka's hand, lying white as milk on Mitya's red shirt.

'Nikolay Petrovich! What are you doing?' she murmured and lowered her eyes, then gently raised them again . . . The expression in her eyes was charming as she looked up from under her brows, with a loving, slightly foolish laugh.

Nikolay Petrovich had got to know Fenechka in the following way. Once, three years previously, he had had to spend the night in an inn in a distant district town. He had been pleasantly impressed by the cleanliness of the room he was given and the freshness of the bed linen. 'I wonder if the landlady isn't German,' he had thought. But she turned out to be Russian, a woman of about fifty, neatly dressed, with an attractive, intelligent face and a reserved way of speaking. He started talking to her over tea. He liked her very much. Nikolay Petrovich at that time had just moved into his new home and, not wishing to use serfs, was looking for free servants to hire. The landlady for her part was complaining about how few visitors came to the town and about times being difficult. He offered her the job of housekeeper in his house; she agreed. Her husband had died long ago, leaving her just one daughter, Fenechka. A couple of weeks later Arina Savishna (that was the new housekeeper's name) and her daughter arrived at Marino and were lodged in the wing. Nikolay Petrovich had made a successful choice. No one talked much about Fenechka, who was already seventeen, and she was hardly seen ; she led a quiet, retiring existence, and it was only on Sundays that Nikolay Petrovich noticed her del-

icate profile and white face in a corner of the parish church.
More than a year went by like this.

One morning Arina came into his study and, bowing low,
as she usually did, asked if he could do something to help her
daughter, who had had a spark from the stove in her eye.
Nikolay Petrovich, like all landowners living on their estates,
dabbled in medicine and had even ordered a homoeopathic
medicine chest. He at once told Arina to bring in the patient.
When she learnt the master had summoned her, Fenechka was
very scared but still she followed her mother in. Nikolay
Petrovich took her up to the window and held her head in
both his hands. Having carefully examined her red and
inflamed eye, he prescribed an eyewash, which he made up
himself then and there, and, ripping up his handkerchief, he
showed her how to soak the compress. When he had finished,
Fenechka was about to leave. 'Kiss the master's hand, you
stupid girl,' Arina said to her. Nikolay Petrovich wouldn't
give her his hand and, embarrassed himself, kissed her on the
parting of her bowed head. Fenechka's eye soon mended, but
the impression she had made on Nikolay Petrovich didn't pass
so quickly. He kept seeing that pure, delicate, timidly raised
face. He felt that soft hair under the palms of his hands, saw
those innocent, slightly open lips, showing pearly teeth gleam-
ing moistly in the sun. He started looking closely at her in
church and tried to engage her in conversation. At first she
was shy of him, and one evening, seeing him coming towards
her on a narrow footpath people had trampled through a rye
field, she went and hid in the tall, thick rye, full of wormwood
and cornflowers, so he shouldn't catch sight of her. He could
see her head behind the golden lattice of heads of rye, through
which she looked out like a little wild animal, and he shouted
to her in a friendly voice:

'Good evening, Fenechka! I don't bite.'

'Good evening,' she whispered, staying behind her barrier.

She was gradually becoming used to him, though she was
still shy in his presence, when her mother Arina suddenly died
from cholera. Where was Fenechka to go? She had inherited
her mother's love of order, her good sense and her reserve; but

she was so young, so alone; Nikolay Petrovich himself was so kind and gentle . . . There is no need to finish the story . . .

'So my brother came in to see you?' Nikolay Petrovich asked her. 'He just knocked and came in?'

'Yes.'

'Well, that's good. Let me give Mitya a rock.'

And Nikolay Petrovich began to toss him almost up to the ceiling, to the baby's great pleasure and to the no small anxiety of his mother, who at every toss stretched out her arms towards his bare legs.

But Pavel Petrovich went back to his elegant study, with its walls, papered in a handsome dark grey, displaying weapons hung on a multicoloured Persian rug, with its walnut furniture upholstered in dark-green velveteen, a 'Renaissance' bookcase of old black oak and bronze statuettes on a magnificent writing table, with its fireplace[6] . . . He threw himself on a couch, put his hands behind his head and remained motionless, staring at the ceiling almost in desperation. Did he want to conceal the expression on his face from the very walls, or was there another reason? He got up, opened the heavy curtains at the windows and again threw himself down on the couch.

IX

Bazarov too met Fenechka that same day. He and Arkady were walking in the garden, and he was explaining to him why some young trees hadn't rooted, especially the oaks.

'You ought to be planting more silver poplars here, and firs, and limes, I suppose, and putting in some good topsoil. Now that arbour has taken well,' he added, 'because acacia and lilac are good children, they don't need any care. Look, someone's there.'

Fenechka was sitting in the arbour with Dunyasha and Mitya. Bazarov stopped, and Arkady nodded to Fenechka like an old friend.

'Who's that?' Bazarov asked him as soon as they had gone past. 'She's so pretty!'

'Who do you mean?'

'It's obvious. There's only one pretty one.'

Now without embarrassment Arkady explained to him in a few words who Fenechka was.

'Aha!' said Bazarov. 'Your father knows what's good for him. I like your father, I really do! Good for him. But I should meet her,' he added and walked back to the arbour.

'Yevgeny!' Arkady shouted after him in a fright. 'For God's sake be careful.'

'Don't be so worried,' said Bazarov. 'I've been around, I've lived in cities.'

When he came up to Fenechka he took off his cap.

'May I introduce myself,' he began, bowing politely, 'I'm a friend of Arkady Nikolaich – and a peaceable fellow.'

Fenechka got up from the bench and looked at him silently.

'What a splendid little boy!' Bazarov went on. 'Don't worry, I haven't yet brought bad luck[1] to anyone. Why are his cheeks so red? Is he teething?'

'Yes,' said Fenechka, 'four teeth have come through, and now his gums are swollen again.'

'Show me . . . don't be scared, I'm a doctor.'

Bazarov took the baby in his arms, and to the amazement of both Fenechka and Dunyasha Mitya offered no resistance and wasn't frightened.

'I see, I see . . . It's fine, all's well. He'll have a good mouth of teeth. Tell me if anything happens. And is your own health good?'

'Yes, thank God.'

'Thank God indeed, that's the best thing. And how's yours?'

Dunyasha, a girl who was very prim in the house but full of fun once outside the gates, just answered him with a snort of laughter.

'Excellent. Here's your champion back.'

Fenechka took the baby into her arms.

'He was so quiet with you,' she said in a low voice.

'All children are with me,' answered Bazarov, 'I have a secret.'

'Children know who loves them,' remarked Dunyasha.

'They do,' Fenechka added. 'Now Mitya just won't go into some people's arms.'

'Will he come to me?' asked Arkady who, having stood at a distance for a while, now had come up to the arbour.

He beckoned to Mitya, but Mitya threw back his head and began to cry, to Fenechka's great embarrassment.

'Another time, when he's got used to me,' Arkady said indulgently, and the two friends went off.

'What's her name?' asked Bazarov.

'Fenechka . . . Fedosya,' answered Arkady.

'And her father's? One should know that too.'

'Nikolayevna.'

'*Bene.*[2] I like her for not being too embarrassed. I suppose some people would have criticized her for that. What nonsense! What's there to be embarrassed about? She's a mother – and she's right.'

'She is right,' said Arkady, 'but my father . . .'

'He's right too,' Bazarov interrupted.

'No, I don't find that.'

'You obviously don't like there being another little heir.'

'You ought to be ashamed to think I'd have such thoughts!' Arkady answered angrily. 'I don't find my father wrong from that point of view; I consider he should marry her.'

'Oh-ho!' Bazarov said calmly. 'What nobility of spirit! You still attach some significance to marriage. I didn't expect that from you.'

The friends took several steps in silence.

'I've seen your father's whole set-up,' Bazarov began again. 'The cattle are poor, and the horses in bad shape. The buildings too aren't up to much, and the labourers look complete and utter idlers; and the bailiff is either a fool or a rogue: which – I haven't yet worked out properly.'

'You're being severe today, Yevgeny Vasilyevich.'

'And the good muzhiks will absolutely swindle your father. You know the proverb "The Russian muzhik will have God himself for his breakfast."'

'I'm beginning to agree with my uncle,' said Arkady. 'You have a decidedly poor opinion of Russians.'

'Who cares! The Russian's sole virtue lies in his having a very low opinion of himself. The important thing is that twice two makes four, and everything else is a load of nonsense.'

'And is nature a load of nonsense?' said Arkady, looking pensively into the distance at the many colours of the fields in the mellow and beautiful light of the sun, which was now low in the sky.

'Nature too is nonsense – in your meaning of the word nature. Nature isn't a temple but a workshop, and man is a workman in it.'

At that very moment the lingering notes of a cello came to them. Someone was playing Schubert's *Erwartung*,[3] with feeling if with a hand that lacked practice, and the sweet melody filled the air like the smell of honey.

'What's that?' said Bazarov with surprise.

'It's my father.'

'Your father plays the cello?'

'Yes.'

'How old is your father?'

'Forty-four.'

Bazarov suddenly roared with laughter.

'What are you laughing at?'

'For pity's sake! A man of forty-four, a *pater familias*,[4] living in the province of *** – and he plays the cello.'

Bazarov went on laughing, but Arkady, for all the reverence he bore his master, this time didn't even smile.

X

About two weeks went by. Life at Marino followed its regular pattern: Arkady relaxed, and Bazarov worked. Everyone in the house had become used to him, to his informal manners, to his brusque and laconic way of speaking. Fenechka in particular felt so much at ease with him that one night she had him woken: Mitya had convulsions, and Bazarov came and in his usual way, laughing a bit, yawning a bit, sat in her room for a couple of hours and helped the little boy. Pavel Petrovich on the other hand grew to hate Bazarov with a passion: he thought him arrogant, insolent, cynical, vulgar; he suspected Bazarov had no respect for him, almost despised him – him, Pavel Kirsanov! Nikolay Petrovich was a bit scared of the young 'nihilist' and wondered whether he had a good influence on Arkady; but he found pleasure in listening to him and being present at his physics and chemistry experiments. Bazarov had brought a microscope with him and fiddled about with it for hours. The servants too had become attached to him although he teased them: they still felt he was one of them and not a 'master'. Dunyasha was happy to giggle with him and surreptitiously gave him significant glances as she ran past him like a little quail. Pyotr, an extraordinarily conceited and stupid fellow, always anxiously wrinkling up his forehead, whose entire virtue lay in an obsequious manner, in being able to spell out his words and in frequently brushing his coat – he too smirked and beamed if ever Bazarov paid him any attention. The farm boys ran after the 'dokhtoor' like puppies. Only old Prokofyich didn't like him, serving him his food at table with a gloomy face. He called him a 'horse-knacker' and a 'crook', and said that Bazarov with his side whiskers looked a real pig in a bush. Prokofyich in his own way was just as much an aristocrat as Pavel Petrovich.

Now came the best days in the year – the first days of June. The weather was lovely. It's true there was another threat of cholera in the distance, but the people of the province of *** were already used to its visits. Bazarov would get up very early and go off a mile or two away, not for a walk – he couldn't abide walks without a purpose – but to collect grasses and insects. He sometimes took Arkady with him. On the way back they usually argued, and Arkady was usually the loser although he spoke more than his friend.

Once for some reason they were late back. Nikolay Petrovich went out into the garden to meet them and when he got as far as the arbour he suddenly heard the quick footsteps and voices of the two young men. They were walking on the other side of the arbour and couldn't see him.

'You don't know my father well enough,' said Arkady.

Nikolay Petrovich concealed himself.

'Your father's a good fellow,' said Bazarov, 'but he's a pensioner from another age, he's had his day.'

Nikolay Petrovich listened carefully . . . Arkady made no reply.

'The pensioner' stood motionless for a couple of minutes and went off home.

'The other day I saw he was reading Pushkin,' Bazarov meanwhile went on. 'Do please explain to him that that's no good. He isn't a boy. It's time he gave up that nonsense. And what a thing to be a romantic in this day and age! Give him something sensible to read.'

'Like what?' asked Arkady.

'Well, first, I think, Büchner's *Stoff und Kraft*.'[1]

'I quite agree,' Arkady said approvingly. '*Stoff und Kraft* is popularly written . . .'

'So you and I've become "pensioners",' Nikolay Petrovich said to his brother that day after dinner as they sat in Pavel Petrovich's study. 'We've had our day. In the end maybe Bazarov's right. But I have to say I find one thing painful: I had hoped that Arkady and I would find ourselves getting closer and fonder of each other, but it appears I've got left behind, he's gone off ahead of me, and we can't understand each other.'

'But why has he got ahead? And what sets him so far apart from us?' Pavel Petrovich exclaimed impatiently. 'All this has been knocked into his head by this signor, this nihilist. I loathe the little quack. In my opinion he's just a charlatan. I am sure that for all his frogs he hasn't progressed very far even in physics.'

'No, dear Brother, don't say that. Bazarov is a clever man and knows a lot.'

'And that repellent self-esteem,' Pavel Petrovich interrupted again.

'Yes,' Nikolay Petrovich remarked, 'self-esteem he does have. But it seems one can't do without it. Only this is what I don't understand. I think I do everything to keep up with the times. I've settled my peasants, set up a farm so I am even known as a "red" all over the province. I read, I study, I generally try to be up to the demands made on me by the modern world – and they say I've had my day. So, Brother, I myself am beginning to think I may well have done.'

'Why?'

'This is why. Today I was sitting and reading Pushkin . . . I remember, my eye had been caught by "The Gypsies"[2]. . . Suddenly Arkady came up to me and without a word, with an expression of tender compassion, he gently removed my book, as one does to a child, and put in front of me another book, a German one . . . he smiled and went off, taking Pushkin.'

'Really! What book did he give you?'

'This one.'

And Nikolay Petrovich took out of the back pocket of his coat the ninth edition of Büchner's famous pamphlet.

Pavel Petrovich turned over some pages.

'Hm!' he grunted. 'Arkady Nikolayevich is bothering about your education. So have you tried to read it?'

'I have.'

'And . . .?'

'Either I'm stupid or it's all nonsense. It must be I'm stupid.'

'But you haven't forgotten your German?' Pavel Petrovich asked.

'I understand German.'

Pavel Petrovich again turned over some pages and looked at his brother with a frown. Neither of them said anything.

'Oh, by the way,' Nikolay Petrovich began again, clearly wanting to change the subject of conversation. 'I had a letter from Kolyazin.'

'Matvey Ilyich?'

'Yes. He's come to *** to do an inspection of the province.[3] He's become a bigwig now and writes to me that as a relation he wants to see us and invites us both with Arkady to town.'

'Will you go?' asked Pavel Petrovich.

'No. And will you?'

'I won't either. That's all I need – to traipse thirty miles for a glass of something. Mathieu wants to show off to us in all his glory. To hell with him! He'll get enough provincial flattery and will survive without ours. What's so great about Privy Councillor![4] If I'd gone on in that stupid service career I'd have been a general aide-de-camp by now.[5] And then you and I are pensioners.'

'Yes, dear Brother. I can see it's time to order our coffins and cross our arms over our breast,' Nikolay Petrovich said with a sigh.

'Well, I won't give in so quickly,' his brother muttered. 'That medical person and I will have another set-to, I foresee it.'

The set-to occurred that very evening over tea. Pavel Petrovich had come into the drawing room all ready for the fray, in a decisive and irritable mood. He was just looking for a pretext to attack the enemy; but the pretext was long in coming. Bazarov generally didn't talk much in front of the 'Kirsanov old gentlemen' (as he called the two brothers), and that evening he was feeling out of sorts and drank cup after cup in silence. Pavel Petrovich was all on fire with impatience; at last his desires were fulfilled.

The name of a neighbouring landowner came up. 'Useless creature, aristocratic trash,' calmly commented Bazarov, who had come across him in St Petersburg.

'May I ask you a question?' Pavel Petrovich began, and his lips began to tremble. 'By your way of thinking do the words "useless creature" and "aristocrat" mean one and the same thing?'

'I said "aristocratic trash",' said Bazarov, lazily taking a sip of tea.

'You did indeed. But I assume that you have the same opinion of aristocrats as you have of aristocratic trash. I feel it my duty to inform you that I do not share that opinion. I venture to say that everyone knows me to be a liberal man, a lover of progress; but that is precisely why I respect aristocrats – real aristocrats. Remember, my dear sir,' (at these words Bazarov looked up at Pavel Petrovich) 'remember my dear sir,' he repeated acidly 'the aristocrats of England. They do not give up one iota of their rights, and that is why they respect the rights of others; they demand what is due to them, and that is why

they themselves perform what is due *from them*. The aristocracy gave England freedom and maintains it.'

'We've heard that old story many times,' Bazarov countered,
'but what do you want to demonstrate by that?'

'By *thert*, my dear sir, I want to demonstrate,' (Pavel Petrovich when he got angry deliberately mispronounced *that* in an
affected way although he knew very well that proper usage
didn't admit it. This idiosyncrasy was the remnant of traditions
going back to the time of Alexander I. The great men of the
day, on the rare occasions when they spoke their mother tongue,
would use such corruptions of language to show we are Russians through and through, at the same time we are noblemen
who are licensed to ignore school rules) 'by *thert* I want to
demonstrate that, without a sense of one's own dignity, without
self-respect – and in the aristocrat these feelings are highly
developed – there is no solid foundation for the public . . . for
the *bien public*,[6] for the edifice of society. Character, my dear
sir, is the key; man's character must be firm as a rock, because
on it everything is built. I know very well, for example, that
you see fit to ridicule my habits, my clothes, even my personal
fastidiousness – but all this comes from a sense of self-respect,
from a sense of duty, yes, sir, yes, duty. I live in the country, in
the back of beyond, but I don't let myself go, I have respect for
the human being I am.'

'Excuse me, Pavel Petrovich,' said Bazarov, 'there you are
respecting yourself and sitting with your arms folded. What
does that do for the *bien public*? Without self-respect you'd be
doing exactly the same.'

Pavel Petrovich went pale.

'That's a quite different question. It certainly doesn't suit me
to explain to you now why I'm sitting with my arms folded, to
use your phrase. I want only to say that aristocracy is a principle, and in our day and age only amoral and worthless people
can live without principles. I said that to Arkady the day after
he came here and I say it again now to you. Don't you think so,
Nikolay?'

Nikolay Petrovich nodded in assent.

'Aristocracy, liberalism, progress, principles,' Bazarov was saying meanwhile, 'goodness, what a lot of foreign . . . and useless words! A Russian doesn't need them, even if they come free.'

'What does a Russian need then, in your opinion? To listen to you, we are in any case living beyond the bounds of humanity, outside its laws. But really – the logic of history demands . . .'

'What's that logic to us? We'll get on without it.'

'How?'

'Like this. I hope you don't need logic to put a bit of bread into your mouth when you're hungry. What good are all these abstractions to us?'

Pavel Petrovich raised his hands.

'After that remark I don't understand you. You insult the Russian people. I do not understand how one can fail to acknowledge principles and rules! What guides you, then?'

'Uncle, I've already told you we don't recognize any authority,' Arkady intervened.

'We are guided by what we recognize as useful,' said Bazarov. 'The most useful course of action at present is to reject – and we reject.'

'You reject everything?'

'Everything.'

'What? Not just art, poetry . . . but also . . . I hardly dare say it . . .'

'Everything,' Bazarov repeated with an air of ineffable calm.

Pavel Petrovich stared at him. He hadn't expected that answer, and Arkady even went red from pleasure.

'Come now,' said Nikolay Petrovich. 'You reject everything, or more precisely, you destroy everything . . . But one must also build.'

'That's not our concern . . . First one must clear the ground.'

'The present condition of the people demands it,' Arkady said seriously. 'We must meet those demands, we don't have the right to satisfy personal egoism.'

It was clear that Bazarov didn't like this last sentence, it gave off a whiff of philosophy, i.e. romanticism, for he called philosophy as well by that name; but he didn't see the need to contradict his young pupil.

'No, no!' Pavel Petrovich exclaimed in a sudden burst of temper. 'I don't want to believe that you gentlemen know the Russian people properly, that you represent their needs, their aspirations! No, the Russian people aren't what you imagine them to be. They have a hallowed respect for traditions, they are patriarchal, they can't live without faith . . .'

'I won't argue with that,' interrupted Bazarov, 'I am even prepared to agree that on *that* you are right.'

'But if I am right . . .'

'That still proves nothing.'

'Proves precisely nothing,' Arkady repeated with the confidence of an experienced chess player who has foreseen an obviously dangerous move from his opponent and so is not at all thrown by it.

'What do you mean proves nothing?' Pavel Petrovich stuttered in astonishment. 'So you're going against your own people?'

'And what if I am?' exclaimed Bazarov. 'Those people think that when it thunders it's the Prophet Elijah going about the heavens in a chariot. So? Am I to agree with them? You talk of the people being Russian, but aren't I Russian myself?'

'No, you are not Russian after all you've just said! I cannot recognize you as a Russian.'

'My grandfather ploughed the soil,' Bazarov replied with arrogant pride. 'Ask any one of your peasants which of us – you or me – he would first recognize as a fellow countryman. You can't even talk to them.'

'And you talk to them and at the same time you hold them in contempt.'

'What of that, if they deserve contempt! You disapprove of my way of thinking, but why do you assume it's just accidental, that it doesn't come out of that very same national spirit you're so keen on?'

'What! So what we really need are nihilists!'

'Needed or no, that's not for us to judge. You too regard yourself as serving some purpose.'

'Gentlemen, gentlemen, please, no personal remarks!' Nikolay Petrovich exclaimed, getting up from his seat.

Pavel Petrovich smiled and, putting his hand on his brother's shoulder, made him sit down again.

'Don't worry,' he said. 'I won't lose control of myself, precisely because of that sense of dignity which Mr . . . which the doctor mocks so cruelly. Now let me say this,' he went on, again addressing Bazarov, 'perhaps you think that you are teaching something new? You're wrong to think that. The kind of materialism you preach has been in vogue several times and it has always turned out to be groundless . . .'

'Another foreign word,' Bazarov interrupted. He was beginning to get angry and his face took on an ugly, almost copper colour. 'In the first place, we preach nothing, we're not like that . . .'

'What do you do then?'

'This is what we do. At first, not so long ago, we were saying that our civil servants take bribes, that we have no roads, no trade, no proper courts of justice . . .'

'Yes, yes, you're denouncers – I think that's the term. I too agree with many of your denouncements, but . . .'

'But then we realized that to witter away about the sores on the face of society just isn't worth doing, it only leads to trivial and doctrinaire thinking. We came to see that our so-called progressives and denouncers are good for nothing, that we're spending our time on nonsense, talking about some kind of art, unconscious creativity, parliamentarianism, the bar and God knows what else, when what's at stake is people's daily bread, when we're suffocating under the crudest superstition, when all our public companies are going bankrupt solely because there aren't enough honest men, when the liberation[7] the government is so concerned with will probably bring us little benefit because our muzhiks are happy to rob themselves in order to go and drink themselves silly in a tavern.'

'Very well,' Pavel Petrovich interrupted. 'You've made up your mind about all that and have decided not to do anything serious about it.'

'We've decided not to do anything serious about it,' Bazarov repeated gloomily.

He suddenly became angry with himself for having spoken so openly in front of this gentleman.

'And you just want to hurl abuse?'

'Exactly.'

'And that's called nihilism?'

'And that's called nihilism,' Bazarov repeated again, this time in a particularly insolent tone.

Pavel Petrovich narrowed his eyes slightly.

'So that's how things are!' he said in a strangely calm voice. 'Nihilism is to bring succour to all our woes, and you, you are our saviours and heroes. But why do you abuse others, just like those denouncers of what's wrong? Don't you talk just as much hot air as everyone else?'

'If there's one thing we're not guilty of, it's that,' Bazarov muttered between his teeth.

'Well then, are you taking action? Or planning to take action?'

Bazarov didn't reply. Pavel Petrovich began to tremble but controlled himself at once.

'Hm! . . . Taking action, destroying . . .' he went on. 'But how can one destroy without even knowing why?'

'We destroy because we're a force,' said Arkady.

Pavel Petrovich looked at his nephew and gave a smile.

'Yes, a force. And one that doesn't have to give an account of itself,' said Arkady, standing straighter.

'Wretched boy!' cried Pavel Petrovich, quite unable to contain himself any longer. 'If you'd only think what you are supporting in Russia with your second-rate phrase! No, it would try the patience of an angel! A force! There is a force in a savage Kalmuck and in a Mongol – but why do we need it? Civilization is our road, yes, yes, sir, it is. We value the fruits she bears. And don't tell me those fruits are worthless. The humblest dauber, *un barbouilleur*,[8] the cheap pianist who gets five kopecks for an evening, they all bring more benefit than you do, because they are representatives of civilization and not of crude Mongol force! You imagine yourselves to be advanced – only to sit in a Kalmuck cart! A force! And lastly, do remember this, you men of force – there are just four and a half of you, but the rest are millions strong. They won't let you trample their most hallowed beliefs underfoot. They will crush you!'

'Even if they crush us, that's the way we have to go,' said Bazarov. 'We shall see what we shall see. We're not as few as you suppose.'

'What? Do you seriously think you can cope, cope with an entire nation?'

'Moscow, you know, was burnt down by a penny candle,'[9] answered Bazarov.

'Yes, yes. First, you show us almost Satanic pride, then ridicule. This, this is what grabs the interest of the young, this is what rules the hearts of inexperienced boys! There's one here sitting next to you, he almost worships you, just look at him.' (Arkady turned away and frowned.) 'And this infection has already spread far and wide. I'm told our painters in Rome don't set foot in the Vatican. They think Raphael[10] almost an idiot because he is an "authority", but they themselves are disgustingly feeble and unproductive, their own imagination doesn't go beyond *A Maiden at the Fountain*,[11] try as they will! And the maiden is execrably painted. You think they're heroes, don't you?'

'I think,' Bazarov objected, 'that Raphael isn't worth a brass farthing, and that they are no better than him.'

'Bravo! Bravo! Do listen, Arkady . . . That's how the modern young should talk! And indeed, if you think about it, they are bound to follow you! Previously young people had to study; they didn't want to be thought ignoramuses and so they were forced to work. But now they only have to say "Everything in the world is rubbish" – and the world's their oyster. The young are happy. And with reason, they were once simply dimwits but now they've become nihilists.'

'Now you've been let down by your vaunted sense of personal dignity,' Bazarov said calmly while Arkady went red and his eyes flashed. 'Our argument has gone too far . . . I think we'd better stop it. And I'll be prepared to agree with you,' he added standing up, 'when you show me a single institution in our society, in the private or public sphere, which doesn't demand total, unsparing rejection.'

'I will show you millions of such institutions,' exclaimed Pavel Petrovich, 'millions of them! The peasant commune, for example.'[12]

A cold smile curled Bazarov's lips.

'Now, on the subject of the commune,' he said 'you'd better have a chat to your brother. I think he's now come to know from experience what the commune is like, and its collective responsibility, and the temperance movement, and little things of that sort.'

'Then what about the family, the family as it exists among our peasants!' Pavel Petrovich shouted.

'I think you'd better not look into that question either in too much detail. I imagine you've heard of incest between men and their sons' wives? Listen, Pavel Petrovich, give yourself a couple of days, you won't hit on anything right away. Review all the classes of our society and think very carefully about each one, while Arkady and I go and . . .'

'Mock everything,' Pavel Petrovich continued.

'No, dissect frogs. Come on, Arkady. Goodbye, gentlemen!'

The two friends went out. The brothers remained alone and at first just looked at each other.

At last Pavel Petrovich spoke. 'There you see modern youth! Those are our heirs!'

'Our heirs,' Nikolay Petrovich repeated with a heavy sigh. During the whole argument he'd been sitting as if he were on hot coals, only giving the odd furtive, pained glance at Arkady. 'Do you know, Brother, what I've remembered? I once had a quarrel with our dead mamma. She shouted and wouldn't listen to me. In the end I said to her, "You can't understand me; we belong to two different generations." She was terribly offended, but I thought to myself, "What's one to do? The pill is bitter but it has to be swallowed." Now our turn has come, and our heirs can say to us, "You don't belong to our generation. Swallow the pill."'

'You are much too indulgent and modest,' Pavel Petrovich objected. 'On the contrary I am convinced that you and I have much more right on our side than these young gentlemen, although perhaps our language may be slightly old-fashioned, *vieilli*,[13] and we don't have that arrogant self-assurance . . . And the modern young are so affected! You ask one, do you want red or white wine. "I have an habitual preference for red!" he answers in a bass voice and with such a pompous expression, as if the whole universe were looking at him at that moment . . .'

'Do you want any more tea,' said Fenechka, putting her head round the door. She hadn't been brave enough to come into the drawing room while she could hear the argument.

'No, you can tell them to take the samovar away,' said Nikolay Petrovich, getting up to greet her. Pavel Petrovich brusquely said '*bon soir*'[14] to him and went off to his study.

XI

Half an hour later Nikolay Petrovich went into the garden, to his favourite arbour. His thoughts were gloomy. For the first time he recognized how far he and his son had grown apart. He foresaw that with every day the distance between them would become greater and greater. So there had been no point in his having spent whole days during those winters in St Petersburg poring over the most recent publications; no point in his listening carefully to the conversations of the young; no point in his pleasure at getting a word in during their heated discussions. 'My brother says we are right,' he thought, 'and setting all vanity aside, I do myself think they are further from the truth than we are, but at the same time I feel they have something which we don't, some advantage over us . . . Youth? No, not just youth. Doesn't their advantage lie in their being less marked by class than we are?'

Nikolay Petrovich sunk his head and rubbed his face with his hand.

'But to reject poetry?' he thought again. 'Not to have a feeling for art, for nature . . .?'

And he looked around him as if trying to understand how it was possible not to have a feeling for nature. Evening was now coming on. The sun had gone behind a small aspen wood which lay a quarter of a mile from his garden and cast its seemingly unending shadow over the motionless fields. A peasant was trotting on his white horse down a narrow, dark track which ran by the wood; although he was riding in shade, his whole figure was clearly visible down to a patch on his shoulder; his horse's legs moved with a brisk regularity that was pleasing to the eye. For their part the sun's rays went into the wood and, penetrating the undergrowth, bathed the trunks of the aspens in such a warm light that they looked like the trunks of fir trees; their foliage went almost dark blue while above them rose the azure sky tinged pink by the sunset. Swallows were flying high; the wind had dropped; lingering bees lazily, sleepily buzzed on the lilac blooms; a column of moths danced above a single protruding branch. 'My God, how beautiful it is!' thought Nikolay Petrovich, and some favourite lines of poetry were about to spring to his lips when he remembered Arkady and *Stoff und Kraft* and fell silent. He continued to sit there and continued to indulge in the pleasurable, melancholy sport of solitary reverie. He liked to dream – living in the country had developed that propensity in him. It was not so long ago that he was dreaming like this while waiting for his son at the inn, but since then a change had happened, relationships that weren't quite clear had now been defined . . . so very clearly!

He thought again of his dead wife, but not as he had known her for many years, a good and careful housewife, but as a girl with a slender waist, an innocently curious gaze and tightly plaited hair above a child's neck. He remembered seeing her for the first time. He was then still a student. He met her on the stairs of the apartment where he was living. He bumped into her by accident, turned round to apologize and could only mumble '*Pardon, monsieur*';[1] she bowed her head, smiled and ran off as if she was frightened; then at the turn of the stairs, she gave him a quick look, put on a serious face and blushed. And then his first shy visits, the half words, half smiles, the doubts and sorrow and outbursts, and finally the breathless happiness . . . Where had all that gone? She became his wife, he was happy as few men on earth are . . . 'But why,' he thought, 'couldn't those first sweet moments last for ever and never die?'

He didn't try to clarify his thoughts for himself, but he felt that he wanted to keep hold of that time of happiness with something more powerful than memory; he wanted palpably to feel his Mariya by him again, to feel the warmth of her body and her breath, and he already sensed that above him . . .

'Nikolay Petrovich,' came Fenechka's voice from near by, 'where are you?'

He shuddered. He felt no pain or guilt . . . He didn't admit even the possibility of any comparison between his wife and Fenechka, but he regretted she'd thought of looking for him. Her voice at once reminded him of his grey hairs, his age, his present state . . .

The enchanted world into which he had entered, rising out of the cloudy waters of the past, shivered – and vanished.

'I'm here,' he answered, 'I'm coming, you go in.' 'There's the voice of class' was the thought that flashed through his mind. Fenechka silently looked at him in the arbour and disappeared, and he noticed with surprise that night had fallen since he had started to dream. Everything round him was dark and quiet, and he saw before him Fenechka's pale little face. He got up and was about to return home; but the emotions in his breast couldn't settle, and he started to walk slowly around the garden, now pensively looking at the ground underfoot, now raising his eyes to the sky with its swarm of twinkling stars. He walked a long time, till he was almost exhausted, but the anxiety in him, a vague, questing, sad feeling, still hadn't gone. How Bazarov would have laughed at him if he knew what was going on in his mind! Arkady himself would have censured him. Here he was, a man of forty-four, an agronomist and landowner, in tears, tears for no reason. It was a hundred times worse than the cello.

Nikolay Petrovich went on walking and couldn't bring himself to go back into the house, into that peaceful and cosy nest, welcoming him with all its lit windows. He hadn't the strength to leave the darkness, the garden, the feeling of fresh air on his face, that melancholy, that sense of uneasiness . . .

He met Pavel Petrovich at the bend of a path.

'What's the matter with you?' Pavel Petrovich asked him.

'You're pale as a ghost. You're not well. Why don't you go to bed?'

Nikolay Petrovich briefly explained to him his state of mind and went away. Pavel Petrovich walked to the end of the garden and he too started thinking and he too lifted his eyes to the sky. But his fine, dark eyes reflected nothing but the light of the stars. He wasn't a romantic by temperament, and his soul, drily fastidious and passionate, misanthropic *à la française*, had no room for dreams . . .

'Do you know what?' Bazarov said to Arkady that same evening. 'I've had a splendid idea. Your father was saying today he'd had an invitation from that grand relative of yours. Your father isn't going. Why don't you and I slip away to *** – he was asking you as well. The weather here's turned pretty bad, but we can have a nice trip and look at the town. We'll get five or six days' fun, and that's it!'

'And will you come back here?'

'No, I must go and see my father. You know, he's twenty miles from ***. I haven't seen him or my mother for a long time. I must give the old people some pleasure. They're good souls, especially my father – he's such a curious character. And I'm all they've got.'

'And will you stay with them long?'

'I doubt it. I should think I'll get bored.'

'But you'll come and see us on the way back?'

'I don't know . . . I'll see. So that's agreed? Are we off?'

'I suppose so,' Arkady said lazily.

At heart he was delighted with his friend's proposal but he felt he had to hide his feelings. He wasn't a nihilist for nothing!

The next day he and Bazarov left for ***. The young people of Marino were sad at their going; Dunyasha even burst into tears . . . but the 'old gentlemen' breathed more easily.

XII

The town of ***, to which our friends had set off, was under a 'young' governor, a man who was both a progressive and a tyrant – something that is happening all over Russia. During the first year of his administration he managed to quarrel not only with the marshal of nobility,[1] a retired Guards staff captain, a breeder of horses and a great host, but also with his own officials. The ensuing row finally took on such proportions that the ministry in St Petersburg found it necessary to send down a trusty pair of hands to sort things out on the spot. The choice of the powers that be fell on Matvey Ilyich Kolyazin, the son of the Kolyazin who had once been the Kirsanov brothers' guardian. He was another of the 'young ones', i.e. he had only recently had his fortieth birthday but was already on the road to political success and wore the star of an order on each side of his chest. One, it's true, was a foreign order, and not a very distinguished one. Like the governor, in whose case he had come to adjudicate, he had the reputation of a progressive, and though he was already a high-flyer he was not like most high-flyers. He had the highest opinion of himself, and his vanity knew no bounds, but he behaved simply, looked benignly, listened indulgently and laughed with such good nature that on first meeting he could be taken for a 'good fellow'. However, when it was called for, he knew how to 'shake things up', as the phrase goes. 'Energy is essential,' he would say then, '*l'énergie est la première qualité d'un homme d'état.*'[2] But for all that he usually lost out and any official with a bit of experience could ride all over him. Matvey Ilyich spoke with great respect of Guizot[3] and tried to impress on all and sundry that he wasn't one of the tribe of out-of-date bureaucrats, slaves to routine, and that no important manifestation in society could escape him . . . Words like that all came easily to his lips. He even followed developments in modern literature – if only with a kind of pompous insouciance, just as a grown man meeting a crocodile of urchins in the street will sometimes join them. In reality Matvey Ilyich hadn't progressed much beyond the politicians of Alexander I's[4] time, who, when preparing themselves for a *soirée* at Madame Svechina's[5] (who was then living in St Petersburg), would read a page of Condillac[6] in the morning. Only his methods were more modern. He was an adroit courtier, a great schemer – and nothing else. He knew nothing about business, he wasn't intelligent, but he did know how to look after his own interests. In that no one could hold him back – and that's the main thing after all.

Matvey Ilyich received Arkady in the way of most enlightened high officials – amiably, even playfully. However, he expressed surprise when he learnt that the relations he had invited had stayed behind in the country. 'Your *papá* was always an eccentric,' he said, playing with the tassels of his magnificent velvet dressing-gown. All of a sudden he turned to a young official, all very properly buttoned up in his undress uniform, and exclaimed, with a worried air, 'What is it?' The young man, who had lost his tongue from the long silence, got up and looked at his boss with incomprehension. But Matvey Ilyich, having confounded his subordinate, was no longer paying him any attention. Our high-ranking officials generally like to confound their subordinates; the methods they use to achieve this aim are various. One such, which is widely used – 'is quite a favourite',[7] as the English say – is this: the official suddenly ceases to understand the simplest words, as if he were deaf. For example, he asks what day it is.

There comes a very polite reply: 'Today is Friday, Your Excellenc-c-c-cy.'

'Eh? What? What's that? What did you say?' the dignitary repeats nervously.

'Today is Friday, Your Excellenc-c-cy.'

'What? What? What's Friday? What Friday?'

'Friday, Your Excellenc-ccc-ccc-cy, the day of the week.'

'Come now, are you trying to teach me?'

For all his liberal reputation Matvey Ilyich remained a high-ranking official.

'I advise you, my friend, to go and call on the governor,' he said to Arkady. 'You must understand I'm not giving you this advice out of any adherence to old-fashioned ideas about the need to go and pay court to the powers that be, but simply because the governor is a decent fellow. Also you probably want to get to know local society . . . you're not, I hope, going to be a recluse. And he's giving a big ball the day after tomorrow.'

'Will you be at the ball?' Arkady asked.

'He's giving it for me,' Matvey Ilyich said almost regretfully. 'Do you dance?'

'I do, only badly.'

'That doesn't matter. There are some pretty girls here, and a young man should be ashamed of not dancing. Again I don't say this out of any old-fashioned ideas. I absolutely don't think the seat of the brain has to lie in the feet, but Byronism is comical, *il a fait son temps.*'[8]

'But, Uncle, it's not out of any Byronism that I don't . . .'

'I'll introduce you to the local young ladies, I'll take you under my wing,' Matvey Ilyich interrupted and gave a complacent laugh. 'You'll be at home there, won't you?'

A manservant came in and announced the arrival of the president of the revenue department, an old gentleman with sugary eyes and wrinkled lips, who had an extraordinary love of nature, especially on a summer's day, when, in his words, 'every little bee takes a bribe from every little flower . . .' Arkady went away.

He found Bazarov at the inn where they were staying and spent a long time persuading him to go to the governor's. 'It can't be helped,' Bazarov said finally. 'I've started something and I have to carry it through! We came to look at the gentry – so let's do that!' The governor received the young men affably but he didn't ask them to sit down nor did he sit himself. He was always in a hurry and bustling about. In the morning he put on his close-fitting uniform and a very tightly tied cravat, he didn't give himself time to finish food or drink, he was always 'the man in charge'. In the province he had the nickname of Bourdaloue[9] – the reference wasn't to the famous French preacher but to *burdá*, hogwash. He invited Arkady and Bazarov to his ball and two minutes later invited them a second time, thinking now they were brothers and calling them Kaysarov.

They were walking home from the governor's when suddenly a shortish man, in a Slavophile's[10] Hungarian jacket, leapt out of a passing droshky and rushed up to Bazarov with a cry of 'Yevgeny Vasilyich!'

'Aha, it's you, Herr Sitnikov,' said Bazarov, continuing to walk along the pavement. 'What brings you here?'

'Imagine, it's just by chance,' he answered and, turning to the droshky, waved an arm five times and shouted, 'Follow us, you follow us! My father has some business here,' he went on, jumping over a gutter, 'so he asked me to . . . I heard today you were here and I've already been to your place . . .' (Indeed the friends, on returning to their room, had found there a visiting card with the corners turned down[11] and with Sitnikov's name on one side in French, on the other in Slavonic script.) 'I hope you're not coming from the governor's.'

'Don't say that, we've just left him.'

'Ah! In that case I too will go and see him . . . Yevgeny Vasilyich, do introduce me to your . . . to him . . .'

'Sitnikov, Kirsanov,' Bazarov muttered, without stopping walking.

'Most gratifying,' Sitnikov began, smirking and walking sideways and quickly pulling off his extremely elegant gloves. 'I've heard so much . . . I'm an old friend of Yevgeny Vasilyich's and can even say his pupil. I owe him my regeneration . . .'

Arkady looked at Bazarov's pupil. A worried and vacant expression came over the small if perfectly pleasant features of his well-groomed head; his little eyes, which looked as if they'd been stuck into his head, had a fixed and anxious stare, and he had an anxious laugh, short and wooden.

'Believe me,' he went on, 'when I first heard Yevgeny Vasilyich say one shouldn't recognize any authority, I felt such ecstasy . . . as if I'd seen the light!' "Here," I thought, "at last I've found a man!" Now, Yevgeny Vasilyich, you've absolutely got to go and see a lady here – she's wholly capable of understanding you, and a visit from you will be a real treat for her. I think you may have heard of her.'

'Who's that?' Bazarov said reluctantly.

'Kukshina, Eudoxie, Yevdoksiya Kukshina. She's a remarkable character, *émancipée*[12] in the true meaning of the word, a progressive woman. Do you know what? Let's go now and see her together. She lives two steps from here. We'll have lunch there. Have you had lunch yet?'

'No, not yet.'

'Very good then. You must understand she's separated from her husband, she isn't attached to anyone.'

'Is she attractive?' asked Bazarov.

'N . . . no, I can't say that.'

'So why the devil are you inviting us to go and see her?'

'Always making a joke . . . She'll give us a bottle of champagne.'

'So that's the point! Now one can see a practical man. By the by, is your pa still in the state liquor business?'[13]

'Yes, he is,' Sitnikov said hurriedly and gave a shrill laugh. 'So, do we have a deal?'

'I really don't know.'

'You wanted to look at people, so go,' Arkady said in a low voice.

'And what about you, Mr Kirsanov?' Sitnikov went on. 'You must come too, we can't go without you.'

'How can we all barge in together?'

'It doesn't matter! Kukshina is a wonderful woman.'

'Will there be a bottle of champagne?' asked Bazarov.

'There'll be three bottles!' cried Sitnikov. 'I'll guarantee that.'

'What with?'

'My own head.'

'I'd rather have your pa's wallet. Anyway, let's go.'

XIII

Avdotya Nikitishna (or Yevdoksiya) Kukshina lived in a small gentry house, like one in Moscow, in a street of the town of * * * that had recently burnt down. We know our provincial towns have a fire every five years. By the door, above a crookedly

pinned-up visiting card, was a bell handle, and the visitors were
met in the hall by a woman in a cap, half maidservant, half
lady companion – a clear sign of the progressive aspirations of
the hostess. Sitnikov asked if Avdotya Nikitishna was at
home.

'Is that you, *Victor*?' came a high-pitched voice from the
adjoining room. 'Come in.'

The woman in the cap vanished at once.

'I'm not alone,' said Sitnikov and, jauntily throwing off his
topcoat – beneath it he had on a kind of old Russian-style loose
jacket – he gave a cocky glance at Arkady and Bazarov.

'It doesn't matter,' the voice answered. '*Entrez*.'[1]

The young men went in. The room into which they came
was more like a study than a drawing room. Dusty tables were
piled with papers, letters and fat Russian journals (mostly
uncut). There were white cigarette ends scattered all over the
place. Half reclining on a sofa was a lady. She was still young,
fair-haired and a bit dishevelled, and wore a rather untidy silk
dress. She had big bracelets on her short little arms and a lace
scarf on her head. She got up from the sofa and, loosely pulling
over her shoulders a velvet coat lined with yellowing ermine,
she drawled out, 'Good morning, Victor,' and shook Sitnikov's
hand.

'Bazarov, Kirsanov,' he said curtly, imitating Bazarov's introduction.

'Welcome,' answered Kukshina and, fixing her round eyes
on Bazarov – between them was a poor little red turned-up
nose – she added, 'I know you,' and shook hands with him as
well.

Bazarov frowned. Though there was nothing especially
repellent in the emancipated woman's plain little figure, the
expression of her face made an unpleasant impression on the
viewer. It made you want to ask her, 'What's the matter with
you? Are you hungry? Or bored? Or shy? Why are you so
tense?' Something inside was always nagging away at her, as it
was with Sitnikov. Her speech and her movements were very
fluent and at the same time clumsy. She clearly thought of herself as a good-natured and simple being, but, whatever she

might be doing, she always seemed to want to be doing something else. Everything about her came over as 'done on purpose', as children say – i.e. as affected and artificial.

'Yes, yes, I know you, Bazarov,' she repeated. (She had the habit, characteristic of provincial and Moscow ladies, of calling men by their surnames from the first day she met them.) 'Would you like a cigar?'

'A cigar's all very well,' Sitnikov interrupted. He was already sprawled in an armchair with his leg in the air. 'But give us some lunch, we're terribly hungry. And tell her to open a bottle of champagne for us.'

'You sybarite,' said Yevdoksiya and laughed. (When she laughed, her top gums showed above her teeth.) 'Bazarov, don't you think he's a sybarite?'

'I like the comforts of life,' Sitnikov said pompously. 'That doesn't stop me being a liberal.'

'Yes, it does, it does!' cried Yevdoksiya. However, she told her handmaiden to produce lunch and the champagne. 'What's your opinion about this?' she added, turning to Bazarov. 'I'm sure you share my view.'

'No, I don't,' Bazarov countered, 'a bit of meat is better than a bit of bread, even from the point of view of chemical analysis.'

'Do you study chemistry? It's my passion. I've even invented a plastic myself.'

'You've invented a plastic?'

'Yes, me. Do you know what for? To make dolls, so their heads don't break. I'm a practical woman too, you know. But it's not quite ready yet. I still must read a bit of Liebig. By the way have you read Kislyakov's article on women's work in *Moskovskiye vedomosti*?[2] Do please read it. You must be interested in the question of women? What about schools? What does your friend do? What's his name?'

Mrs Kukshina let fall her questions one after the other with an affected carelessness and didn't wait for an answer. Spoilt children talk like that to their nannies.

'My name is Arkady Nikolaich Kirsanov,' said Arkady, 'and I don't do anything.'

Yevdoksiya burst out laughing.

'That's so charming! Why aren't you smoking? Victor, you know I'm cross with you.'

'Why?'

'Someone told me you'd again started to speak well of George Sand.[3] How can you compare her to Emerson?[4] She has no ideas about education or about physiology or about anything. I'm sure she hasn't even heard of embryology, and in this day and age how can you do without it?' (At this juncture Yevdoksiya even gestured with her hands apart.) 'Oh what an amazing article Yelisevich[5] wrote about that! That gentleman's a genius.' (Yevdoksiya constantly used the word 'gentleman' for 'man'.) 'Bazarov, come and sit next to me on the sofa. Perhaps you don't know it, but I'm terribly scared of you.'

'Why is that? I'm curious to know.'

'You're a dangerous gentleman, you're so critical. My God! It's ridiculous, I'm talking like some lady landowner in the sticks. By the way, I really am a landowner. I look after my estate myself, and just imagine, my steward Yerofey is an amazing type, Fenimore Cooper's Pathfinder[6] in the flesh. There's something so spontaneous in him! I have settled here for good. The town's unbearable, isn't it? But what can one do?'

'It's just a town,' said Bazarov coolly.

'Everyone's interests are so petty, that's what's so terrible! I used to spend the winters in Moscow . . . but now my revered spouse, Monsieur Kukshin, lives there. And Moscow now . . . I don't know . . . isn't the same. I am thinking of travelling abroad. Last year I was all ready to go.'

'To Paris, I imagine?' asked Bazarov.

'To Paris and to Heidelberg.'

'Why Heidelberg?'

'Heavens above, Bunsen's[7] there.'

Bazarov couldn't find an answer to that.

'Pierre Sapozhnikov . . . do you know him?'

'No, I don't.'

'Heavens, Pierre Sapozhnikov . . . he's still always at Lidiya Khostatova's.'

'I don't know her either.'

'Well, he was going to be my escort. Thank God, I am free, I have no children . . . What am I saying – *Thank God!* But it hardly matters.'

Yevdoksiya rolled a cigarette in her fingers that were stained yellow from tobacco, licked it with her tongue, sucked it and lit up. The maid came in with a tray.

'Ah, here's lunch. Will you have something first? Victor, uncork the bottle. That's your specialty.'

'It is, it is,' Sitnikov muttered and again gave his shrill laugh.

'Are there any attractive women here?' Bazarov asked, drinking down his third glass.

'There are,' Yevdoksiya answered, 'but they're all so empty-headed. For example, *mon amie*[8] Odintsova isn't bad. A pity her reputation is a bit . . . However, it wouldn't matter, but there is no freedom of opinion, no breadth, none . . . of that kind of thing. We've got to change the whole system of education. I've already been thinking about that. Our women are very badly educated.'

'You won't be able to do anything with them,' said Sitnikov. 'One should despise them, and I do despise them, utterly and completely!' (The ability to despise and to voice that scorn Sitnikov found a most agreeable feeling; he was given to attacking women in particular, without suspecting that in a few months his fate would be to crawl before his wife just because she had been born a Princess Durdoleosova.) 'There's not one who would be capable of understanding our conversation. There's not one worthy of being the subject of discussion by serious men like us!'

'But they absolutely don't have to understand our conversation,' said Bazarov.

'Who are you talking about?' asked Yevdoksiya.

'Attractive women.'

'What! That means you share Proudhon's[9] view.'

Bazarov proudly drew himself up.

'I don't share anybody's views. I have my own.'

'Down with authority!' shouted Sitnikov, delighted at the

opportunity of expressing himself forcibly in front of a man he idolized.

'But Macaulay[10] himself . . .' Kukshina began.

'Down with Macaulay!' Sitnikov thundered. 'Are you standing up for those pathetic women?'

'No, I'm not standing up for them, but for the rights of women, which I've sworn to defend to the last drop of my blood.'

'Down with . . .' Here Sitnikov stopped. 'But I don't deny them,' he added.

'No, I can see you're a Slavophile!'[11]

'No, I'm not a Slavophile, although of course . . .'

'You are, you are! You are a Slavophile. You're a disciple of the *Domostroy*.[12] You only need a whip in your hand!'

'A whip's a good thing,' commented Bazarov, 'only we've just come to the last drop . . .'

'Of what?' Yevdoksiya interrupted.

'Of champagne, dear Avdotya Nikitishna – not of your blood.'

'I can't listen calmly when people attack women,' Yevdoksiya continued. 'It's terrible, terrible. Instead of attacking them you'd do better to read Michelet's *De l'Amour*.[13] It's a wonder. Gentlemen, let's talk of love,' Yevdoksiya went on, languidly letting her arm fall on to a squashed sofa cushion.

A sudden silence fell.

'No, why talk about love?' said Bazarov. 'But you just mentioned Odintsova . . . I think that was the name? Who is this lady?'

'An absolute charmer!' chirped Sitnikov. 'I'll introduce you. Clever, rich and a widow. Sadly she's not yet very progressive. She ought to get to know our Yevdoksiya better. Eudoxie, I drink your health! Chin-chin! "*Et toc, et toc, et tin-tin-tin! Et toc, et toc, et tin-tin-tin!*"[14]

'Victor, you're a naughty boy.'

Lunch went on for a long time. The first bottle of champagne was followed by a second, a third and even a fourth . . . Yevdoksiya spouted without drawing breath. Sitnikov kept up with her. They talked a lot: is marriage a prejudice or a crime;

are all people born the same, or not; what exactly is personality. It all ended with Yevdoksiya, red in the face from the wine she had drunk, striking the keys of an out-of-tune piano with her stumpy nails. She started singing in a hoarse voice, first gipsy songs, then Seymour Schiff's romance 'Drowsy Granada slumbers'.[15] And Sitnikov wrapped a scarf round his head and acted the dumbstruck lover as she sang:

> 'And join my lips to thine
> With burning kisses.'

Eventually Arkady could stand no more. 'Gentlemen, this has become some kind of Bedlam,' he said aloud.

Bazarov, who had only occasionally contributed a sarcastic remark to the conversation – he was more interested in the champagne – yawned loudly, got up and went out with Arkady without saying goodbye to the hostess. Sitnikov rushed after them.

'Well, well, what do you think?' he asked them, darting obsequiously from one to the other. 'I told you, she's a remarkable personality! That's the kind of woman we need more of! In her own way she's a phenomenon of high morality.'

'And is that establishment of your pa's another phenomenon of high morality?' said Bazarov, calling Sitnikov 'thou' for the first time and pointing at a tavern they passed at that moment.

Sitnikov again gave his shrill laugh. He was very ashamed of his background and didn't know whether to feel flattered or offended by Bazarov's unexpected mode of address.

XIV

The governor's ball took place some days later. Matvey Ilyich was indeed the 'hero of the feast'. The marshal of the nobility told all and sundry that he had come especially out of respect for him. As for the governor, even at the ball and even standing still, he nonetheless continued to be 'in charge of things'. Matvey Ilyich's affability was only matched by the stateliness of his manners. He flattered everyone – some with a hint of superciliousness, others with a hint of deference. He showered compliments on the ladies '*en vrai chevalier français*'[1] and kept repeating a powerful, booming laugh – as befits a great man. He patted Arkady on the back and loudly addressed him as 'dear nephew', and bestowed on Bazarov, dressed up in a rather old tail coat, a distracted but well-meaning sideways look and a vague but friendly roar, in which one could only make out 'I' and '-stremely'. He gave Sitnikov a finger and smiled at him, although he was already turning away his head. He even gave Kukshina an '*Enchanté!*'[2] – she had appeared at the ball without a crinoline[3] and wearing dirty gloves, but with a bird of paradise in her hair. There were masses of people and no lack of partners for the ladies. The civilians tended to crowd along the walls, but the officers were keen dancers, especially one of them who had spent some six months in Paris and there had learnt various exciting exclamations like '*Zut*', '*Ah fichtrrre*', '*Pst, pst, mon bibi*' and so forth. He pronounced them perfectly, with true Parisian chic, and at the same time said '*si j'aurais*' instead of '*si j'avais*' and '*absolument*' in the sense of 'certainly'[4] – in a word he expressed himself in that Russo-French dialect which the French laugh at so when they don't feel the need to reassure our fellow countrymen that we speak their language like angels, '*comme des anges*'.

As we know Arkady danced badly and Bazarov didn't dance at all. They both installed themselves in a corner, where they were joined by Sitnikov. He looked around him insolently with a scornful smile, making malicious comments. Suddenly his expression changed and, turning to Arkady, he said with a kind of embarrassment, 'Odintsova is here.'

Arkady looked round and saw a tall woman in a black dress standing in the door of the ballroom. He was struck by the dignity of her bearing. Graceful was the way she held her bare arms beside her slender figure, and graceful the light sprays of fuchsia that drooped from her lustrous curls on to the slope of her shoulders. The brilliant eyes below a white and slightly prominent forehead were serene and intelligent, serene but not pensive, and a barely perceptible smile played around her lips.

'Do you know her?' Arkady asked Sitnikov.

'Intimately. Do you want me to introduce you?'

'Please . . . after this quadrille.'

Bazarov too noticed Odintsova.

'Who is that person?' he said. 'She doesn't look like the other women.'

When the quadrille was over, Sitnikov took Arkady up to Odintsova. But he couldn't have known her that intimately. He stumbled over his words, and she looked at him with some amazement. However, her expression became welcoming when she heard Arkady's surname. She asked him if he was the son of Nikolay Petrovich.

'I am indeed.'

'I've seen your father a couple of times and have heard a great deal about him,' she went on. 'I'm very pleased to meet you.'

At that moment an aide-de-camp rushed up to her and invited her to dance a quadrille. She accepted.

'Do you dance?' Arkady asked her politely.

'I do. And why do you think I don't? Or do you think I'm too old?'

'I'm sorry, how could you imagine . . . In that case may I book you for the mazurka?'

Odintsova gave him an indulgent smile.

'Certainly,' she said and looked at Arkady, without condescension but as married sisters look at their very young brothers.

Odintsova was only slightly older than Arkady. She was twenty-eight, but in front of her he felt himself a schoolboy, a student, as if the difference in years between them was much greater. Matvey Ilyich came majestically towards her and made a speech of compliments. Arkady withdrew but continued to watch her. He didn't take his eyes off her during the quadrille. She talked just as easily with her partner as with the great man, gently moving her head and eyes from side to side and a couple of times laughing quietly. Her nose was a little thick, like most Russians', and her complexion wasn't quite clear. For all that Arkady decided he had never encountered such a lovely woman. He kept on hearing the sound of her voice, he thought the very folds of her dress fell differently from those of the other ladies, more gracefully and more fully, and all her movements were extraordinarily fluid and at the same time natural.

When the first sounds of the mazurka struck up and Arkady sat down beside his partner, he felt a bit shy inside himself and, as he tried to make conversation, he just stroked his hair and couldn't come up with a single word. But his shyness and confusion didn't last long. Odintsova's calm communicated itself to him. In less than a quarter of an hour he was freely talking about his father, his uncle, life in St Petersburg and in the country. Odintsova listened to him with polite interest, slightly opening and closing her fan. His talk was interrupted when her partners called her out. (Sitnikov asked her twice.) She came back, sat down again and took up her fan, not even out of breath, and Arkady resumed his chatter, full of the happiness of being near her, of talking to her, looking into her eyes, at her noble brow, at her whole attractive, serious and intelligent face. She herself didn't say much, but her words showed a certain knowledge of life. From a number of her remarks Arkady concluded that this young woman had managed to acquire a great deal of experience in her emotions and her thoughts . . .

'Who were you standing with,' she asked him, 'when Mr Sitnikov brought you up to me?'

'Did you notice him?' Arkady asked in his turn. 'Don't you find he has a fine face? That's Bazarov, my friend.'

Arkady started to talk about his 'friend'.

He talked about him in such detail and with such passion that Odintsova turned towards him and looked at him searchingly. The mazurka was now coming to a close. Arkady was sorry to leave his partner. He had happily spent with her something like an hour! It's true that the whole time he constantly felt that she was being nice to him, that he ought to be grateful to her . . . but young hearts aren't humiliated by such a feeling.

The music stopped.

'Merci,' said Odintsova, getting up. 'You promised to visit me. Do bring your friend too with you. I'll be very curious to see a man who is bold enough to believe in nothing.'

The governor came up to Odintsova, announced that dinner

was ready and gave her his arm with an anxious expression. As she left, she turned and gave Arkady a final smile and nod. He bowed low and followed her with his eyes (how elegant he found her waist, encased in the silvery sheen of black silk!), and, as he thought, 'At this moment she's already forgotten about my existence,' he felt in his heart a kind of pleasing resignation.

'Well then?' Bazarov asked as soon as Arkady returned to him in their corner. 'Did you enjoy yourself? A gentleman was just telling me that lady's a bit of oh-ho-ho. However, I think that gentleman's an idiot. But do you think she really is a bit of oh-ho-ho?'

'I don't quite understand what that means,' answered Arkady.

'Come on! What an innocent!'

'If it's that, I don't understand your gentleman. I agree Odintsova is very nice – but her manner is so cold and severe that . . .'

'Still waters . . . you know!' said Bazarov. 'You say she's cold. That's what makes her tasty. Don't you like ice-cream?'

'Maybe,' Arkady stammered. 'I can't judge of that. She wants to meet you and asked me to bring you to see her.'

'I can imagine the portrait you gave of me! But you did well. Take me. Whatever she is, provincial star or progressive woman like Kukshina, she's got a pair of shoulders like I haven't seen for ages.'

Bazarov's cynicism grated on Arkady, but, as often happens, he took up with his friend something different from what had actually displeased him . . .

'Why won't you admit of freedom of opinion in women?' he said in a low voice.

'Because, my friend, I've observed that the women who think freely are hideous.'

The conversation ended on that. The two young men left immediately after supper. Kukshina gave them a nervous and angry laugh (even if it was rather a timid one). Her vanity was deeply wounded by the fact that neither had paid her any attention. She stayed at the ball later than anyone and danced a

Parisian-style polka-mazurka with Sitnikov after 3 a.m. That edifying spectacle closed the governor's ball.

XV

'. . . Let's see what species of mammal this person belongs to,' Bazarov said to Arkady the next day as together they were climbing the stairs of the hotel where Odintsova was staying. 'My nose tells me something here's not quite right.'

'I'm surprised at you,' exclaimed Arkady. 'What's this? You – you Bazarov – supporting the kind of narrow morality which . . .'

'What a funny fellow you are!' Bazarov interrupted coolly. 'Surely you know that in our language – *our* language – "not quite right" means the opposite? It means there's gain to be had here. Didn't you yourself say today that she made a strange marriage, although in my view marrying a rich old man isn't at all strange but, on the contrary, very sensible. I don't believe town gossip, but I like to think, in the words of our learned governor, that it is justified.'

Arkady made no reply and knocked on the door of the apartment. A young footman in livery led the two friends into a big room, poorly furnished, like all Russian hotel rooms, but full of flowers. Odintsova herself soon appeared, wearing a simple morning dress. In the spring sunshine she looked even younger. Arkady introduced Bazarov to her and was secretly surprised to observe that he was awkward, whereas Odintsova remained quite calm, as she had been the day before. Bazarov himself was aware of his awkwardness, and he was cross. 'Just look at you! You're scared of this bloody woman!' he thought and, sprawled in his chair like a Sitnikov, he began to speak with exaggerated assurance. Odintsova didn't take her bright eyes from his face.

Anna Sergeyevna Odintsova was the daughter of Sergey Nikolayevich Loktev, a man celebrated for his speculations, his gambling and his looks, who, after maintaining a very

public existence in St Petersburg and Moscow for about fifteen years, finally lost everything at the tables and had to go
to live in the country, where he soon died. He left a minute
inheritance to his two daughters, Anna, who was twenty, and
Katerina, who was twelve. Their mother, who came from the
impoverished princely family of Kh–, had died in St Petersburg
while her husband was still going strong. Anna's situation after
her father's death was very hard. Her brilliant Petersburg
education hadn't prepared her for coping with estate and
domestic chores, or for the boredom of country life. She knew
absolutely no one in the whole neighbourhood, and she had
no one from whom to take advice. Her father had tried to
avoid contact with the neighbours; he despised them and they
despised him, each in their own way. However, she didn't lose
her head and at once wrote and sent for her mother's sister,
Princess Avdotya Stepanovna Kh–ya, a proud and ill-tempered
old woman who, as soon as she had settled in her niece's house,
took all the best rooms for herself. She groused and grumbled
from morning till night and even on her walks in the garden
she was always accompanied by her only serf, a glum footman
in a worn pea-green livery with blue braid and a tricorne hat.
Anna patiently put up with all her aunt's caprices, occupied
herself in the meantime with her sister's education and seemed
to have already reconciled herself to the thought of fading
away in the depths of the country . . . But fate had decreed for
her otherwise. She happened to catch the eye of one Odintsov,
a very wealthy man of forty-six or so, an eccentric and hypo-
chondriac, fat, heavy and depressive, but for all that far from
stupid and a good man. He fell in love with her and offered her
his hand. She consented to be his wife – and he lived with her
for about six years and, dying, left her all his fortune. Anna
Sergeyevna didn't leave the estate for about a year after his
death; then she and her sister went off abroad. But she went
only to Germany. She missed home and came back to live in
her beloved Nikolskoye, which was about twenty-five miles
from the town of ***. There she had a magnificent, richly furnished house and a beautiful garden with hothouses: her late
husband had denied himself nothing. Anna Sergeyevna went

to the town very seldom, mostly on business and then only for
short visits. She wasn't liked in the province; her marriage to
Odintsov had given rise to a terrible amount of talk; people
told all manner of silly stories about her, averring that she had
helped her father in his swindles, that she had gone abroad for
a very good reason, out of the necessity of concealing the
unfortunate consequences of . . . 'You know what of, don't
you?' the indignant gossips would conclude. It was said of her,
'She's been through fire and water'; and a famous wit in the
province would usually add, 'And through copper piping too.'
All these rumours reached her, but she let them flow past her:
she was a free spirit and quite strong-minded.

Odintsova sat leaning against the back of her armchair and
listened to Bazarov, one arm resting on the other. Unusually
for him he talked quite a lot and was clearly making an effort
to impress Anna Sergeyevna: this again surprised Arkady. He
couldn't decide if Bazarov was achieving his aim. It was difficult to read Anna Sergeyevna's thoughts from her face: she
kept the same expression, amiable and refined. Her lovely
eyes were luminous with attention, but their depths were not
stirred. Bazarov's posing in the first moments of the visit made
an unpleasant impression on her, like a bad smell or a grating
noise, but she immediately understood that he was embarrassed, and that even flattered her. Only vulgarity repelled
her, and no one could have accused Bazarov of vulgarity. That
day there were continual surprises for Arkady. He expected
Bazarov to talk to Odintsova, as an intelligent woman, about
his convictions and opinions: she herself had expressed her
wish to listen to a man 'who is bold enough to believe in
nothing'. But instead Bazarov talked of medicine and homoe-
opathy and botany. It was apparent that Odintsova hadn't
wasted her time in her solitude: she had read a number of
good books and she spoke good Russian.[1] She began talking
about music but, seeing that Bazarov had no time for art, she
quietly returned the conversation to botany, although Arkady
was on the point of holding forth on the meaning of folk
tunes. Odintsova continued to treat him like a younger
brother: she seemed to appreciate in him the good heart and

ingenuousness of youth – and nothing more. The conversation – measured, wide-ranging and lively – went on for over three hours.

At last the two friends got up and began to take their leave. Anna Sergeyevna looked at them warmly, gave each of them her beautiful white hand and, after a moment's thought, said with a wavering but positive smile:

'Gentlemen, if you're not afraid of being bored, come and see me in Nikolskoye.'

'Anna Sergeyevna, what are you saying?' exclaimed Arkady. 'I'd be particularly happy to . . .'

'What about you, Monsieur Bazarov?'

Bazarov just bowed – and Arkady had a final surprise: he noticed his friend was blushing.

'Well?' he said to Bazarov in the street. 'Do you still think she's a bit of oh-ho-ho?'

'God knows! She really has frozen herself up!' Bazarov responded, and added after a moment's silence, 'A duchess, a sovereign lady. She just needs to have a train behind her and a crown on her head.'

'Our duchesses don't speak Russian like that.'

'She's had some difficult times, my friend. She's eaten the same bread as we have.'

'But still she's a delight,' said Arkady.

'And what a splendid body!' Bazarov went on. 'I'd like to see it now on the dissecting table.'

'For God's sake, Yevgeny, stop it! That's disgusting.'

'Calm down, don't be so dainty. I said – she's first class. We must go and see her.'

'When?'

'Why not the day after tomorrow? What is there for us to do here? Drink champagne with Kukshina? Listen to your cousin, the liberal statesman? . . . Let's get on the road the day after tomorrow. Also my father's little property is not far from there. Isn't Nikolskoye on the *** road?'

'Yes.'

'*Optime.*[2] Let's not waste time. Only fools waste time – and know-alls. I say to you, a splendid body!'

Two days later the two friends were on the road to Nikol-skoye. It was a bright day, not too hot, and the well-fed little post-horses trotted smoothly along, their braided and plaited tails swinging gently. Arkady looked at the road and smiled, without knowing why.

'You must congratulate me,' Bazarov exclaimed suddenly. 'Today is the 22nd of June, my saint's day. Let's see how he looks after me. They're expecting me at home today,' he added, lowering his voice . . . 'Well, they'll have to wait, it doesn't matter!'

XVI

The mansion where Anna Sergeyevna lived stood on the slope of an open hill a short distance from a yellow-painted church with a green roof, white columns and above the main entrance a fresco in the 'Italian' style representing the Resurrection of Christ. The eye was particularly caught by the muscular con-tours of a swarthy warrior in a spiked helmet reclining in the foreground. Beyond the church stretched two long rows of vil-lage houses, their chimneys sticking up here and there above the thatched roofs. The manor house was built in the same style as the church, the style we call Alexandrine.[1] The house too was painted yellow, and had a green roof, white columns and a pediment with a coat of arms. The province architect had been responsible for both buildings, much to the taste of the late Odintsov, who couldn't stand 'pointless and whimsical innova-tions', as he called them. The house was flanked on both sides by the dark trees of an old garden, and an avenue of clipped firs led to the entrance.

Two strapping liveried footmen met our friends in the hall, and one of them at once ran off to fetch the butler. The butler, a portly man in a black frock coat, soon appeared and directed the guests up a carpeted staircase to their particular room, where there were already two beds and everything necessary for their toilet. It was clear that order reigned in the house:

everything was clean, everything had an official smell, like in a minister's reception room.

'Anna Sergeyevna asks you to come down to her in half an hour,' said the butler. 'Meanwhile do you need anything?'

'Nothing, my good sir,' said Bazarov, 'but would you be very kind and bring me a glass of vodka.'

'Of course, sir,' the butler replied, not without some surprise, and went off, his boots squeaking as he went.

'What style, what *grand genre*!' said Bazarov. 'I think that's what you call it. A duchess, that's what she is.'

'A fine duchess,' retorted Arkady, 'who right away offers an invitation to such mighty aristocrats as you and me.'

'Me especially, doctor to be, son of a doctor, grandson of a sexton . . . You knew my grandfather was a sexton?. . . Like Speransky,'[2] Bazarov added with a grimace, after a short silence. 'Still, the lady really does know how to indulge herself! Shouldn't we put on tails?'

Arkady just shrugged his shoulders . . . but he too felt a bit awkward.

Half an hour later Bazarov and Arkady went down to the drawing room. It was a large and lofty room, furnished with some luxury but without much taste. The usual formal row of furniture stood along the walls. The wallpaper, gold-patterned on a brown background, had been ordered by the late Odintsov from Moscow, from his friend and commission agent, a wine merchant. Above the central sofa hung the portrait of a flabby, fair-haired man – who seemed to look at the guests with unfriendly eyes. 'That must be *himself*,' Bazarov whispered to Arkady and added, wrinkling his nose, 'Why don't we run away?' But at that moment the hostess came in. She wore a light wool dress, and, with her hair smoothly combed back behind her ears, her fresh, clean face had a girlish look.

'Thank you for keeping your promise,' she began. 'Now be my guests for a while. It's really quite nice here. I'll introduce you to my sister, she plays the piano rather well. Monsieur Bazarov, you don't care but, Monsieur Kirsanov, I think you like music. Apart from my sister my old aunt lives with me. And there's a neighbour who sometimes comes to play cards. That's all of our society. And now let's sit down.'

Odintsova pronounced the whole of this little speech with particular clarity as if she had learnt it off by heart. Then she turned to Arkady. It turned out her mother had known Arkady's and had even been a confidante when she had been in love with Nikolay Petrovich. Arkady spoke with warmth about his dead mother. Meanwhile Bazarov began to look through some picture albums. 'I've become so tame,' he thought to himself.

A beautiful borzoi bitch with a sky-blue collar ran into the drawing room, her feet clacking over the parquet, and she was followed by a girl of about eighteen, dark-complexioned and black-haired, with a slightly rounded but attractive face and small dark eyes. In her hands she held a basket of flowers.

'Here is my Katya,' said Anna Sergeyevna, indicating her with a movement of her head.

Katya gave them a small curtsey, sat down by her sister and began to sort the flowers. The borzoi, which was called Fifi, came up to each of the guests, wagging her tail, and thrust her cold muzzle into their hand.

'Did you pick all these yourself?' Anna Sergeyevna asked.

'I did,' answered Katya.

'And is Aunt coming to tea?'

'Yes.'

When Katya spoke she had a very attractive smile, shy and open, accompanied by a curiously stern upward look. Everything in her spoke of the springtime of youth – her voice, the down on her face, her rosy hands with white circular marks on the palms, her slightly narrow shoulders . . . She kept on blushing and taking quick breaths.

Anna Sergeyevna turned to Bazarov.

'Yevgeny Vasilyevich,' she began, 'you're looking at pictures out of politeness. It doesn't interest you. Better come over here and let us have a good talk about something or other.'

Bazarov came over.

'What would you like to talk about?' he said.

'Whatever you choose. I warn you, I'm terribly argumentative.'

'Are you?'

'Yes. That seems to surprise you. Why is that?'

'Because, in so far as I can judge, your temperament is calm and cold, but argument needs passion.'

'How have you got to know me so soon? First, I am impatient and persistent – you should ask Katya – and, second, I'm very easily carried away by passion.'

Bazarov looked at Anna Sergeyevna.

'Maybe. You know best. And so, you want an argument. Let's begin. I was looking at the views of Saxon Switzerland[3] in your album, and you said to me that that can't interest me. You said that because you assume I have no artistic sense – and indeed I have none. But those views could interest me from a geological point of view, for example in connection with the formation of mountains.'

'Excuse me, as a geologist you should be consulting a book, a specialist work, rather than a picture.'

'A drawing can present to me visually what a book needs ten whole pages to explain.'

Anna Sergeyevna didn't reply.

'And so do you really not have a drop of artistic sense?' she said, putting her elbows on the table and with this movement bringing her face nearer to Bazarov. 'How can you do without it?'

'But may I ask why it's needed?'

'If only to be able to get to know people and to study them.'

Bazarov smiled.

'First, for that we have life experience. And second I tell you it's a waste of effort studying separate individuals. All human beings are like one another, in their souls as much as their bodies. Each of us has an identically constructed brain, spleen, heart, lungs. And the so-called moral qualities are the same in us all; small variations have no significance. A single human specimen is enough to judge them all. People are like trees in a forest. No botanist is going to study each individual birch tree.'

Katya, who was unhurriedly arranging the flowers, looked up at Bazarov in bewilderment – and meeting his bold, roving gaze, she flushed red to her ears. Anna Sergeyevna shook her head.

'Trees in a forest,' she repeated. 'So, in your opinion, there is no difference between a stupid man and an intelligent one, between a good man and a bad one?'

'No, there is. As there is between a sick man and a healthy one. The lungs of a consumptive aren't in the same condition as yours or mine, although they are identically made. We know approximately the causes of bodily ailments, and moral diseases come from bad education, from all kinds of rubbish people's heads have been crammed with since childhood – in a word, from the shameful state of society. Reform society, and you'll have no more diseases.'

Bazarov said all this looking as if he was thinking to himself, 'I really don't care whether you believe me or not!' He slowly stroked his side whiskers with long fingers and let his eyes roam the corners of the room.

'And do you suppose,' said Anna Sergeyevna, 'that, when society is reformed, there'll be no stupid or bad people?'

'At least in a properly ordered society it won't matter if a man is stupid or intelligent, bad or good.'

'Yes, I understand. They'll have an identical spleen.'

'Quite so, madame.'

Anna Sergeyevna turned to Arkady.

'And what do you think, Arkady Nikolayevich?'

'I agree with Yevgeny,' he answered.

'Gentlemen, you astonish me,' said Anna Sergeyevna, 'but we'll talk more about this. Now I can hear my aunt coming to have tea. We must spare her ears.'

Anna Sergeyevna's aunt, Princess Kh–ya, a thin little woman with a face pinched in like someone making a fist, staring malevolent eyes and a grey wig, came in and, barely greeting the guests, sank into a velvet easy chair on which no one except for her had the right to sit. Katya put a footstool under her feet. The old woman didn't thank her, didn't even look at her, but moved her hands about under the yellow shawl which enveloped most of her puny body. The princess liked the colour yellow: her cap had bright-yellow ribbons.

'Did you sleep well, Auntie?' Anna Sergeyevna asked, raising her voice.

'That dog's in here again,' was the old woman's grumbling reply, and, seeing that Fifi had made two tentative steps in her direction, she cried, 'Shoo, shoo!'

Katya called Fifi and opened the door for her. Fifi happily rushed out, hoping that someone would take her for a walk, but, left alone outside the door, she began to scratch and whine. The princess frowned and Katya was about to go out . . .

'I think tea must be ready,' said Anna Sergeyevna. 'Gentlemen, come. Auntie, would you like to have tea?'

The princess got up from her chair without a word and left the drawing room first. Everyone followed her into the dining room. A page in Cossack livery noisily pulled back from the table another favourite cushioned chair, into which the princess sank. Katya, who was pouring the tea, served her first in a cup with a painted coat of arms. The old woman put honey in her cup (she thought that to take tea with sugar was both sinful[4] and expensive, although she herself didn't spend a penny on anything) and suddenly asked in a croaking voice:

'What does *Prince* Ivan say in his letter?'

No one answered her. Bazarov and Arkady soon made out that no one paid her any attention for all their politeness to her. 'They keep her for show – spawn of princes,' thought Bazarov. After tea Anna Sergeyevna suggested going for a walk. But it began to drizzle, and the whole company, with the exception of the princess, returned to the drawing room. The neighbour who liked playing cards arrived. His name was Porfiry Platonych; he was a plump gentleman, very polite and full of smiles, with grey hair and short, well-turned little legs. Anna Sergeyevna, who more and more was talking to Bazarov, asked him if he would like to play with them an old-fashioned round of *préférence*.[5] Bazarov agreed, saying he had to become prepared for the duties of a country doctor that lay ahead for him.

'Be careful,' said Anna Sergeyevna. 'Porfiry Platonych and I will destroy you. And, Katya,' she added, 'you play something for Arkady Nikolayevich. He loves music and we too can listen.'

Katya unwillingly went to the piano; and Arkady, although he did indeed love music, unwillingly followed her. He thought Anna Sergeyevna was dismissing him and, like every young man of his age, he felt stirring in his heart a confused and painful feeling like some foretaste of love. Katya raised the lid of the piano and, without looking at Arkady, asked in a low voice:

'What would you like me to play you?'

'Whatever you like,' Arkady answered indifferently.

'What kind of music do you like best?' Katya said again without moving.

'Classical music,' Arkady answered in the same tone of voice.

'Do you like Mozart?'

'Yes, I do.'

Katya got out Mozart's Fantasy in C-Minor.[6] She played very well, although a little severely and drily. She sat firm and upright, not taking her eyes off the music and with her lips pressed firmly together, and it was only at the end of the sonata that her cheeks began to glow and a little lock of loosened hair fell over her dark eyebrows.

The last part of the sonata made a particular impression on Arkady, the part where, amidst the enchanting gaiety of the light-hearted melody, there is a surge of such anguished, almost tragic grief . . . But his thoughts occasioned by the sounds of Mozart were not of Katya. Looking at her, he only thought, 'This girl really plays quite well, and she's not bad-looking either.'

Having finished the sonata, Katya asked, without taking her hands from the keys, 'Have you had enough?' Arkady stated that he wouldn't presume to impose on her any more and began talking to her about Mozart. He asked her if she had chosen this sonata herself, or had somebody recommended it to her. But Katya gave him monosyllabic answers: she just *hid*, she went into herself. When that happened to her, it took a long time before she came out. Her actual face took on then an obstinate, almost obtuse expression. She was not exactly shy but mistrustful and a bit scared of the sister who brought her up – something of course which the latter did not suspect. To keep face Arkady was reduced to calling to Fifi, who had come back, and stroking her head with an amiable smile. Katya went back to doing her flowers.

Meanwhile Bazarov paid fine after fine. Anna Sergeyevna played a masterly game of cards; Porfiry Platonych too could hold his own. Bazarov was the loser; although his loss was insignificant, it still wasn't very pleasant for him. At supper Anna Sergeyevna again brought up the subject of botany.

'Let's go for a walk tomorrow morning,' she said to him. 'I want to learn from you the Latin names of wild plants and their properties.'

'Why do you need Latin names?' asked Bazarov.

'One needs order in everything,' she replied.

'What a wonderful woman Anna Sergeyevna is,' Arkady exclaimed when he was alone with his friend in the room they'd been given.

'Yes,' answered Bazarov, 'that's a lady with a brain. And she's seen life.'

'In what sense do you mean, Yevgeny Vasilyich?'

'In a good sense, my friend Arkady Nikolaich, in a good sense! I am sure too that she manages her estate really well. But she isn't the real wonder, that's her sister.'

'What? That little dark girl?'

'Yes, that little dark girl. There is something fresh and untouched and timid and silent, anything you like. There is someone worth bothering with. You can make out of her whatever you want. The other one's been around.'

Arkady didn't answer Bazarov, and each went to bed with his own particular thoughts in his head.

Anna Sergeyevna too thought of her guests that night. She had liked Bazarov – for his unpretentiousness and for the very bluntness of his views. She saw in him something new she hadn't come across before and she was curious.

Anna Sergeyevna was a rather strange being. Having no prejudices, having no real beliefs even, she stopped before nothing, but she didn't move in any particular direction. Many things she saw clearly, many things engaged her interest, and nothing fully satisfied her: she probably didn't want complete satisfaction. Her mind was questing and indifferent at one and the same time: her doubts were never sufficiently allayed for her to forget them, but they never grew so as to cause her alarm. If she hadn't been rich and independent, perhaps she would have joined the fray and known passion . . . But she had an easy life, although she was sometimes bored, and she went on living day after unhurried day, only occasionally prey to anxiety. Rainbow colours sometimes flashed before her eyes, but when they faded she was relieved and didn't regret them. Her imagination even went beyond the bounds of what the laws of conventional morality regard as permissible; but even then the blood just went on coursing quietly through the veins of her calm, lovely and graceful body. At times, as she left her scented bath, all warm and pampered, she would ponder the insignificance of life, its sorrow, its toil and evil . . . A rush of courage would fill her spirit, and she would be fired by a noble impulse; but a draught would come in through a half-open window, and Anna Sergeyevna would shrink and complain and almost get angry, and at that moment she only wanted one thing – for that horrid wind to stop blowing.

Like all women who haven't managed to know love she wanted something without herself knowing exactly what. In fact she didn't really want anything although she thought she wanted everything. She had barely been able to tolerate the late Odintsov (she had married him out of calculation although she probably wouldn't have done so if she hadn't recognized he was a good man) and she experienced a secret revulsion for all men, whom she thought of as nothing more than messy, heavy, flabby, limp and tiresome creatures. Somewhere abroad she had once met a young, handsome Swede with a chivalrous expression, honest blue eyes and an open brow; he had made a strong impression on her, but that hadn't kept her from returning to Russia.

'What a strange man that doctor is!' she thought as she lay in her splendid bed on her lace pillows under a light silken coverlet . . . Anna Sergeyevna had inherited from her father a bit of his taste for luxury. She had dearly loved her father, with all his sins but a kind heart; he worshipped her, joked with her as a friend and equal, trusted her completely and took her advice. Her mother she barely remembered.

'What a strange man the doctor is!' she repeated to herself. She stretched, smiled and put her hands behind her head. Then she scanned a couple of pages of a silly French novel, dropped the book – and fell asleep, all clean and cold in her clean and scented sheets.

The next morning Anna Sergeyevna and Bazarov went off botanizing immediately after breakfast and returned just before dinner. Arkady didn't go anywhere and spent an hour or so with Katya. He wasn't bored with her, and she herself volunteered to play yesterday's sonata again. But when Odintsova came back, his heart tightened for a moment . . . She walked through the garden with slightly weary steps, her cheeks were flushed, and her eyes shone more than usual from under her round straw hat. She was turning round in her fingers the stem of a wild flower, a light shawl had slipped down to her elbows, and the broad grey ribbons of her hat lay on her breast. Bazarov walked behind her confidently and easily, as usual, but Arkady didn't like the expression on his face – though it was cheerful, even affectionate. Muttering 'Good day!' Bazarov went off to his room, and Anna Sergeyevna distractedly shook Arkady's hand and also walked on past him.

'Good day!' thought Arkady. 'As if we hadn't seen each other today?'

XVII

It's a known fact that time sometimes flies like a bird and sometimes creeps along like a worm. But it's best for a man if he doesn't notice whether it's passing quickly or slowly. That's how Arkady and Bazarov spent a fortnight at Odintsova's. It was partly helped by the order she had established in the house and in her life. She maintained it rigidly and made others observe it. Everything during the day took place at a known time. In the morning, at eight precisely, the whole company gathered for tea. From tea till lunch everyone did what he wanted while the hostess was busy with her steward (the estate was run on a quit-rent basis), her butler and her head house-keeper. Before dinner the company assembled again to talk or read. The evenings were given over to walking, cards and music. At half past ten Anna Sergeyevna withdrew to her room, gave her orders for the following day and went to bed. Bazarov didn't like this measured, slightly formal regularity of everyday life; he claimed, 'It's as if you were going along on rails': liver-ied footmen and dignified butlers offended his democratic sen-sibility. He found that if things had gone that far, they might as well sit down to dinner like the English, in white tie and tails. He once had it out with Anna Sergeyevna on this subject. Her way of behaving was such that anyone would be quite open about what they thought in front of her. She heard him out and said, 'From your point of view you are right – and maybe in this case I am playing the grand lady. But one can't live in the country without order; otherwise one would be overcome by boredom.' And she went on acting in her own way. Bazarov grumbled, but the reason that he and Arkady had such a com-fortable time at Odintsova's was because everything in her house 'went along as if it was on rails'.

With all this a change took place in both young men from the very first days of their stay at Nikolskoye. Bazarov, whom Anna Sergeyevna clearly liked though she seldom agreed with him, felt a sense of disquiet he hadn't had before: he was easily irritated, was reluctant to talk, looked angrily about him and couldn't sit still, as if something were nagging him. And Arkady, who had finally decided he was in love with Anna Sergeyevna, began to indulge in quiet despair. However, this despair didn't prevent him from becoming close to Katya: it even helped him to be on affectionate and friendly terms with her. '*She* doesn't appreciate me! So that's that! . . . But here is a kind being who doesn't reject me,' he thought, and his heart again tasted the pleasure of high-minded generosity. Katya dimly felt he was seeking some kind of solace in her company, and didn't deny either him or herself the innocent pleasure of a friendship that was both timid and trusting. In front of Anna Sergeyevna they didn't speak to one another: Katya always shrank under her sister's sharp eyes, and Arkady – as is right for a man in love – when he was near the object of his love, couldn't pay attention to anything else. But he was at ease with Katya on her own. He felt it was beyond his power to engage Anna Sergeyevna's interest; he was shy and became flustered when he was alone with her; and she didn't know what to say to him; he was too young for her. On the other hand with Katya Arkady felt at home; he was indulgent with her and didn't stop her sharing with him what she had learnt from music, reading novels, poetry and other nonsense, without himself noticing or acknowledging that this nonsense interested him. For her part Katya didn't stop his melancholy pose. Arkady felt good in Katya's company, and Anna Sergeyevna in Bazarov's, and so it usually happened that after a short time together both couples would go off by themselves, especially during their walks. Katya *adored* nature, and Arkady liked nature too although he didn't dare admit it. Anna Sergeyevna was fairly indifferent to nature, like Bazarov. Since now our friends were apart almost the whole time, that too had consequences: their relationship started to change. Bazarov stopped talking to Arkady about Odintsova, he even stopped criticizing her 'aristocratic little ways'. It's true he continued to praise Katya and only advised Arkady to control her tendency towards sentimentality, but his praise was cursory and his advice stiff. In general he chatted to Arkady much less than before . . . as if he were avoiding him, were ashamed of him . . .

Arkady noticed all this but kept his thoughts to himself.

The real reason for this whole change lay in the feelings that Odintsova had inspired in Bazarov – feelings which tormented and maddened him and which he would have denied with a scornful laugh and a cynical curse if anyone had even remotely hinted at the possibility of what had happened to him. Bazarov was a great lover of women and of feminine beauty, but love in the ideal or, in his word, romantic, sense he called rubbish, unforgivable folly; he considered chivalrous love a kind of deformity or disease, and several times he expressed his surprise that Toggenburg hadn't been consigned to a lunatic asylum with the whole pack of Minnesingers and troubadours.[1] 'If you like a woman,' he would say, 'try and get what you want; but if you can't, well, you can't; just go away – there are other fish in the sea.' He liked Anna Sergeyevna: the stories that went around about her, the freedom and independence of her thinking, her indubitably positive feelings towards him – everything seemed to be in his favour; however, he soon realized that with her you wouldn't get 'what you want', but to his amazement he hadn't the strength to turn away from her. As soon as he started to think of her, his blood was on fire; he could easily have coped with that, but something else had taken root in him, something he had absolutely no time for, which he always used to mock, which offended all his pride. In his conversations with Anna Sergeyevna he expressed his scornful indifference to all things romantic even more than before; but when he was on his own he recognized with indignation that he had become a romantic. Then he would take himself off to the woods and walk there with big strides, breaking off branches in his path and muttering curses at her and at himself; or he would go up into the hayloft in the barn and, stubbornly closing his eyes, would try to fall asleep, in which of course he didn't always succeed. He would suddenly imagine those chaste arms some day twined in an embrace round his neck, those proud lips responding to his kisses, those wise eyes tenderly – yes, tenderly – meeting his, and his head would spin and for a moment he would forget himself – until his anger flared up again. He caught himself in all manner of 'shameful' thoughts as if a devil were playing with him. He sometimes thought that Anna Sergeyevna too had changed, that her expression signified something particular, that perhaps . . . But then he would usually stamp his foot and grind his teeth and shake his fist.

However, Bazarov wasn't completely wrong. He had caught Odintsova's imagination, he interested her, she thought about him a lot. When he wasn't there she didn't pine, she didn't wait for him to come, but his coming at once enlivened her; she was glad to spend time alone with him and was glad to talk to him even when he made her angry or attacked her taste and her elegant ways. She seemed to want to study her own self while putting him to the test.

One day, as they were walking in the garden, he suddenly announced in a glum voice that he was going to leave and go to his father's village . . . She went pale as if she'd been stabbed in the heart – so painfully that she was surprised and for a long time afterwards thought about what that might mean. Bazarov hadn't made this announcement to test her and see what happened. He never played games. That morning he had seen Timofeich, his father's bailiff who had looked after him as a child, a shrewd and agile old man with faded yellow hair, a weather-beaten red face and screwed-up, running eyes. Timofeich had unexpectedly appeared before Bazarov in his short jacket of thick grey-blue cloth, belted with a bit of strap, and tarred boots.

'Well, old friend, greetings!' exclaimed Bazarov.

'Greetings, Yevgeny Vasilyevich, sir,' the old man began and gave a happy smile, which wrinkled up his entire face.

'Why've you come? Did they send you for me?'

'How can you think that, sir?' Timofeich stammered (remembering the strict instructions his master had given him when he left). 'I was going to town on master's business and heard Your Honour was here, so I dropped in on the way, that is – just to have a look at Your Honour, otherwise I wouldn't bother you!'

'Don't tell lies,' Bazarov interrupted him. 'Is this your way to town?'

Timofeich hesitated and didn't reply.

'Is my father well?'

'He is, thank God.'

'And my mother?'

'Arina Vlasyevna is well, thanks to the Lord.'

'I suppose they're waiting for me.'

The old man put his little head to one side.

'Oh, Yevgeny Vasilyevich, how could they not! Believe me, my heart bleeds when I look at your parents.'

'Very well then! Don't get carried away. Tell them I'll soon be there.'

'Yes, sir,' Timofeich answered, with a sigh.

Having gone out of the house, he pulled down his cap over his forehead with both hands, got up into the wretched fast droshky he had left at the gates and went off at a trot, only not in the direction of the town.

That evening Anna Sergeyevna was sitting in her room with Bazarov while Arkady was walking up and down the big drawing room, listening to Katya play the piano. The princess had gone to her rooms upstairs; she generally couldn't stand guests, and in particular these 'new lunatics' as she called them. In the public rooms she just sulked, but in her own quarters with her maid she sometimes got so carried away with abuse that her cap and wig jumped about on her head. Anna Sergeyevna knew all that.

'How can you think of leaving?' she began. 'What about your promise?'

Bazarov shivered.

'What promise?'

'Have you forgotten? You were going to give me some chemistry lessons.'

'What can I do? My father is expecting me, and I can't hold back any longer. However, you can read Pelouse and Frémy's *Notions générales de Chimie*.[2] It's a good book and clearly written. You'll find in it all you need.'

'But do you remember you told me a book cannot replace – I've forgotten how you phrased it, but you know what I mean . . . do you remember?'

'What can I do?' Bazarov repeated.

'Why leave?' said Anna Sergeyevna, lowering her voice.

He looked at her. She leant her head against the back of her chair and crossed her arms, which were bare to the elbow, on her breast. She looked paler in the light of a single lamp with a cut paper shade. She was completely shrouded in the soft drapery of a voluminous white dress: the tips of her feet, which were also crossed, were only just visible.

'But why stay?' Bazarov replied.

She turned her head a little.

'Why? Aren't you enjoying yourself here? Or do you think you won't be missed?'

'I'm sure I won't be.'

For a moment Anna Sergeyevna didn't say anything.

'You're wrong to think that. But I don't believe you. You couldn't be serious saying it.' Bazarov continued to sit without moving. 'Yevgeny Vasilyevich, why aren't you saying anything?'

'What should I be saying to you? In general there's no point in missing people, certainly not me.'

'Why is that?'

'I'm a down-to-earth, uninteresting man. I don't know how to talk.'

'You're fishing for compliments, Yevgeny Vasilyevich.'

'I don't do that. Don't you yourself know that I can't enter the elegant side of life, that side you so value?'

Anna Sergeyevna bit the corner of her handkerchief.

'You can think what you like, but I'll be bored when you go.'

'Arkady will be staying behind.'

She slightly shrugged her shoulders.

'I'll be bored,' she said again.

'Really? At all events you won't be bored for long.'

'What makes you think that?'

'Because you yourself told me that you only get bored when the order of your life is disturbed. You've organized your life with such faultless regularity that there can be no room in it for boredom or distress . . . for any painful feeling.'

'You find me faultless . . . that is, in the regularity of my life?'

'Absolutely! For example – in a few minutes' time it'll strike ten, and I know in advance you'll ask me to leave.'

'No, I won't, Yevgeny Vasilyich. You can stay. Open that window . . . I feel there's no air.'

Bazarov got up and gave the window a push. It opened at once with a noise . . . He wasn't expecting it to open so easily – and his hands were shaking. The dark and gentle night entered the room with its almost black sky, the soft murmur of the trees and the fresh smell of free, clean air.

'Pull down the blind and sit down,' said Anna Sergeyevna. 'I want to chat to you before you go. Tell me something about yourself. You never talk about yourself.'

'Anna Sergeyevna, I try and talk to you about useful things.'

'You're very modest . . . But I'd like to learn something about you, about your family, about your father, for whom you're leaving us.'

'Why is she talking like this?' thought Bazarov.

'All that has absolutely no interest,' he said aloud, 'especially for you. We're humble people . . .'

'And you think I'm an aristocrat?'

Bazarov raised his eyes to her.

'Yes,' he said with exaggerated emphasis.

She smiled.

'I see you don't know me very well, although you claim all men are like one another and there is no point in studying them. One day I'll tell you the story of my life . . . But first you'll tell me yours.'

'I don't know you very well,' Bazarov repeated. 'Perhaps you're right; perhaps everyone effectively is a riddle. You, for example. You shun society, it wears you down – and then you invite two students to come and stay. Why, with your intelligence, with your beauty, do you live in the country?'

'What? What did you say then?' Anna Sergeyevna interrupted him animatedly. 'With my . . . beauty?'

Bazarov frowned.

'It doesn't matter,' he mumbled, 'I meant to say I don't really understand why you've gone to live in the country.'

'You don't understand . . . However, do you have a way of explaining it to yourself?'

'Yes, I do . . . I suppose you stay the whole time in the same place because you are spoilt, because you're very fond of comfort and convenience, and are pretty indifferent to everything else.'

She smiled again.

'You really don't want to think I'm capable of passion.'

Bazarov looked at her with a frown.

'Out of curiosity perhaps, but not otherwise.'

'Really? Well, now I understand why we get on so well. You're just the same as me.'

'We get on so well . . .' Bazarov said in a low voice.

'Yes! . . . But I forgot that you want to leave.'

Bazarov got up. A lamp was feebly burning in the dark, scented, secluded room. The blind stirred lightly and let in the irritating freshness of the night and its mysterious rustling. Anna Sergeyevna didn't move but she was gradually overcome by a hidden emotion . . . which communicated itself to Bazarov. He suddenly felt himself alone with a young and beautiful woman . . .

'Where are you going?' she said slowly.

He didn't reply and sat down again on his chair.

'And so you think me an effete, spoilt creature, with no troubles,' she went on in the same tone of voice and keeping her eyes fixed on the window. 'But I know about myself that I'm very unhappy.'

'You're unhappy! Why? Surely you can't attach any importance to worthless gossip?'

She frowned. She was annoyed that he had misunderstood her.

'That gossip doesn't even make me laugh, Yevgeny Vasilyevich, and I am too proud to let it worry me. I am unhappy because . . . because I have no desire, no urge to live. You're looking at me distrustfully, you're thinking – there's the "aristocrat" speaking, all dressed in lace, sitting in her velvet chair. I am quite open: I like what you call comfort, and at the same time I don't have much wish to live. Reconcile that contradiction as you choose. But of course all that to you is romanticism.'

Bazarov shook his head.

'You're healthy, independent, rich: what else? What more do you want?'

'What more do I want?' she repeated and sighed. 'I'm very tired, I'm old, it seems to me I've been alive for a long time. Yes, I'm old,' she went on, slowly pulling the edge of her mantilla over her bare arms. Her eyes met Bazarov's and she went slightly red. 'I have already so many memories behind me: life in St Petersburg, riches, then poverty, then my father's death, marriage, then the usual trip abroad . . . I have many memories, but nothing worth remembering, and ahead of me lies a long, long road, and no goal . . . I don't want to take that road.'

'Are you so disillusioned?' asked Bazarov.

'No,' she said after a pause, 'but I'm not satisfied. I think that if I could form a strong attachment to something . . .'

'You want to love,' Bazarov interrupted her, 'but you can't. That's where your unhappiness comes from.'

Anna Sergeyevna began to examine the sleeves of her mantilla.

'Can't I love?' she said.

'No! Only I was wrong to call that unhappiness. On the contrary, one should feel for someone to whom that thing happens.'

'To whom what happens?'

'Love.'

'And how do you know that?'

'From hearsay,' Bazarov said crossly.

'You're flirting,' he thought, 'you're bored and you're playing with me from having nothing to do while I . . .' His heart really felt as if it was bursting.

'Besides, perhaps you're too demanding,' he said, leaning right forward and playing with the fringe of his chair.

'Maybe I am. For me it's all or nothing. A life for a life. What I give I expect to be given – no regrets and no return. Otherwise better not.'

'Well then,' said Bazarov, 'those are fair conditions, and I am surprised you haven't yet . . . found what you want.'

'But do you think it's easy to surrender oneself completely to something?'

'It's not easy once you start reflecting on it, and playing a waiting game, and putting a price on yourself, that is valuing yourself, but if you don't reflect, it's very easy to surrender yourself.'

'How should one not value oneself? If I have no price, who needs my devotion?'

'That's not my concern now. It's for someone else to work

out what's my price. The important thing is to be able to surrender oneself.'

Odintsova leant forward in her chair.

'You speak,' she began, 'as if you'd had experience of all this.'

'It just came to mind, Anna Sergeyevna. You know, all this
isn't my kind of thing.'

'But you would know how to surrender yourself?'

'I don't really know, I don't want to boast.'

Odintsova said nothing, and Bazarov fell silent. The sounds
of the piano came to them from the drawing room.

'Why is Katya playing so late?' she said.

Bazarov got up.

'Yes, it really is late, it's time for us to go to bed.'

'Wait a moment. Where are you hurrying off to? . . . I need
to tell you one thing.'

'What?'

'Wait a moment,' she whispered.

Her eyes came to rest on Bazarov. She seemed to be examining him attentively.

He walked across the room, then suddenly came right up to
her, quickly said 'goodbye', gripped her hand so hard she almost
screamed and went out. She lifted her fingers, still all squeezed
together, to her lips, blew on them and then jumped up from
her chair and hurried towards the door as if to bring Bazarov
back . . . A maid came into the room with a carafe on a silver
tray. Anna Sergeyevna stopped, told her to leave and sat down
again, and again became lost in her thoughts. Her hair became
unloosened and fell on her shoulders like a dark serpent. The
lamp went on burning in Anna Sergeyevna's room for a long
time, and for a long time she sat without moving, just occasionally moving her fingers over her arms, which were being gently
nipped by the night chill.

Two hours later Bazarov came back to his bedroom, his
boots all wet with the dew, looking dishevelled and gloomy. He
found Arkady at the writing table, with a book in his hands, his
coat still buttoned right up.

'Haven't you gone to bed yet?' he said almost with annoyance.

'Did you sit up a long time with Anna Sergeyevna?' said
Arkady, not answering his question.

'Yes, I sat with her the whole time you and Katerina
Sergeyevna were playing the piano.'

'I wasn't playing . . .'Arkady began and then fell silent. He
felt tears coming into his eyes and he didn't want to cry in front
of his mocking friend.

XVIII

The following day, when Anna Sergeyevna came down to tea,
Bazarov sat for a long time hunched over his cup, then suddenly looked up at her . . . She turned to him, as if he had
pushed her, and he thought her face had become slightly paler
overnight. She soon went to her room and only reappeared at
lunch. It had been raining all morning, and there was no possibility of going for a walk. The whole company assembled in
the drawing room. Arkady got the latest issue of a journal and
started to read aloud. The princess, in her usual way, at first
looked surprised, as if he had done something indecent, and
then gave him a malevolent stare; but he didn't pay her any
attention.

'Yevgeny Vasilyevich,' said Anna Sergeyevna, 'let's go to my
room . . . I want to ask you . . . Yesterday you mentioned to me
the title of a textbook . . .'

She got up and moved towards the door. The princess looked
around, making a face which meant 'Look, look how shocked
I am!' and gave Arkady another stare, but he raised his voice
and, exchanging a look with Katya, by whom he was sitting,
continued to read.

Anna Sergeyevna walked quickly to her study. Bazarov
briskly followed her, without raising his eyes from the ground,
and it was only his ears that caught the delicate swish and rustle of her silk dress gliding before him. She dropped into the
same chair she had sat in the evening before, and Bazarov took
his place of yesterday.

'What is the name of that book?' she began after a short silence.

'Pelouse et Frémy, *Notions générales* . . .' Bazarov answered. 'But I can also recommend to you Ganot's *Traité élémentaire de physique expérimentale*.[1] In that the illustrations are clearer, and generally speaking this textbook . . .'

She held out her hand.

'Yevgeny Vasilyevich, forgive me, but I didn't ask you in here to talk about textbooks. I wanted to come back to our conversation of yesterday. You went out so suddenly . . . Will this bore you?'

'I am at your service, Anna Sergeyevna. But what were we talking about yesterday?'

She gave Bazarov a sideways look.

'I think we were talking about happiness. I was telling you about myself. Now I just used the word "happiness". Tell me, why is it that even when we enjoy, for example, music, or a good party, or conversation with sympathetic people, why is it that all that seems to be a hint of some infinite happiness existing somewhere else rather than a real happiness, that is one we own ourselves? Why? Or perhaps you don't feel anything of the kind?'

'You know the proverb "the grass is always greener on the other side of the hill",' replied Bazarov, 'and you yourself said yesterday that you're not satisfied. But really such thoughts don't enter my head.'

'Perhaps they seem ridiculous to you?'

'They don't, but they don't enter my head.'

'Really? You know, I'd very much like to know what *you* think about.'

'What? I don't understand you.'

'Listen, for a long time I've been wanting to talk to you about this. I don't need to tell you – you know it yourself – you're no ordinary man; you're still young – you have your whole life in front of you. What are you preparing yourself for? What future awaits you? I mean to say – what goal do you want to reach, where are you going, what are your innermost feelings? In a word, who are you, what are you?'

'You astonish me, Anna Sergeyevna. You know that I am

studying the natural sciences, and as for who I am . . .'

'Yes, who are you?'

'I have already stated to you that I am a future district doctor.'

Anna Sergeyevna made an impatient movement.

'Why do you say that? You yourself don't believe it. Arkady could give me an answer like that, but not you.'

'How does Arkady . . .?'

'Stop it! Is it possible that you'd be satisfied with such a modest occupation, and aren't you yourself always claiming medicine has no meaning for you? A district doctor? You, with your pride? You are giving me that answer to fob me off, because you have no trust in me. But do you know, Yevgeny Vasilyich, I could understand you: I was poor and proud like you; I underwent maybe the same experiences as you.'

'All that is very fine, Anna Sergeyevna, but you must excuse me . . . I am generally not accustomed to baring my heart, and there is such a distance between you and me . . .'

'What distance? Are you going to tell me again that I am an aristocrat? Enough of that, Yevgeny Vasilyich; I think I have proved to you . . .'

'Yes, and besides,' Bazarov interrupted her, 'why all this talking and thinking about a future which very largely doesn't depend on us? If we have the chance to do something, well and good, but if we don't, then we can be thankful we did without all the pointless chatter about it beforehand.'

'You call conversation with a friend chatter . . . Or perhaps you don't consider me, as a woman, worthy of your trust? Since you despise us all.'

'I don't despise you, Anna Sergeyevna, and you know that.'

'No, I don't know anything . . . but let's make an assumption: I understand your not wanting to talk about the future of your work; but with all that's going on inside you at this moment . . .'

'Going on inside me!' Bazarov repeated. 'As if I were some kind of state or society! At all events it's completely without interest; and also can a man say out aloud everything that is "going on" inside him?'

'But I don't see why you can't speak out everything in your heart.'

'Can *you*?' asked Bazarov.

'Yes, I can,' Anna Sergeyevna answered after a brief hesitation.

Bazarov bowed his head.

'You're more fortunate than me.'

Anna Sergeyevna gave him an inquiring look.

'As you choose,' she went on, 'but all the same something tells me that there is a reason for our having become close to one another, that we will be good friends. I am sure that your, what should I call it, your tenseness, your reserve will eventually disappear.'

'So you've noticed reserve in me . . . what did you also call it . . . tenseness?'

'Yes.'

Bazarov got up and went to the window.

'And you would like to know the reason for that reserve, you would like to know what is going on inside me?'

'Yes,' Anna Sergeyevna said again, with a fear she didn't yet understand.

'And you won't be angry?'

'No, I won't.'

'You won't?' Bazarov was standing with his back to her. 'So you must know that I love you, foolishly, madly . . . That's what you've got out of me.'

Anna Sergeyevna held both her arms out in front of her while Bazarov pressed his forehead against a window pane. He was choking; his whole body was visibly trembling. But it wasn't the tremor of a young man's shyness he was feeling, nor the pleasurable terror of a first declaration of love. It was passion fighting in him, a strong and oppressive passion – one that looked like anger and was perhaps indeed akin to it. Anna Sergeyevna felt both frightened of him and sorry for him.

'Yevgeny Vasilyich,' she said, and in spite of herself there was tenderness in her voice.

He quickly turned round, devoured her with his eyes and, grabbing both her arms, pulled her to his breast.

She didn't escape from his arms at once; but a moment later she was already standing far from him in a corner, and from there she looked at him. He rushed towards her . . .

'You haven't understood me,' she whispered hurriedly in fright. If he'd taken one more step, it seemed she would have screamed . . . Bazarov bit his lip and went out.

Half an hour later a maid gave Anna Sergeyevna a note from Bazarov; it consisted of a single line: 'Must I leave today – or can I stay until tomorrow?' 'Why must you leave? I didn't understand you – and you haven't understood me' was Anna Sergeyevna's reply to him, and she herself thought: 'And I didn't understand myself.'

She didn't appear again till dinner and kept pacing up and down in her room, her hands behind her back, from time to time stopping before a window or before the mirror and slowly rubbing a handkerchief over her neck, which felt as if it had a burning patch on it. She kept on asking herself what had made her get that admission out of him (to use Bazarov's phrase), and if she hadn't suspected anything . . . 'I am to blame,' she said aloud, 'but I couldn't have foreseen this.' She became lost in her thoughts and blushed when she remembered the almost animal expression on Bazarov's face when he dashed towards her . . .

'Or maybe?' she suddenly said and stopped her pacing and shook her curls . . . She caught sight of herself in the mirror; her head thrown back and the enigmatic smile of her half-closed, half-open eyes and lips seemed to be telling her in that moment something which made her feel embarrassed . . .

'No,' she decided finally, 'God knows where that might have led, one mustn't play about with this, after all, peace of mind is the best thing in the world.'

Her peace of mind was not disturbed; but she became melancholy and even wept once without knowing why, only not from being insulted. She didn't feel herself to have been insulted: it was more that she felt herself guilty. Under the influence of various confused feelings, and the consciousness of life moving on, and a desire for novelty, she had made herself go up to a limit and had made herself look beyond it – and she had seen beyond not even an abyss but emptiness . . . or ugly things.

XIX

For all Anna Sergeyevna's self-control, for all her being above pre-judice, she still felt awkward when she came into the dining room for dinner. But dinner went quite successfully. Porfiry Platonych came and told various stories; he had just come back from the town. He told them among other things that Governor Bourd-aloue had instructed his officials on special assignments to wear spurs in case he should send them somewhere on horseback, in the interests of speed. Arkady had a discussion with Katya in a low voice and paid diplomatic court to the princess. Bazarov main-tained a stubborn and gloomy silence. Anna Sergeyevna a couple of times looked – openly, not covertly – at his stern and bitter face, with lowered eyes, with the mark of scornful determination stamped on every feature, and thought to herself: 'No . . . no . . . no . . .' After dinner she and the rest of the company went into the garden and, seeing that Bazarov wanted to talk to her, she took a few steps to one side and stopped. He drew near her, though with-out raising his eyes even now, and said in a dull voice:

'Anna Sergeyevna, I must apologize to you. You can't not be angry with me.'

'No, I'm not angry with you, Yevgeny Vasilyich,' she answered, 'but I'm disappointed.'

'So much the worse. In any case I am punished enough. My situation is extremely silly – you must agree. You wrote to me, why must you leave? But I cannot and do not want to stay. Tomorrow I won't be here.'

'Yevgeny Vasilyich, why are you . . .'

'Why am I leaving?'

'No, that wasn't what I meant.'

'One can't bring back the past, Anna Sergeyevna . . . and sooner or later this was bound to happen. Consequently, I have to leave. I can see only one condition under which I could stay; but that condition can never be. Excuse my impertinence, but you don't love me, do you, and you can't ever love me.'

For a second Bazarov's eyes flashed from under his dark brows.

Anna Sergeyevna didn't answer him. 'I am frightened of this man,' was the thought that went quickly through her mind.

'Goodbye, madame,' Bazarov said, as if he had guessed her thought and went towards the house.

Anna Sergeyevna quietly followed him and, calling Katya, took her arm. She didn't leave her side the whole evening. She wouldn't play cards and did little but laugh, which didn't at all accord with her pale and troubled expression. Arkady was perplexed and watched her, as young people do, that is he kept asking himself, 'What does this mean?' Bazarov had shut himself in his room. However, he did come back for tea. Anna Sergeyevna wanted to say a kind word to him but she didn't know how to open the conversation . . .

An unforeseen circumstance rescued her: the butler announced the arrival of Sitnikov.

It is difficult to find the words to describe the flying entrance of the young progressive. Having decided with his customary bravado to go to the country and visit a woman he barely knew, who had never invited him, but who according to his intelligence had staying with her these clever friends of his, he was scared witless all the same; instead of producing ready-prepared excuses and greetings, he mumbled out some rubbish about Yevdoksiya Kukshina having sent him to inquire about Anna Sergeyevna's health, and also about Arkady Nikolayevich having always talked to him about her in such glowing terms . . . At this point he stumbled and got so confused that he sat down on his own hat. However, since no one showed him the door and since Anna Sergeyevna introduced him to her aunt and sister, he soon recovered himself and chattered away for all he was worth. The appearance of vulgarity often serves a purpose in life: it reduces the tension in strings that are drawn too tight and calms down feelings that are overly confident or forgetful, reminding them how closely related vulgarity is to them. With Sitnikov's coming everything somehow became cruder – and simpler. Everyone even had more appetite for supper and went off to bed half an hour earlier than usual.

'I can now say to you what you once said to me,' said Arkady, lying in bed, to Bazarov, who also had undressed: '"Why are you so gloomy?" You must have carried out some sacred duty.'

For some time the two young men had developed a kind of bantering between themselves that was only easy on the surface: that is always a sign of secret dissatisfaction or suppressed suspicions.

'Tomorrow I'm going to see my old man,' said Bazarov.

Arkady raised himself and leant on his elbow. He was both surprised and for some reason pleased.

'Aha!' he said. 'So that's what making you gloomy?'

Bazarov yawned.

'Ask too many questions . . .'

'And what does Anna Sergeyevna . . .?' Arkady went on.

'What has Anna Sergeyevna got to do with it?'

'I mean, will she let you go?'

'I'm not her servant.'

Arkady became thoughtful, and Bazarov got into bed and turned his face to the wall.

Some minutes of silence passed.

'Yevgeny!' Arkady exclaimed at last.

'What?'

'I'll leave tomorrow with you.'

Bazarov didn't answer.

'Only I'll go home,' Arkady went on. 'We'll travel together as far as the hamlet of Khokhlovsk, and there you can take horses from Fedot. I'd like to meet your parents but I'm afraid I'd be a nuisance to them and to you. You'll be coming later to stay with us again, won't you?'

'I've left my things with you,' Bazarov answered without turning round.

'Why doesn't he ask me why I am going?' Arkady thought. 'And just as suddenly as he is. Really, why am I going, and why is he?' he went on in his thoughts. He couldn't find a satisfactory answer to his own question, and his heart was full of a kind of bitterness. He felt it would be difficult for him to leave this way of life to which he'd become so accustomed; but for him to stay on his own was a bit odd. 'Something must have happened between them,' he said to himself. 'What's the point of my hanging around her after he's gone? I'll really get on her nerves, and I'll lose everything else.' He began to visualize Anna Sergeyevna; then gradually another face eclipsed the beautiful features of the young widow.

'I'll miss Katya too!' he whispered into his pillow – on to which he had already shed a tear . . . Suddenly he shook his head and said loudly:

'Why the hell has that idiot Sitnikov showed up?'

Bazarov first shifted in bed and then said this:

'My friend, I see you're still pretty thick. The Sitnikovs of this world are essential to us. You've got to understand I absolutely need idiots like that. The gods need someone to do the dirty work!'

'Oho!' Arkady thought to himself, and for a moment the boundless scope of Bazarov's egotism now opened up to him. 'So you and I are gods! That is, you are – aren't I one of the idiots?'

'Yes, you're still pretty thick,' Bazarov repeated glumly.

Anna Sergeyevna expressed no particular surprise when Arkady told her the next day that he was leaving with Bazarov. She seemed distracted and tired. Katya silently gave him a serious look, the princess even crossed herself[1] underneath her shawl in such a way that he couldn't but notice it. But Sitnikov was thrown into a panic. He had just come down to breakfast in a new outfit (not a Slavophile one this time). The previous day he had astonished the manservant assigned to him by the quantities of linen he had brought with him. Now his friends were abandoning him! He danced about a bit, rushed around like a driven hare on the edge of a wood – and suddenly announced, in a kind of frightened shriek, that he too was going to leave. Anna Sergeyevna didn't stop him.

'I have a very quiet carriage,' the wretched young man added, turning to Arkady. 'I can give you a lift, and Yevgeny Vasily-evich can take your *tarantas*, so it'll be that much easier.'

'But really, it's quite out of your way, and it's a long way to my home.'

'It doesn't matter, it doesn't matter. I've a lot of time to spare, and I've got business round there.'

'Vodka business?' Arkady asked rather too scornfully.

But Sitnikov was in such despair that, unusually for him, he didn't even laugh.

'I assure you, my carriage is extremely quiet,' he muttered, 'and there'll be room for everyone.'

'Don't say no and disappoint Monsieur Sitnikov,' said Anna Sergeyevna . . .

Arkady looked at her and bowed his head low.

The guests left after breakfast. Saying goodbye to Bazarov, Anna Sergeyevna gave him her hand and said:

'We'll meet again, won't we?'

'As you wish,' answered Bazarov.

'In that case we will.'

Arkady went out first on to the porch and got into Sitnikov's carriage. The butler deferentially helped him, and Arkady could gladly have hit him or burst into tears. Bazarov settled himself in the *tarantas*. When they got to Khokhlovsk, Arkady waited for Fedot, the innkeeper, to harness the horses. He went up to the *tarantas*, gave Bazarov a smile as he used to and said:

'Yevgeny, take me with you. I want to come and stay with you.'

'Get in,' said Bazarov through his teeth.

When Sitnikov, who was walking round the wheels of his carriage gaily whistling, heard this, he could only gawp in astonishment while Arkady coolly took his belongings out of the carriage, got in next to Bazarov – and, with a polite bow to his former fellow-traveller, shouted, 'Let's be off!' The *tarantas* rolled on and soon disappeared from view . . . This time Sitnikov was really thrown and gave his driver a look, but the driver was playing with his whip around the tail of one of the side-horses. Then Sitnikov jumped into the carriage, and, shouting to two passing muzhiks to 'Put your caps back on, idiots!', he made his way to the town, where he arrived very late. The next day at Kukshina's he really went for those two 'awful arrogant louts'.

When Arkady got into the *tarantas* next to Bazarov, he gripped his hand firmly and for a long while didn't say anything. Bazarov seemed to understand and to appreciate both

the handshake and the silence. The previous night he had neither slept nor smoked, and he had eaten next to nothing for
some days. His cap was pulled down over his forehead, empha-
sizing his profile below it, drawn and melancholy.

'Well, my friend,' he said at last, 'give me a cigar . . . And
would you look, is my tongue yellow?'

'It is,' Arkady answered.

'Thought so . . . and the cigar tastes bad. The engine's falling
apart.'

'You really have changed recently,' said Arkady.

'It doesn't matter. I'll get over it. One thing's tiresome – my
mother's so soft-hearted: if you don't eat ten times a day and
put on a paunch, she gets all upset. My father's fine, he's been
everywhere himself and has had a tough and varied life. No, I
can't smoke,' he added, tossing his cigar into the dust of the
road.

'How far is it to your place, fifteen miles?' Arkady asked.

'Yes, fifteen miles. But why don't you ask this wise fellow?'

He pointed to the muzhik sitting on the box, Fedot's driver.

But the wise fellow answered, 'Who knows – they haven't
measured the miles round here,' and went on muttering curses
at his shaft-horse for 'kicking with her noddle', that is, tossing
her head.

'Yes, yes,' Bazarov went on, 'let that be a lesson to you, my
young friend, an instructive example. It's the devil's own mess!
Every man is hanging on a thread, any moment an abyss can
open up beneath him, but he still has to go and think up all
manner of troubles for himself and ruin his life.'

'What are you hinting at?' Arkady asked.

'I'm not hinting at anything, I'm saying straight out that you
and I have both behaved very stupidly. What's the point of talking about it! But I've noticed in the clinic that the patient who
gets angry with his pain always manages to overcome it.'

'I don't fully understand you,' said Arkady. 'I don't think
you've got anything to complain about.'

'If you don't fully understand me, then I'll tell you this: in my
view – it's better to break stones on the road than for a woman
to get control of even the tip of your finger. That's just a load of

. . .' Bazarov almost uttered his favourite word 'romanticism' but refrained and said 'nonsense'. 'You won't believe me now, but I tell you that you and I went into a world of women and we liked it. But getting out of that sort of world is like plunging into cold water on a hot day. A man should never become involved in such nonsense; in the words of an excellent Spanish saying, a man should be fierce. Now, you there, my clever friend,' he added, turning to the muzhik sitting on the box, 'do you have a wife?'

The muzhik turned, showing the two friends his flat features and short-sighted eyes.

'A wife? Yes, I do. Of course I have a wife.'

'Do you beat her?'

'Do I beat my wife? Occasionally. But not without a reason.'

'Very good. Well, and does she beat you?'

The muzhik gave a tug at the reins.

'What a thing to say, sir. Making a joke of everything . . .' He was visibly offended.

'Do you hear that, Arkady Nikolayevich? But you and I were beaten . . . that's what it means to be educated.'

Arkady gave a forced laugh, but Bazarov turned away his head and didn't open his mouth for the whole of the rest of the journey.

The fifteen miles seemed to Arkady like thirty. But finally the little village where Bazarov's parents lived came into sight on the slope of a low hill. Next to the village in a young birch wood stood a little thatched manor house. Two muzhiks were standing by the first village hut, quarrelling. 'You're a big swine,' said one to the other, 'worse than a little piglet.' 'And your wife's a witch,' the other retorted.

'This familiarity,' Bazarov said to Arkady, 'this playful language should lead you to the conclusion that my father's peasants aren't too badly treated. And there he is coming out on to the porch of his house. That's him, it's him – I can see his face. But hey, hey! How grey he's gone, poor old fellow!'

XX

Bazarov leant out of the *tarantas*, while Arkady looked over his friend's shoulder and saw standing on the porch of the little manor house a tall thin man with untidy hair and a fine, aquiline nose, dressed in an old uniform coat worn open. He was standing legs apart, smoking a long pipe and screwing up his eyes against the sun. The horses stopped.

'You've come at last,' Bazarov's father said, continuing to smoke although his chibouk pipe was shaking between his fingers. 'Well, get out, get out and let's have a kiss.'

He began to embrace his son . . . 'Yenyusha, Yenyusha' – they could hear a tremulous woman's voice. The door opened and there appeared on the porch a small, plump old woman in a white cap and a multi-coloured jacket. She exclaimed, stumbled and probably would have fallen if Bazarov hadn't held her. She at once put her chubby little arms round his neck, pressed her head to his chest, and there was silence. They could only hear her broken sobs.

Old Bazarov took a deep breath and screwed up his eyes even more than before.

'Well, that's enough, Arisha, that's enough! Stop it,' he said, exchanging a look with Arkady, who was standing stock-still by the *tarantas*, while the muzhik on the box even turned away his head. 'That's quite out of order! Stop it, stop it!'

'Oh, Vasily Ivanych,' the old woman mumbled, 'it's been so long since my boy, my darling Yenyushenka . . .' and without removing her arms she moved her wrinkled face, all wet with tears and full of tenderness, away from Bazarov and then again pressed her head against him.

'Well, yes, of course, it's all in the nature of things,' said Vasily Ivanych, 'only it'd be better if we went inside. Yevgeny's brought a guest here. You must excuse us,' he added, turning to Arkady, with a small click of his heels, 'you understand, feminine frailty, well . . . and a mother's heart too . . .'

However, his own lips and eyebrows were twitching, and his

chin trembled . . . but it was obvious he wanted to control himself and to appear almost unmoved. Arkady bowed.

'Come on, Mother, really,' said Bazarov and led the exhausted old woman into the house. Having put her into a comfortable chair, he again gave his father a quick hug and introduced Arkady to him.

'I am so pleased to meet you,' said Vasily Ivanych, 'only you mustn't be too critical of us. I have a simple house, army style. Arina Vlasyevna, do please calm down. Pull yourself together. This gentleman who's come to stay is going to think badly of you.'

'Sir,' said the old woman through her tears, 'I don't have the honour of knowing your name . . .'

'Arkady Nikolaich,' Vasily Ivanovich proclaimed, prompting in a low voice.

'You must forgive my silliness.' The old woman blew her nose and, leaning her head first right then left, she carefully wiped one eye after the other. 'Forgive me. You see, I thought I would die without seeing again my da. . .a. . ,arling.'

'But you have now, madame,' Vasily Ivanovich interrupted. 'Tanyushka,' he said, turning to a barefoot girl of about thirteen in a bright-red cotton dress, who had timorously put her head round the door, 'bring your mistress a glass of water – and mind you bring it on a tray – and may I invite you, gentlemen,' he added with a kind of old-fashioned playfulness, 'into a half-pay veteran's study?'

'Yenyushechka, let me give you just one more hug,' Arina Vlasyevna moaned. Bazarov bent down towards her. 'You've become so handsome!'

'Handsome or not,' said Vasily Ivanovich, 'but as people say, he's a real *homme fait*.[1] And now, Arina Vlasyevna, I hope that, having sated your mother's heart, you'll also think of feeding your dear guests, because, as you know, you can't get nightingales to sing on just stories.'

The old woman got up from her armchair.

'The table will be laid right away, Vasily Ivanych. I'll run round to the kitchen myself and tell them to put on the samovar.

You'll have everything, just everything. It's three years I haven't seen him, three years I haven't given him anything to eat or drink – that's hard.'

'Well, mistress, see to it all and don't let us down. Gentlemen, please follow me. And here's Timofeich come to greet you, Yevgeny. And I think he's pleased to see you, the old rascal. What? You're pleased to see him, aren't you, old rascal? Be so good as to follow me.'

And Vasily Ivanovich bustled ahead, scraping and shuffling along in his worn-down slippers.

His whole small house consisted of six tiny rooms. One of them, to which he took our friends, was called the study. A table with massive legs, piled with papers that were black with dust as if they had been smoked, took up the entire space between the two windows. On the walls hung Turkish rifles, whips, a sabre, a couple of maps, some kind of anatomical drawings, a portrait of Hufeland,[2] a monogram woven out of hair in a black frame and a diploma framed under glass. A leather couch, in places worn through and torn, stood between two huge cupboards of Karelian birch: their shelves were crammed higgledy-piggledy with books, boxes, stuffed birds, tins and glass flasks. In a corner stood a broken electrical machine.

'I warned you, my dear guest, that we live here like in army camp, so to speak . . .'

'Stop it, why are you apologizing?' Bazarov interrupted. 'Kirsanov knows very well that we're not rich as Croesus and that you don't live in a palace. Where are we going to put him, that's the problem?'

'Excuse me, Yevgeny, I've got an excellent room in the wing. He'll be very comfortable there.'

'So you've got a wing now?'

'Of course, where the bathhouse is,' Timofeich interjected.

'That is, next door to the bathhouse,' Vasily Ivanovich quickly interrupted. 'It's summer now . . .[3] I'll go round there and give the orders. And, Timofeich, you bring in his things. Yevgeny, you of course will be getting my study. *Suum cuique.*'[4]

'That's what he's like. The funniest old fellow and the very best,' Bazarov added as soon as Vasily Ivanovich had gone out. 'Just as odd a fellow as yours, but in a different way. He talks a great deal.'

'And I think your mother's a lovely woman,' said Arkady.

'Yes, she has no pretensions. You just see what a dinner she'll give us.'

'We didn't expect you today, sir. They didn't bring the beef,' said Timofeich, who had just dragged in Bazarov's trunk.

'We'll do without beef, if there isn't any there's nothing we can do. They say poverty isn't a vice.'

'How many serfs does your father own?' Arkady suddenly asked.

'The property isn't his but my mother's. As far as I remember, fifteen.'

'They're twenty-two in all,' said Timofeich crossly.

They heard the shuffling of slippers, and Vasily Ivanovich appeared again.

'Your room will be ready to receive you in a few minutes,' he solemnly announced, 'Arkady . . . Nikolaich? I think I've got your name right. And here is your servant,' he added, pointing to a boy who had come in with him, with a closely cropped head and wearing a dark-blue tunic that had gone at the elbows and borrowed boots. 'His name is Fedka. I say once again, although my son tells me not to, don't be too critical. But he can fill a pipe. You do smoke?'

'Yes, but usually I smoke cigars,' Arkady answered.

'You're so sensible. I myself have a preference for cigars, but in our remote parts it's exceptionally difficult to obtain them.'

'That's enough whingeing from you,' Bazarov interrupted again. 'Better sit down here on the couch and let me have a look at you.'

Vasily Ivanovich laughed and sat down. He was very like his son in features, only his forehead was lower and his mouth a little wider, and he kept moving the entire time and shrugging his shoulders as if his clothes were too tight under the arms; he blinked and coughed and fidgeted with his fingers, whereas his son displayed a kind of relaxed immobility.

'Whingeing!' Vasily Ivanovich repeated. 'Yevgeny, don't think I want to make our guest feel sorry for us by saying we live so far out in the sticks. On the contrary, I'm of the opinion that for a thinking man there's no such thing as the sticks. At least I try in so far as I am able not to let the grass grow under my feet, as people say, not to lag behind the times.'

Vasily Ivanovich took out of his pocket a new yellow silk handkerchief which he'd gone to get as he hurried to Arkady's room, and went on speaking, waving the handkerchief in the air.

'I'm not talking now of the fact, for example, that I have made painful sacrifices. I've put my peasants on quit-rent[5] and given them the land in return for half the crop. That I thought my duty, and in this case common sense dictated it, although other landowners don't even think about that. I'm talking of science, of education.'

'Yes, I see you have the *Friend of Health*[6] from 1855,' Bazarov remarked.

'An old colleague sends it on to me out of friendship,' Vasily Ivanovich said quickly, 'but we do have, for example, some notion of phrenology,' he added, addressing himself, however, more to Arkady and pointing to a small white plaster head in the cupboard, divided up into numbered squares. 'We've heard too of Schönlein and Rademacher.'[7]

'Do folk in the province of *** still believe in Rademacher?'

Vasily Ivanovich coughed.

'In the province of . . . Of course, gentlemen, you know better. How can we keep up with you? You've come to take our place. In my day too there was a Hoffman, a humoral pathologist, and a Brown with his "Vitalism",[8] who seemed very funny, but they too once had their day. In your eyes some new man has taken their place, whom you worship, but in twenty years' time he too probably will be laughed at.'

'I'll say to you as a consolation,' said Bazarov, 'that now we generally laugh at medical science and don't acknowledge any masters.'

'How is that? Don't you want to be a doctor?'

'I do, but one thing doesn't stand in the way of the other.'

Vasily Ivanovich poked his middle finger into his pipe, in which there still was some hot ash.

'Well, maybe, maybe – I'm not going to argue. So what am I? A retired army doctor, *voilà tout*,[9] who's now become an agronomist. I served in your grandfather's brigade,' (again he addressed Arkady) 'yes, yes, I've seen a lot in my time. I've mixed in every kind of society, there's no one I haven't met! I . . . this man whom you see in front of you has taken the pulse of Prince Wittgenstein and of Zhukovsky.[10] And the men of 14 December from the Army of the South[11] – you understand whom I'm talking about' (and here Vasily Ivanovich meaningfully pursed his lips) '– I knew them all, every one. Well, that was nothing to do with me. I just know how to use a lancet, and that's it! But your grandfather was very respected, a true soldier.'

'Come on, he was a real dolt,' Bazarov said lazily.

'Oh, Yevgeny, your language! Please . . . Of course, General Kirsanov wasn't one of the . . .'

'Enough of him,' Bazarov interrupted. 'As we were driving up here I was pleased to see your little birch wood, it's come on well.'

Vasily Ivanovich livened up.

'And just look at my little garden now! I've planted every tree myself. I have fruit, and soft fruit, and all kinds of medicinal herbs. You young gentlemen may be very clever, but still old Paracelsus[12] expressed a hallowed truth: "*In herbis, verbis et lapidibus* . . ."[13] I've given up practising, you know, but a couple of times a week I have to get up to my old tricks. If they come for advice, one can't send them out on their ear. Sometimes the poor come for help. And there are no doctors here at all. One of my local neighbours, a retired major, also acts as a doctor – think of that. I ask whether he's studied any medicine . . . I am told, no, he hasn't, he's more of a philanthropist . . . Ha ha, a philanthropist! Eh? That's good! Ha ha! Ha ha!'

'Fedka, fill me a pipe,' Bazarov said grimly.

'Another doctor here comes to see a patient,' Vasily Ivanovich went on with a kind of desperation, 'but the patient's already gone *ad patres*.[14] The servant won't let the doctor in and says,

"You're not needed now." The doctor wasn't expecting that, he's nonplussed and asks, "So, did your master have the hiccoughs before he died?" "He did, sir." "Did he hiccough a lot?" "Yes, he did, a lot." "Ah – that's good." So back he goes. Ha ha ha!'

The old man was the only one to laugh. Arkady gave a smile. Bazarov just stretched. The conversation went on this way for about an hour. Arkady managed to go to his room, which turned out to be the bathhouse's changing room, but very comfortable and clean. Eventually Tanyusha came in and announced dinner was ready.

Vasily Ivanovich was the first to get up.

'Gentlemen, let's go in! I am truly sorry if I've bored you. Perhaps my good lady will satisfy you more than I have.'

The dinner, though prepared in haste, turned out to be excellent, even abundant. Only the wine had gone off a bit, as they say: the almost black sherry, which Timofeich had bought from a merchant he knew in the town, had a taste which was a mixture of copper and resin. And the flies too were a problem. Usually a house boy kept them away with a big branch of foliage; but on this occasion Vasily Ivanovich had sent him off for fear of censure from the younger generation.

Arina Vlasyevna had managed to smarten up her appearance: she had put on a tall cap with silk ribbons and a blue fringed shawl. She burst into tears again as soon as she saw her Yenyusha, but her husband didn't have to reprove her: she herself quickly wiped away her tears so as not to stain her shawl.

Only the young men ate. The master and mistress had had their dinner long before. Fedka served, clearly bothered by his unfamiliar boots, and he was helped by a woman with one eye and a masculine face, Anfisushka by name, who performed the duties of housekeeper, poultrywoman and laundress. Throughout the dinner Vasily Ivanovich paced up and down the room and with a completely happy, even blissful expression on his face talked about the grave misgivings he felt about the policies of Napoleon III and the complexity of the Italian question.[15] Arina Vlasyevna paid no attention to Arkady and didn't press food on him. Leaning her round head on her hand – her full cherry-red lips and the small birthmarks on her cheeks and brow emphasized its sweet-naturedness – she didn't take her eyes off her son and kept on sighing; she was dying to know how long he had come for but she was frightened to ask him. 'What if he says for two days,' she thought, and her heart froze. After the roast Vasily Ivanovich disappeared for a moment and came back with an opened half-bottle of champagne. 'You see,' he exclaimed, 'even though we live at the back of beyond, on high days and holidays we have the wherewithal for enjoyment!' He poured out three goblets and a tiny glass, proposed the health of 'our guests beyond price' and drank down his goblet in one, army fashion, and he made Arina Vlasyevna drink the tiny glass to the last drop.

When it was the turn of the preserves,[16] Arkady, who couldn't abide sweet things, nonetheless felt it his duty to sample four different kinds, all freshly made, all the more so because Bazarov flatly declined and lit up a cigar right away. Then tea came on the scene, with cream and butter and pretzels. Then Vasily Ivanovich took them all into the garden to admire the beauty of the evening. Walking past a bench, he whispered to Arkady:

'I like to philosophize in this spot and watch the sunset. That's just the thing for a hermit. And further on, over there, I've planted a few trees, Horace's[17] favourites.'

'What kind of tree?' asked Bazarov, who had overheard.

'Acacias, of course.'

Bazarov started yawning.

'I suppose it's time for the travellers to go to the arms of Morpheus,'[18] said Vasily Ivanovich.

'You mean it's time to sleep!' said Bazarov. 'That's sound thinking. It's time indeed.'

Saying goodnight to his mother, Bazarov kissed her on the forehead, and she embraced him and surreptitiously, behind his back, made the sign of the cross over him three times. Vasily Ivanovich took Arkady to his room and wished him 'that health-giving repose I used to enjoy at your happy age'. And indeed Arkady slept very well in his changing room: it smelt of mint, and two crickets chirped soporifically to each other behind the stove. Vasily Ivanovich left Arkady to go to his study. He curled up on the couch at his son's feet and was going to chat to him; however, Bazarov immediately asked him to go, saying he was sleepy, but he didn't sleep till dawn. Eyes wide open, he stared angrily into the darkness: childhood memories had no power over him while he hadn't yet had time to be free of his recent bitter experiences. Arina Vlasyevna first prayed her fill, then she talked for a long, long time to Anfisushka, who, standing stock-still before her mistress and fixing her single eye on her, communicated to her all her own observations and thoughts about Yevgeny Vasilyevich. The old woman had become quite giddy from happiness, and wine, and cigar smoke. Her husband started to talk to her and threw up his hands.

Arina Vlasyevna was a true Russian gentlewoman of olden time. She should have lived two hundred years before, in the days of old Muscovy. She was extremely devout and sensitive, believed in all kinds of portents, fortune-telling, spells and dreams. She believed in holy idiots,[19] house spirits, wood goblins, unlucky encounters, the evil eye, folk medicines, Maundy Thursday salt,[20] and in the imminence of the world's end. She believed that if the candles at the Easter midnight service didn't go out, then there'd be a good crop of buckwheat, and that mushrooms stop growing if seen by a human eye. She believed the devil likes being where there is water and that every Jew bears a blood-red mark on his breast. She was afraid of mice, grass-snakes, frogs, sparrows, leeches, thunder, cold water, draughts, horses, billy goats, redheads and black cats, and thought crickets and dogs unclean creatures. She didn't eat veal or pigeon or crab or cheese or asparagus or Jerusalem artichokes or rabbits or watermelons (because a cut-open watermelon reminds one of the head of John the Baptist), and she only mentioned oysters with a shudder. She liked her food – and kept strict fasts. She slept ten hours out of the twenty-four – and didn't go to bed at all if Vasily Ivanovich had a headache. She hadn't read a single book except *Alexis, or The Cottage in the Wood*,[21] wrote one or at most two letters a year and had a good understanding of housekeeping, of drying food and making preserves, although she touched nothing with her own hands and generally didn't like to move from her seat.

Arina Vlasyevna was very kind-hearted and in her own way not at all stupid. She knew that in the world there are the masters, who have to give orders, and the ordinary people, who have to serve – and so she wasn't offended by obsequiousness or bows to the ground;[22] but she treated the lower orders kindly and gently, she let no beggar go by without a donation and never condemned anyone, though she did sometimes gossip. In her youth she had been very pretty, she played the clavichord and could speak a little French; but in the course of many moves of house with her husband (whom she had married against her will) she had lost her figure and forgotten her music and French. She loved her son and was unutterably frightened of him. She had given over the management of the estate to Vasily Ivanovich – and now had nothing to do with any of it. She cried out, fanned herself with her handkerchief and raised her eyebrows higher and higher in alarm as soon as the old man began to explain about the coming changes and his plans. She was suspicious, was always expecting some great disaster and immediately cried as soon as she thought of something sad. Women like that are now a dying breed. God knows whether one should rejoice at that!

XXI

Having got out of bed, Arkady opened the window – and the first thing he saw was Vasily Ivanovich. In a Bukharan dressing-gown held together with a handkerchief, the old man was digging hard in the vegetable garden. He noticed his young guest and, leaning on his spade, called out:

'Your very good health! How did you sleep?'

'Really well,' Arkady answered.

'And here I am as you can see, like a modern Cincinnatus,[1] digging a bed for late turnips. The time has now come – and thank God for that! – when everyone must earn his substance with his own hands. It's no use relying on others: one must work oneself. After all Jean-Jacques Rousseau[2] was right. Half an hour ago, my dear sir, you would have seen me in a quite different position, I had a peasant woman complaining of the cramps – that's what they call it, but in our terms dysentery – and I . . . how shall I say it? . . . I gave her some opium. And I took out another woman's tooth. I offered to give her ether . . . but she refused. All this I do gratis – *en amateur*.[3] However, there's nothing extraordinary in my doing this. Because I'm a plebeian, a *homo novus*[4] – I'm not a noble with a family tree, like my good lady . . . But why don't you come here into the shade and breathe in the morning cool before we have our tea?'

Arkady went and joined him.

'Once more, welcome!' Vasily Ivanovich exclaimed, raising his hand in a military salute to the greasy skull-cap which covered his head. 'I know you're accustomed to luxury and pleasure, but even the great of this world don't scorn a little while spent under a cottage roof.'

'Excuse me,' cried Arkady, 'what sort of a great man am I? And I'm not accustomed to luxury.'

'Now, now,' Vasily Ivanovich objected with a friendly grin, 'although I've now been put on the archive shelf, I too have been around in the world, rubbing along – I can tell a bird by the way it flies. And in my own way I am a psychologist and physiognomist. If I didn't have that, let me call it talent, I'd have gone to the wall long ago, as a little man I'd have been quite rubbed out. Without wanting to compliment you, I'll say this – the friendship I observe between you and my son makes me truly happy. I met him just now. In his usual way, which you probably know, he jumped out of bed very early and has gone off somewhere in the locality. May I be inquisitive – how long have you known my Yevgeny?'

'Since last winter.'

'Really. And may I ask you something else – but let's sit down – may I ask you, speaking as a father, to tell me frankly – what do you think of my Yevgeny?'

'Your son is one of the most remarkable men I have ever met,' Arkady answered animatedly.

Vasily Ivanovich's eyes opened wider, and his cheeks flushed slightly. The spade fell from his hands.

'So you think . . .' he began.

'I am convinced,' Arkady went on, 'that a great future is waiting for your son, that he'll make your name famous. I've been convinced of that since our very first meeting.'

'How . . . how was that?' Vasily Ivanovich barely managed to get the words out. His lips were parted in an ecstatic smile, which didn't leave them.

'Do you mean, how did we meet?'

'Yes . . . and generally . . .'

Arkady began to recount and to speak of Bazarov with even greater passion and enthusiasm than on the evening when he danced the mazurka with Odintsova.

Vasily Ivanovich listened and listened, he blew his nose, rolled his handkerchief between both hands, coughed, passed his hands through his hair – and finally couldn't contain himself: he leant over to Arkady and kissed him on the shoulder.[5]

'You have made me completely happy,' he said, still smiling. 'I must tell you that I . . . worship my son. I won't mention my old lady – of course she has a mother's feelings! But I don't dare to speak out what I feel in front of him because he doesn't like that. He is the enemy of all emotional talk. There are many who criticize him for hardness and see in that a sign of pride and insensitivity; but people like him can't be measured by the normal rule, can they? For example, someone else in his situation would have gone on taking from his parents. But can you imagine, he hasn't taken a spare penny from us in his life, as God's my witness!'

'He is a selfless, honourable man,' said Arkady.

'Selfless indeed. And, Arkady Nikolaich, I not only worship him, I am proud of him, and all my vanity lies in the hope that some day his biography will contain the following words: "The son of a simple army doctor, who early saw his true nature and spared nothing for his education . . ."' The old man's voice broke.

Arkady pressed his hand.

'What do you think?' Vasily Ivanovich asked after a moment of silence. 'He won't win that fame you forecast for him in the field of medicine, will he?'

'No, of course not in medicine, though in that respect he'll be one of our leading scientists.'

'Then in what, Arkady Nikolaich?'

'It's difficult to say now, but he will be famous.'

'He will be famous!' the old man repeated and became absorbed in his thoughts.

'Arina Vlasyevna has told me to ask you to come and have tea,' announced Anfisushka, passing by with a huge dish of fresh raspberries.

Vasily Ivanovich roused himself.

'And will there be chilled cream with the raspberries?'

'Yes, sir, there will.'

'Make sure it is chilled! Don't be polite, Arkady Nikolaich, take more of them. Why hasn't Yevgeny come?'

'I'm here.' Bazarov's voice came from Arkady's room.

Vasily Ivanovich turned round.

'Aha! You wanted to visit your friend, but you were late, *amice*,[6] and he and I have already had a long conversation. Now we must go and have tea, your mother's calling. By the by, I must have a word with you.'

'What about?'

'There's a little muzhik here, he's suffering from icterus.'

'You mean jaundice?'

'Yes, a chronic and very resistant icterus. I've prescribed him centaury and St John's wort, I've made him eat carrots and given him soda. But all these are just *palliatives*, one needs something more effective. Though you mock medicine, I am sure you can give me some useful advice. But we'll talk about this later. Now let's go and have tea.'

Vasily Ivanovich got up nimbly from the bench and sang the following lines from *Robert le Diable*:[7]

'It is our rule, my friends, it is our rule –

To live by joy, by jo-o-oy alone!'

'He is full of beans!' Bazarov remarked, moving from the window.

It was midday. The sun was hot, and there was just a thin veil over the sky of whitish clouds. Everything was quiet, only the village cocks gaily crowed to one another, inspiring in everyone who heard them a strange feeling of sleepiness and languor; and from somewhere high in the crown of the trees came the plaintive call of a young hawk, on and on. Arkady and Bazarov were lying in the shade of a small haystack, having spread out beneath them a couple of armfuls of crackling-dry but still green and fragrant hay.

'That aspen,' said Bazarov, 'reminds me of my childhood. It grows on the edge of a pit, all that remains from a brick shed, and I was convinced then that the pit and the aspen possessed a special magic talisman. I was never bored when I was by them. I didn't understand then that the reason I wasn't bored was that I was a child. Well, now I'm a grown man and the talisman doesn't work.'

'How much time in all did you spend here?' Arkady asked.

'Two years at a go. After that we came for short visits. We led a wandering existence – usually trailing from town to town.'

'And has this house been standing long?'

'Yes. It was built by my grandfather, that is my mother's father.'

'What was your grandfather?'

'The devil only knows. Some of kind of major adjutant. He served with Suvorov[8] and always used to tell stories about crossing the Alps. All lies, I should think.'

'So that's why you have a portrait of Suvorov hanging in the drawing room. I love little houses like yours, that are old and warm and have a kind of special smell to them.'

'Yes, of lamp oil and sweet clover,' Bazarov pronounced with a yawn. 'And the flies in these dear little houses . . . Pfui!'

'Tell me,' Arkady began after a short silence, 'they weren't hard on you as a child, were they?'

'You can see what kind of people my parents are. They're not very strict.'

'Do you love them, Yevgeny?'

'Yes, Arkady, I do!'

Bazarov was silent for a moment.

'Do you know what I am thinking about?' he said eventually, putting his arms behind his head.

'No. What?'

'I am thinking what a good life my parents have on this earth. My father at sixty fusses about, talks of "palliatives", treats his patients, is all magnanimous with his peasants – in short he has a ball. And my mother too has a good time, her day is so crammed with all kinds of things to do, with ohs and ahs, that she has no time to think. While I . . .'

'While you?'

'While I think that here I am lying under a haystack . . . The tiny area I occupy is so minute by comparison with the rest of space, where I don't exist, which doesn't bother with me. And the span of time I'll be able to live out is so insignificant before the eternity where I haven't been and where I will not be . . . Yet in this atom, in this mathematical dot blood is circulating, a brain is functioning and wanting something too . . . What a monstrous state of affairs! What nonsense!'

'Can I say something to you – what you are saying applies in general to everyone . . .'

'You're right,' Bazarov went on. 'I meant that they, that is my parents, are busy and don't worry about their own insignificance, they don't find it's obnoxious . . . while I just feel bored and angry.'

'Angry? Why angry?'

'Why? What do you mean why? Have you forgotten?'

'I remember it all, but still I don't think you have the right to be angry. You're unhappy, I agree, but . . .'

'Ah, I see, Arkady Nikolayevich, your understanding of love is like all modern young people's: cluck, cluck, cluck, little chick, but as soon as the chick begins to get close, you're off! I'm not like that. But that's enough on that subject. What can't be helped, one should be ashamed of talking about.' He turned on to his side. 'Hey! Here's a splendid ant dragging along a half-dead fly. Go on, boy, go on! Ignore its struggles, take advantage of your right as an animal not to feel any sympathy with it – not like self-destructive creatures like us!'

'You oughtn't to say that, Yevgeny! When did you destroy yourself?'

Bazarov lifted his head.

'That's the one thing I'm proud of. I didn't destroy myself, and a woman isn't going to destroy me. Amen! That's the end of that! You won't hear another word from me about this.'

The two friends lay a while in silence.

'Yes,' Bazarov began, 'man's a strange being. When you look at a quiet, dull life, like my good parents' life here, cursorily or from a distance, you think – what could be better? Eat, drink and know you're acting in the most correct, most sensible way. But that's not how it is. Boredom descends. You want to engage with people, even if just to shout at them, but still engage with them.'

'One must organize one's life so every moment in it has significance,' Arkady stated thoughtfully.

'Who's talking? Significance, even if it's false, is very nice, and you can make do even with insignificance . . . but petty little problems . . . they're the trouble.'

'Petty problems needn't exist for anyone, provided he refuses to admit them.'

'Hm . . . you're stating an inverted commonplace.'

'What? What do you mean by that term?'

'I mean this. You say, for example, that education is useful. That's a commonplace. But if you say that education is harmful, that's an inverted commonplace. It's a bit flashier, but really it's the same.'

'Where is the truth then, on which side?'

'Where? I'll answer you like an echo – where?'

'You are in a depressed mood today, Yevgeny.'

'Really? I must have caught the sun and I shouldn't eat so many raspberries.'

'In that case it might be a good idea to have a nap,' Arkady remarked.

'Right, only don't look at me. Everyone looks stupid when he's asleep.'

'But what does it matter to you what people think of you?'

'I don't know how to answer you. A real man oughtn't to

care about that. You don't think about a real man, he's to be
obeyed or loathed.'

'That's odd! I don't loathe anyone,' Arkady said, having
thought a moment.

'But I loathe so many. You're so gentle, a softy, you're not going
to loathe anybody! . . . You're shy, you lack self-esteem . . .'

Arkady interrupted: 'So you do have self-esteem, do you?
You have such a high opinion of yourself.'

Bazarov paused.

'When I do meet a man who can hold his own with me,' he
said deliberately, 'then I'll change my opinion of myself. As
for loathing . . . ! For example, today you said as we walked
past the cottage of our village headman Filip, that nice white
one – "There," you said, "Russia will come to a perfect state
when every last muzhik has a house like that, and every one
of us must try and bring that about . . ." But I conceived a
loathing for that last muzhik, Filip or Sidor, for whom I must
work myself to the bone and who won't even say thank you
to me . . . and what do I need his thank you for? Well, he'll be
living in a white cottage while I'll be pushing up the daisies.
So, next point?'

'Yevgeny . . . I've had enough of listening to you today. Willy-
nilly it makes one agree with those who criticize you for lack of
principles.'

'You're talking like your uncle. Principles don't exist – you
haven't grasped that yet! – but sensations do. Everything derives
from sensations.'

'How is that?'

'Like this. Take me, for example. I advocate a negative attitude – by virtue of a sensation. I like negatives, my brain's made
that way – and that's all it is! Why do I like chemistry? Why do
you like apples – also by virtue of a sensation. It's all one and
the same. People won't ever penetrate deeper than that. Not
everyone will tell you this, and I won't tell it to you another
time.'

'So – honesty is a sensation?'

'Of course!'

'Yevgeny!' Arkady began in a sad voice.

'What? You don't like it?' Bazarov interrupted him. 'No, my friend! Once you decide to bring down everything, you cut yourself down as well! . . . But we've talked enough philosophy. "Nature brings on the silence of sleep," as Pushkin said.'

'He never said anything of the kind,' said Arkady.

'Well, if he didn't say it, he could and should have done, as a poet. By the way, Pushkin must have served in the army.'

'Pushkin never was a soldier.'

'Excuse me, he has it on every page – to arms, to arms, for the honour of Russia!'

'What nonsense you're inventing! It's actually slanderous.'

'Slanderous? You are being pompous! What a word you've dug up to scare me with! However much you may slander someone, in reality he deserves something twenty times worse.'

'We'd better have some sleep!' Arkady said crossly.

'With the greatest of pleasure,' answered Bazarov. But neither of them felt like sleeping. Something like hostility had come over the two young men. Five minutes later they opened their eyes and looked at one another in silence.

'Look at that,' Arkady said suddenly. 'There's a maple leaf which has come off and is falling to the ground. Its movements are just like the flight of a butterfly. Isn't that odd? That something so melancholy and dead should be like something so happy and alive.'

'Oh, Arkady Nikolaich, my friend!' exclaimed Bazarov. 'I ask one thing of you: no fine language.'

'I talk as best I can . . . Actually this is tyranny. I have a thought, why can't I say it?'

'Quite so. But why shouldn't I say mine too? I find fine language obscene.'

'So what isn't obscene – abuse?'

'Hey! I see you are really set on following in your uncle's footsteps. How pleased that idiot would be if he heard you!'

'What did you call Pavel Petrovich?'

'I called him what he should be called – an idiot!'

'But you're being intolerable!' cried Arkady.

'Aha! Family feeling speaks,' Bazarov said calmly. 'I've noticed it's very persistent in people. A man is ready to give up everything, to renounce every prejudice, but to admit, e.g., that his brother, who steals people's handkerchiefs, is a thief – is quite beyond him. That's what it is: *my* brother, *mine* – isn't a genius. How can that be?'

'It was only a feeling of fairness in me, not any kind of family feeling,' Arkady retorted angrily. 'But since you don't have that feeling, that *sensation*, you can't pronounce judgement.'

'In other words: Arkady Kirsanov is too elevated for anyone to understand him – I bow down and am silent.'

'Yevgeny, stop it, please. Otherwise we're going to quarrel.'

'Oh, Arkady, do me a favour, do let us for once have a really good quarrel – no holds barred, to the death.'

'But if we do, it'll end in . . .'

'Blows?' Bazarov continued. 'What if it does? Here, in the hay, in these idyllic surroundings, far from the world and the eyes of men – it doesn't matter. But you won't beat me. I'm going to take you now by the throat . . .'

Bazarov spread his long, hard fingers . . . Arkady turned and got ready to resist, as if in play . . . But his friend's expression seemed so full of menace, he saw such a very real threat in the twisted smile on Bazarov's lips and in his angry eyes that in spite of himself he felt afraid . . .

'Ah, that's where you've got to!' At that moment they heard the voice of Vasily Ivanovich, and the old army doctor appeared before the young men, wearing a home-made canvas jacket and a straw hat, also home-made, on his head. 'I've been looking and looking for you . . . But you've chosen an excellent spot and a wonderful pastime. To lie on "mother earth" and look at "the heavens" . . . You know, that has special significance!'

'I look at the heavens only when I want to sneeze,' Bazarov muttered and, turning to Arkady, said in a low voice, 'What a pity he stopped us.'

'Shut up,' Arkady whispered and surreptitiously shook his friend's hand. But no friendship can long stand collisions like that.

'I look at you, my young symposiasts,' Vasily Ivanovich was saying meanwhile, shaking his head and leaning, hands crossed, on an ingeniously turned cane (of his own manufacture) with the figure of a Turk as a handle, 'I look at you – and I have to admire you. You have such strength, such perfect youth, ability, talents! You're just . . . Castor and Pollux!'[9]

'He's now gone off into mythology,' said Bazarov. 'You can see at once he was a fine Latinist in his day! I seem to remember, you got a silver medal for composition, didn't you?'

'Dioscuri, Dioscuri!'[10]

'Now Father, shut up, don't be silly.'

'Once in a while that's allowed,' the old man stammered. 'But I didn't look for you, gentlemen, in order to pay you compliments; but first to tell you that soon we'll be having dinner, and second I wanted to warn you, Yevgeny . . . You're a clever man, you know people, and you know women, and so you'll excuse it . . . Your mother wanted a service held for your coming here. Don't think I'm asking you to attend the service. It's over. But Father Aleksey . . .'

'The reverend?'

'Yes, the priest. He's going to . . . eat with us . . . I wasn't expecting that and even advised against it . . . but it happened . . . he didn't understand me . . . Well, and Arina Vlasyevna . . . But he's a very good and sensible man.'

'So he won't eat my share of dinner?' Bazarov asked.

Vasily Ivanovich laughed.

'Yevgeny, stop it!'

'That's all I ask. I'm prepared to sit down at table with any man.'

Vasily Ivanovich straightened his hat.

'I knew beforehand,' he said, 'that you were above all prejudice. Here I am, an old man, I'm sixty-one, I don't have any prejudices either.' (Vasily Ivanovich didn't admit that he himself had wanted a service . . . He was no less devout than his wife.) 'And Father Aleksey very much wanted to meet you. You'll like him, you'll see. He doesn't mind a game of cards and he even – but that's between us – smokes a pipe.'

'Why not? After dinner we'll get down to whist, and I'll thrash him.'

'Ha ha ha, we'll see! Don't be too sure.'

'So are you up to your old tricks?' Bazarov said with particular emphasis.

A dark flush came over Vasily Ivanovich's bronzed cheeks.

'Aren't you ashamed of yourself, Yevgeny? . . . That's over
and done with. Yes, I'm ready to confess in front of your
friend, I did have that passion when I was young – I did. And
I've paid for it! May I sit down with you? I'm not in the way,
am I?'

'Not at all,' answered Arkady.

Vasily Ivanovich lowered himself on to the hay with a painful grunt.

'Your present abode, gentlemen, reminds me of my army
camp life, of dressing stations – they too were somewhere like
this, by a haystack – and we were thankful to have that.' He
sighed. 'What a lot I've been through in my time. For example,
if you'll allow me, I'll tell you a curious story about the plague
in Bessarabia.'

'For which you got your Vladimir,'[11] Bazarov interrupted.
'We know, we know . . . By the by, why aren't you wearing
it?'

'I told you, I don't go for conventions,' Vasily Ivanovich
muttered (he had had the red ribbon cut off his coat only the
day before) and began to tell the story about the plague. 'Look,
he's gone to sleep,' he whispered suddenly to Arkady with a
friendly wink, pointing at Bazarov. 'Yevgeny, get up!' he added.
'Let's go and have dinner . . .'

Father Aleksey, a handsome large figure of a man, with thick,
carefully combed hair, wearing an embroidered belt over a lilac
silk cassock, turned out to be very clever and quick-witted. He
was quick to take the initiative and give Arkady and Bazarov a
handshake[12] as if he already understood that they didn't need
his blessing, and in general he was completely at ease. He didn't
let himself down, nor did he offend others. He laughed at sem-
inarian Latin and stood up for his bishop. He drank two small
glasses of wine and refused a third. He accepted a cigar from
Arkady but didn't start smoking it, saying he would take it
home. The only not quite pleasant thing about him was that
from time to time he would slowly and carefully bring up his

hand to catch flies on his face and sometimes would actually squash them. He sat down at the green baize card table with a mild expression of pleasure and eventually beat Bazarov soundly, winning off him two and a half roubles in paper money: in Arina Vlasyevna's house they wouldn't dream of keeping a tally in silver[13] . . . She sat by her son as before, leaning her chin on her hand, and only got up to tell them to serve some new delicacy. She was nervous of showing affection to Bazarov, and he didn't give her any encouragement, he didn't invite her caresses. And Vasily Ivanovich had warned her not to 'bother' him too much. 'Young men don't like it,' he repeated to her.

(There's no need to say what kind of dinner was served that day: Timofeich in person had trotted off at daybreak to fetch some special Circassian beef; the bailiff had driven in another direction in quest of burbot, ruff and crayfish; for the mushrooms alone the peasant women were paid 42 copper copecks.)

But Arina Vlasyevna's eyes, which were fixed on Bazarov without moving, didn't just show devotion and tenderness, they showed sorrow too, mixed with curiosity and fear, and also meek reproach.

However, Bazarov didn't bother with working out exactly what lay in the expression of his mother's eyes. He seldom turned towards her, and then only to put a brief question. Once he asked her to give him her hand 'for luck'. She quietly placed her soft hand on his hard, broad palm.

'Well,' she asked after a pause, 'did it help?'

'It was even worse,' he answered with a casual smile.

'He's taking big risks,' Father Aleksey stated, almost with sympathy, stroking his fine beard.

'Napoleon's first rule, Father, Napoleon's first rule,' said Vasily Ivanovich and led an ace.

'That took him to the island of St Helena,' said Father Aleksey and took his ace with a trump.

'Yenyushechka, would you like some blackcurrant drink?' said Arina Vlasyevna.

Bazarov shrugged his shoulders.

'No,' he said the next day to Arkady, 'I'm leaving here tomorrow. It's so dull. I want to work but here I can't. I'll go again to your place. I've left all my experimental stuff there. At least in your house I can shut my door, whereas here my father keeps on saying to me, "My study is at your service – no one is going to bother you," but he himself sticks to me like glue. And I feel a bit ashamed of shutting the door on him. My mother's the same. I can hear her sighing on the other side of the wall, but if I go out to her, I haven't anything to say to her.'

'She'll be very sad,' said Arkady, 'and he will too.'

'I'll come back to them.'

'When?'

'When I go to St Petersburg.'

'I feel especially sorry for your mother.'

'Why? Did she give you some nice berries or something?'

Arkady lowered his eyes.

'You don't know your mother, Yevgeny. She's not just an excellent woman, she's really very intelligent. This morning she chatted to me for half an hour, and was so sensible and interesting.'

'I suppose she went on about me.'

'We didn't only talk about you.'

'Maybe you're right. You're an outsider and can see more. If a woman can keep a conversation going for half an hour, that's a really good sign. But I'm still leaving.'

'It won't be easy for you to break that news to them. They're busy discussing what we're going to be doing in two weeks' time.'

'Yes, it won't be easy. Today the devil tempted me to tease my father. The other day he had one of his quit-rent muzhiks flogged – and he was absolutely right. Don't look at me with such horror, he was absolutely right, because the man was a terrible thief and drunk. Only my father was certainly not expecting me to be "apprised" of this, as they say. He was very embarrassed, and now on top of that I'm going to hurt him . . . It doesn't matter! He'll get over it.'

Bazarov had said, 'It doesn't matter!' – but the whole day went by before he could bring himself to tell Vasily Ivanovich of his plans. Eventually, having already said goodnight to him in the study, he said with a forced yawn:

'Yes . . . I almost forgot to tell you . . .Can you have them send a change of horses over to Fedot's?'

Vasily Ivanovich showed his shock.

'Is Mr Kirsanov leaving us?'

'Yes. And I'm going with him.'

Vasily Ivanovich staggered on his feet.

'You're leaving?'

'Yes . . . I have to. Please tell them about the horses.'

'Very well,' the old man stammered. 'A change of horses . . . very well . . . only . . . only . . . Why are you leaving?'

'I have to go and stay with him a short time. Then I'll come back here.'

'Right! A short time . . . Very well.' Vasily Ivanovich took out his handkerchief and blew his nose, bending down almost to the ground. 'So. That . . . that'll be it. I thought you'd be with us . . . a bit longer. Three days . . . After three years. That's . . . that's not very long. Not very long, Yevgeny!'

'But I've told you I'm coming back soon. I absolutely have to go.'

'You absolutely have to . . . Well then. Duty comes first. So you want me to send the horses? Very well. Of course that's not what Arina and I were expecting. She's just gone and asked our neighbour for flowers to decorate your room.' (Vasily Ivanovich didn't mention that every morning, at first light, standing barefoot in his slippers, he conferred with Timofeich and, pulling out one torn banknote after another, gave him various commissions, with special emphasis on provisions and on red wine, which, as far as he could see, the young men very much liked.) 'The most important thing is liberty. That's my rule . . . no constraints . . . no . . .'

He suddenly stopped and went to the door.

'Father, we'll see each other again soon, we will.'

But Vasily Ivanovich just waved his hand without turning round and went out. Returning to his bedroom, he found his wife in bed and began to pray in a whisper so as not to wake her. But she woke up.

'Is that you, Vasily Ivanych?' she asked.

'Yes, Mother, it is!'

'Have you come from Yenyusha? Do you know, I worry whether he's comfortable sleeping on the couch. I told Anfisushka to give him your army mattress and new pillows. I'd have given him our feather mattress but I remember he doesn't like his bed to be too soft.'

'It doesn't matter, Mother, don't worry. He's fine. Lord, have mercy on us sinners,' he continued, praying in a low voice. Vasily Ivanovich felt sorry for his old woman. He didn't want to tell her of the sorrow that awaited her last thing at night.

Bazarov and Arkady left the next day. From the morning on a gloom came over everyone. Anfisushka dropped dishes. Even Fedka was thrown by events and ended up by taking off his boots. Vasily Ivanovich fussed about more than ever. He was clearly trying to be brave, talking in a loud voice and stamping his feet, but he had a long face and kept avoiding his son's eyes. Arina Vlasyevna cried gently. She would have completely gone to pieces and lost control if early in the morning her husband hadn't lectured her for a whole two hours. When Bazarov, after repeated promises to come back no later than in a month's time, finally tore himself from her clinging embraces and got into the *tarantas*; when the horses started and the harness bell rang and the wheels began to turn; when there was no longer any point in looking after them, and the dust had settled, and Timofeich had scuttled back into his little room, all hunched and stumbling as he went; when the old people were alone in their house which also seemed suddenly to have become shrunken and dilapidated – Vasily Ivanovich, who a few moments before had been bravely waving his handkerchief on the porch, fell into a chair and dropped his head.

'He's, he's deserted us,' he stammered, 'deserted us. He got bored here with us. I'm all alone in the world, like this finger, all alone!' he repeated several times and each time held out his hand in front of him, sticking out his index finger. Then Arina Vlasyevna came next to him and, laying her grey head by his, said, 'What can we do, Vasya! Our son has left the nest. Like a falcon he came to us when he wanted to, and when he wanted to he flew off. And you and I sit side by side and can't move, like mushrooms on a hollow tree. Only I'll be your true one for ever and you'll be mine.'

Vasily Ivanovich took his hands from his face and put his arms round his wife, his helpmeet, in a firm embrace – he hadn't embraced her like that when they were young. She brought him comfort in his grief.

XXII

Our friends travelled to Fedot's in silence, only occasionally exchanging some words of no consequence. Bazarov wasn't altogether pleased with himself. Arkady certainly was not pleased with him. Also he felt in his heart that melancholy which comes on for no reason and which is only known to the very young. The coachman changed the horses, got up on the box and asked, 'Right or left?'

Arkady shivered. The road to the right led to the town, and from there to home, the road to the left led to Odintsova's.

He gave Bazarov a look.

'Yevgeny,' he asked, 'shall we go to the left?'

Bazarov turned away.

'What kind of folly is this?' he mumbled.

'I know it's folly,' Arkady answered. 'But what's the harm? It's not our first time, is it?'

Bazarov pulled his cap down over his forehead.

'You know best,' he said eventually.

'Left!' cried Arkady.

The *tarantas* rolled off in the direction of Nikolskoye. But, having decided on 'folly', the friends maintained a yet more stubborn silence and even seemed angry.

From the very way the butler greeted them on the porch of Anna Sergeyevna's house the friends could have guessed that they had acted stupidly in giving in to a passing whim. They obviously weren't expected. For a longish time they sat in the drawing room, looking quite silly. Finally Anna Sergeyevna came out to them. She greeted them in her normal amiable way but expressed her surprise at their return after such a short time and, in so far as one could judge by the languidness of her speech and movements, was none too pleased by it. They hastened to make it plain that they had only dropped in on their way and after four hours or so would be leaving for town. She confined herself to a mild protest, asked Arkady to give his father her regards, and sent for her aunt. The princess appeared looking very sleepy, which made her wrinkled old face look even crosser than usual. Katya wasn't feeling well and didn't come out of her room. Arkady suddenly felt that he at any rate wanted to see Katya as much as Anna Sergeyevna herself. The four hours went by in trivial talk about this and that; Anna Sergeyevna both talked and listened without a smile. It was only when she actually said goodbye that her earlier friendliness seemed to stir within her.

'I'm feeling out of sorts at present,' she said, 'but pay no attention to that and come again soon – I'm saying that to both of you.'

Both Bazarov and Arkady responded to her with a silent bow, got into the carriage and set off for home without making any further stops. They successfully reached Marino on the evening of the next day. During the whole journey neither one of them as much as mentioned Odintsova's name. Bazarov in particular didn't open his mouth and kept looking sideways, away from the road, with a kind of furious concentration.

Everyone at Marino was overjoyed to see them. His son's prolonged absence was beginning to worry Nikolay Petrovich. He shouted, stamped his feet and bounced up and down on the sofa when Fenechka ran into his room with shining eyes and announced the arrival of the 'young gentlemen'. Pavel Petrovich himself felt some pleasurable excitement and gave a condescending smile as he shook the hands of the returning wanderers. The talk and questions began. Arkady spoke most, especially over dinner, which went on long past midnight. Nikolay Petrovich had served several bottles of porter, which had just been brought from Moscow, and drank quite a bit himself so that his cheeks turned the colour of raspberries and he went on laughing with a kind of half-childish, half-nervous laugh. The general animation infected the servants as well. Dunyasha ran to and fro like a madwoman and kept slamming doors, while even after two in the morning Pyotr was still trying to play a Cossack waltz on the guitar. The strings made a pleasant plaintive sound in the still air, but the cultured valet couldn't produce anything beyond a brief opening trill. Nature had denied him musical talent, like all others.

But meanwhile life at Marino wasn't going too well, and poor Nikolay Petrovich was having a hard time.[1] Troubles with the farm – depressing, stupid troubles – grew daily. Problems with the hired labourers were becoming intolerable. Some were demanding settlements or increases, others left after getting an advance on their wages. Horses went sick and harnesses fell to pieces. Work was carried out sloppily. A threshing machine that had been ordered from Moscow turned out to be useless because of its weight. Another one broke the first time it was used. Half of the cattle byre burnt down because a blind old woman, one of the house serfs, tried to fumigate her cow with a live coal . . . it's true the old woman averred the whole trouble had come about because the master had had the idea of making some extraordinary cheeses and dairy products. The steward became lazy and even started to become fat, as every Russian man does when he starts getting 'free rations'. When he saw Nikolay Petrovich in the distance, to demonstrate his keenness he would throw a stick at a passing piglet or swear at a half-naked urchin, but otherwise he spent most of his time asleep. Peasants who had been put on quit-rent didn't pay on time and stole wood. Almost every night the watchmen caught peasants' horses on the meadows of the 'farm' and sometimes impounded them forcibly. Nikolay Petrovich would impose a fine for the damage to his crops, but matters usually ended with the horses being returned to their owners after a day or two on the master's fodder.

To crown everything the peasants were beginning to quarrel among themselves: brothers demanded a division of property;

their wives couldn't get on together in one house. A fight would flare up, and everyone would suddenly be on their feet as if at an order and rush to the porch of the estate office and get at the master – often with black eyes and drunk – demanding justice and punishment. There was noise and screaming, the snivelling wails of women alternating with the curses of men. Nikolay Petrovich had to sort out the warring parties and shout himself hoarse, knowing in advance that it was still impossible to reach a fair settlement. There weren't enough hands for the harvest. A neighbouring smallholder, looking ever so reasonable, bargained to provide reapers for two roubles a *desyatina*[2] and cheated in the most shameless way. Nikolay Petrovich's own women were asking absurd rates and meanwhile the corn went to seed. One day the mowing wasn't being done, another day the Council of Trustees[3] was threatening and demanding immediate payment of interest in full . . .

'I'm at the end of my tether!' Nikolay Petrovich several times cried out in despair. 'I can't fight myself, my principles don't allow me to send for the local constable, and without the fear of punishment one won't achieve anything!'

'*Du calme, du calme*,'[4] was Pavel Petrovich's comment on this while he himself hummed, frowned and pulled at his moustache.

Bazarov held himself apart from these petty problems, and indeed as a guest it wasn't his role to get involved in other people's business. The day after their arrival at Marino he applied himself to his frogs, his infusoria microscopic specimens and his chemical compounds and kept himself busy with them. Arkady, on the contrary, thought it his duty, if not to help his father, at least to look as if he was prepared to help him. He patiently heard him out and on one occasion gave him some advice, not for it to be followed but to demonstrate his involvement. He felt no antipathy to estate management; he even used to dream about farming activity with pleasure, but then other thoughts began to swarm in his head. To his own surprise Arkady kept constantly thinking of Nikolskoye. Previously he would only have shrugged his shoulders if anyone had said to him that he could get bored under the same roof as Bazarov – and his father's roof at that! – but he actually was bored and longed to be somewhere else. He had the notion of walking till he was exhausted, but even that didn't help.

Talking to his father one day, he learnt that Nikolay Petrovich had a number of quite interesting letters which Odintsova's mother had written some time previously to his late wife, and he gave him no peace until he had got those letters, looking for which Nikolay Petrovich had to rummage in twenty different boxes and trunks. Once he had these semi-decayed papers in his possession, Arkady seemed to calm down, as if he had seen in front of him the goal to which he must go. 'I am saying this to both of you,' he kept whispering – 'she said that herself at the end. I'll go, I'll go, what the devil!' But he remembered the last visit, the cold welcome and his former awkwardness, and shyness overcame him. The 'why not' of youth, the secret desire to know his luck, to try his strength all on his own without the support of another, eventually won through. Ten days hadn't passed since his return to Marino before he was again galloping off to town on the pretext of studying the organization of Sunday schools[5] and from there to Nikolskoye. He nagged the driver continuously and drove there like a young officer into battle: he was both scared and full of cheer, breathless with impatience. 'The main thing is not to think,' he kept repeating to himself. He had got a driver who was quite a lad – he stopped at every tavern, saying, 'I need a quick one' or 'Time for a quick one?'; but, having had his quick one, he didn't spare the horses.

At last there appeared the lofty roofline of the familiar house . . . 'What am I doing?' went suddenly through Arkady's head. 'But I can't go back!' The *troika* of horses sped on together, the driver 'whooped' and whistled. Now the little bridge rumbled beneath their hooves and wheels, then came the avenue of clipped firs . . . There was the flash of a woman's pink dress amid the dark green, and a young face peeped out from under the delicate fringe of a parasol . . . He recognized Katya, and she recognized him. Arkady told the driver to stop the galloping horses, jumped out of the carriage and went to her. 'It's you!' she said and slowly blushed all over her face. 'Let's go to my sister. She's here in the garden. She'll be pleased to see you.'

Katya took Arkady to the garden. Meeting her seemed to him a particularly happy omen. He was overjoyed to see her, just like one of his family. Everything had gone so well – no butler, no announcement. At a turn in the path he saw Anna Sergeyevna. She was standing with her back to him. Hearing footsteps, she quietly turned round.

Arkady might have been embarrassed again, but the first words she uttered reassured him at once. 'How are you, runaway?' she said in her even, friendly voice and came to greet him, smiling and screwing up her eyes against the sun and wind. 'Where did you come across him, Katya?'

'Anna Sergeyevna,' he began, 'I've brought you something you surely didn't expect . . .'

'You've brought yourself, that's best of all.'

XXIII

Bazarov saw Arkady off with a sarcastic expression of regret, letting him know that he wasn't at all deceived about the true purpose of his trip. Bazarov then removed himself completely – he was overcome by a fever for work. He no longer argued with Pavel Petrovich, especially since the latter assumed in his presence an exaggeratedly aristocratic expression and gave vent to his opinions with sounds more than with words. Just once Pavel Petrovich was on the point of crossing swords with the 'nihilist' on the subject of the then fashionable question of the rights of the Baltic barons[1] but he stopped himself, pronouncing with cool politeness:

'But we cannot understand each other; at least I don't have the honour of understanding you.'

'What next!' Bazarov exclaimed. 'A man is capable of understanding everything – how the ether vibrates and what happens on the sun. But to understand how another man can blow his nose differently from the way he blows his own is something beyond his capability.'

'So, is that witty?' Pavel Petrovich inquired and went off.

However, he sometimes asked permission to be present during Bazarov's experiments and once even brought his scented face, washed with some choice concoction, down close to the microscope so he could watch a transparent infusorian swallowing a green speck of dust and carefully chewing it with some very dextrous discs located in its throat. Nikolay Petrovich came to see Bazarov much more often than his brother. He would have come every day, to 'study' as he said, if he hadn't been distracted by his estate problems. He didn't bother the young scientist: he sat down somewhere in a corner of the room and watched attentively, from time to time letting himself put a careful question. During dinner and supper he tried to bring the conversation round to physics, geology or chemistry, since all other subjects, even estate management, not to mention politics, could lead, if not to collision, at any rate to mutual displeasure. Nikolay Petrovich suspected that his brother's hatred for Bazarov had in no way diminished. An insignificant event, among many others, confirmed his suspicions. Cholera had begun to manifest itself here and there in the neighbourhood and even 'carried off' two people from Marino. One night Pavel Petrovich had quite a severe attack. He suffered until morning but would not have any recourse to Bazarov's skills. When he saw him the following day, in answer to Bazarov's question why he hadn't sent for him, he replied, still quite pale but already shaved and with his hair brushed, 'But don't I remember you saying you didn't believe in medicine.' So the days passed. Bazarov worked, determinedly and morosely . . . Meanwhile there was in Nikolay Petrovich's house a being to whom, if he didn't exactly open his heart, he nonetheless willingly chatted . . . That being was Fenechka.

They usually met in the mornings, early, in the garden or the farmyard. He didn't go into her room, and she only once went to his door to ask him whether she should bath Mitya or not. Not only did she trust him, not only did she have no fear of him, she behaved with him more freely and more easily than with Nikolay Petrovich himself. It's difficult to say why this happened. Maybe because she unconsciously sensed in Bazarov the absence of anything aristocratic or superior, which can be both attractive and alarming. He was in her eyes both an excellent doctor and a straightforward man. His presence while she looked after her baby didn't make her nervous and once, when she suddenly felt giddy and a headache coming on, she accepted a spoonful of medicine from him. In front of Nikolay Petrovich she seemed to avoid Bazarov: she did this not out of guile but from some kind of feeling of propriety. She was more frightened of Pavel Petrovich than ever. For some time he had started to watch her, and he used to turn up unexpectedly as if he had sprung out of the ground behind her back in his 'suit', with his sharp-eyed, immobile features and his hands in his pockets. 'It makes a shiver go down your spine,' Fenechka complained to Dunyasha, who in response sighed and thought of another 'unfeeling' man. Bazarov, without suspecting it, had become the *cruel tyrant* of her soul.

Fenechka found Bazarov attractive and he too found her attractive. Even his face became different when he talked to her: it assumed a serene, almost benign expression, and his normal casual manner took on a touch of playful attentiveness. Fenechka became prettier each day. There comes a time in the life of young women when they suddenly begin to blossom and open out like summer roses: that time came for Fenechka. Everything contributed to that, even the July heat which came on then. Dressed in a light white frock, she herself seemed more white and lighter. She wasn't caught by sunburn, but the heat, which she couldn't escape, lightly tinged her cheeks and ears with red and, infusing a gentle indolence over her whole body, had its effect in the dreamy languor of her pretty eyes. She was almost unable to work, her hands just slipped down on her knees. She didn't walk much and kept moaning and complaining with a helplessness that was comical.

'You should bathe more often,' Nikolay Petrovich said to her. He had constructed a big bathing place covered with canvas in his one pond that hadn't completely dried up.

'Oh, Nikolay Petrovich! But one just dies of heat getting to the pond, and one dies of heat coming back. There's no shade in the garden.'

'You're right, there's no shade,' Nikolay Petrovich answered and wiped his brow.

Once after six in the morning Bazarov was returning from a walk and came across Fenechka in the lilac arbour which had long lost its flowers but was still thick and green. She was sitting on the bench. As usual she'd put a white kerchief over her head. Next to her lay a whole bunch of red and white roses, still wet from the dew. He greeted her.

'Ah! Yevgeny Vasilyich!' she said, lifting the edge of her kerchief a little in order to look at him, and as she did it she bared her arm to the elbow.

'What are you doing here?' said Bazarov, sitting down by her. 'Are you making a bouquet?'

'Yes, for the lunch table. Nikolay Petrovich likes it.'

'But it's a long time till lunch. What a huge number of flowers!'

'I've picked them now, otherwise it'll get hot and one won't be able to go out. It's only now one can breathe. I've become quite weak from this heat. I'm worried I'll get ill.'

'You're imagining things! Let me take your pulse.' Bazarov took her hand, found an evenly beating vein and didn't even bother counting the beats. 'You'll live to be a hundred,' he said, letting go her hand.

'Oh, God forbid!' she exclaimed.

'Why? Don't you want to live a long time?'

'But to a hundred! My granny was eighty-five – and she was a real misery! Black and deaf and hunched and always coughing. Just a burden to herself. What kind of life!'

'So it's better to be young?'

'But of course.'

'Why is it better? Tell me!'

'Why? Here I am, young, I can do everything, I can come and go and carry things, and I don't have to ask anyone . . . What can be better?'

'But I don't care if I am young or old.'

'Why do you say you don't care? What you're saying isn't possible.'

'Well, Fedosya Nikolayevna, you judge for yourself what good being young is to me. I live alone, no family or friends . . .'

'That's always up to you.'

'Not altogether! If only someone felt sorry for me.'

Fenechka looked sideways at Bazarov but said nothing.

'What's that book of yours?' she asked after a short pause.

'This? It's a scientific book, quite difficult.'

'And are you still studying? Don't you get bored? I think you know everything already.'

'Obviously I don't. Try and read a bit yourself.'

'But I won't understand any of it. Is it in Russian?' Fenechka asked, taking the massively bound book into both hands. 'It's so fat!'

'Yes, it's in Russian.'

'I still won't understand any of it.'

'But I'm not asking you to understand. I want to look at you and watch how you read. When you read, the end of your nose moves in a very sweet way.'

Fenechka, who was attempting to make sense of an article she had opened the book at – 'On Creosote' – by reading it out in a low voice, burst out laughing and dropped the book . . . it slipped from the bench on to the ground.

'I also like it when you laugh,' said Bazarov.

'Stop it!'

'I like it when you speak. Like a babbling stream.'

Fenechka turned her head away.

'You do go on!' she said, picking at the flowers with her fingers. 'And why do you want to listen to me? You've talked to such clever ladies.'

'Oh, Fedosya Nikolayevna! Believe me, all the clever ladies in the world aren't worth your little elbow.'

'Some more of your nonsense!' Fenechka whispered and pressed her hands together.

Bazarov picked up the book from the ground.

'It's a medical book, why did you drop it?'

'A medical one?' Fenechka repeated and turned towards him. 'Do you know something? Ever since you gave me those drops, do you remember, Mitya sleeps so well! I don't know how to thank you. You're so kind, you really are.'

'But actually doctors should be paid,' Bazarov said with a smile. 'As you yourself know, doctors are mercenary folk.'

Fenechka raised her eyes towards Bazarov; they seemed darker from the whitish reflection falling on the upper part of her face. She didn't know if he was joking or not.

'If that's what you want, we'll gladly . . . I'll have to ask Nikolay Petrovich . . .'

'Do you think I want money?' Bazarov interrupted her. 'No, I don't need money from you.'

'What then?' said Fenechka.

'What?' Bazarov repeated. 'Guess.'

'I haven't got second sight!'

'Then I'll tell you. I want . . . one of those roses.'

Fenechka again burst out laughing and even gestured with her hands. She found Bazarov's wish so funny. She laughed and at the same time felt herself flattered. Bazarov looked fixedly at her.

'If you like, if you like,' she said finally and, leaning down over the bench, she started to sort the flowers. 'What colour shall I give you, red or white?'

'A red one, not too big.'

She stood up straight.

'Here you are, take it,' she said but immediately took back the hand she had held out and, biting her lips, glanced towards the entrance of the arbour and then listened.

'What is it?' Bazarov asked. 'Nikolay Petrovich?'

'No . . . He went off to the fields . . . and I'm not scared of him . . . but now Pavel Petrovich . . . I thought . . .'

'What?'

'I thought he was walking round here. No . . . there's nobody. Take it.' Fenechka gave Bazarov the rose.

'What makes you scared of Pavel Petrovich?'

'He's always making me feel scared. It's not so much what he says, but he gives such strange looks. But you don't like him either. Do you remember, once you were always quarrelling with him? I don't know what your quarrel is about, but I see you can twist him this way and that . . .'

Fenechka showed with her hands how she thought Bazarov twisted Pavel Petrovich.

Bazarov smiled.

'But if he started to get the upper hand,' he asked, 'would you stand up for me?'

'Why would I have to do that? No one is going to beat you.'

'You think so? But I know a hand which, if it wanted to, could knock me down with one finger.'

'Whose hand is that?'

'Don't you know? Smell how sweet's the scent of the rose you gave me.'

Fenechka stretched her neck and brought down her face to the flower . . . The kerchief slipped from her head on to her shoulders, disclosing the soft mass of her black, glossy, slightly disordered hair.

'Wait, I want to smell it with you,' said Bazarov. He bent down and kissed her firmly on her parted lips.

She shivered and pushed his chest away with both hands. But she pushed feebly, and he was able to renew and prolong the kiss.

A dry cough came from behind the lilac. Fenechka instantly moved away to the opposite end of the bench. Pavel Petrovich appeared, bowed slightly, said, 'So you are here,' with a kind of malevolent despondency and went off. Fenechka at once gathered up all the roses and left the arbour. 'You should be ashamed of yourself, Yevgeny Vasilyevich,' she whispered as she left. There was genuine reproach evident in her whisper.

Bazarov recalled another recent episode and he felt a pang of conscience and contempt and vexation. But he immediately shook his head, ironically congratulated himself 'on his formal enrolment into the Philanderers' and went to his room.

But Pavel Petrovich left the garden and walked slowly as far as the wood. There he remained quite a long time, and, when he returned for lunch, Nikolay Petrovich asked him with concern if he was feeling all right, he looked so sombre.

'You know I sometimes have a bilious attack,' Pavel Petrovich quietly answered him.

XXIV

Two hours later he knocked on Bazarov's door.

'I must apologize for disturbing your scientific work,' he began, sitting down on a chair by the window and leaning with both hands on a beautiful cane with an ivory knob (he usually walked without one), 'but I must ask you to give me five minutes of your time . . . no more.'

'All of my time is at your disposal,' Bazarov answered. Something in his face quivered as soon as Pavel Petrovich crossed the threshold of the door.

'Five minutes is enough for me. I have come to put a question to you.'

'A question? About what?'

'Be so good as to hear me out. At the beginning of your sojourn in my brother's house, when I still didn't deny myself the pleasure of conversing with you, I had the occasion of hearing your views on many subjects. But in so far as I can remember, neither between us two nor in my presence did the conversation turn to fighting a duel or to duelling in general. May I ask your opinion on this subject?'

Bazarov, who had got up to meet Pavel Petrovich, sat on the edge of the table and folded his arms.

'My opinion is this,' he said. 'From a theoretical point of view a duel is an absurdity, but from a practical one it's another matter.'

'So you mean, if I have understood you just now, that whatever your theoretical view of duels, in practice you wouldn't allow yourself to be insulted without demanding satisfaction.'

'You have divined my thoughts entirely.'

'That's very good. I am very pleased to hear that from you. Your words remove me from uncertainty . . .'

'From indecision you mean.'

'It's the same thing. I use those phrases to be understood. I . . . am not a seminarist rat. Your words spare me a sad obligation. I have decided to fight you.'

Bazarov opened his eyes wide.

'Fight me?'

'Yes, fight you.'

'But why? Please tell me.'

'I could explain the reason to you,' Pavel Petrovich began, 'but I would prefer to say nothing. In my view, you have no place here. I cannot stand you, I despise you, and if that isn't enough for you . . .'

Pavel Petrovich's eyes lit up. Bazarov's too flashed.

'Very well,' he said. 'Further explanation is unnecessary. You have had the fantastical idea of trying out on me your spirit of chivalry. I could deny you the pleasure, but so be it!'

'I am sincerely obliged to you,' answered Pavel Petrovich, 'and I can now hope that you will accept my challenge without making me resort to violence.'

'Meaning that cane, speaking bluntly?' Bazarov said coolly. 'That's quite fair. There's absolutely no need for you to insult me. That wouldn't be wholly free of risk. You can remain a gentleman . . . I accept your challenge too in a gentlemanly spirit.'

'Excellent,' Pavel Petrovich pronounced and put his cane in a corner. 'We will now say a few words about the conditions of our duel. But first I would like to know if you felt it necessary to resort to the formality of a small quarrel, which could serve as the pretext for my challenge?'

'No, better without formalities.'

'I think so myself. I also consider it inappropriate to go into the real reasons for our conflict. We can't stand one another. What more do we need?'

'What more do we need?' Bazarov repeated ironically.

'As far as the conditions of our duel are concerned, since we won't have seconds – for where would we get them?'

'Where indeed?'

'I have the honour of proposing to you the following: we fight tomorrow, early, let's say at six, beyond the little wood, with pistols, at a distance of ten paces . . .'

'Ten paces? That's right, that's the measure of our mutual hatred.'

'Or else eight,' said Pavel Petrovich.

'Yes, why not.'

'Two shots, and to cover all eventualities each of us puts in his pocket a note putting the blame for his death on himself.'

'Now I don't quite agree with that,' said Bazarov. 'It's becoming a bit like a French novel, a bit improbable.'

'Maybe. However, you will agree that it's unpleasant to lay oneself open to the suspicion of murder.'

'I agree. But there is a way of avoiding that depressing accusation. We won't have seconds, but we could have a witness.'

'Who exactly, if I may ask?'

'Pyotr.'

'Who's Pyotr?'

'Your brother's valet. He's a man standing at the zenith of modern education and will perform his role with all the *comme il faut*[1] necessary on such occasions.'

'My dear sir, I think you are joking.'

'Not at all. Once you have considered my proposal, you will be convinced that it is full of good sense and simplicity. The truth will come out. But I'll undertake to prepare Pyotr appropriately and to bring him to the field of combat.'

'You are continuing to joke,' said Pavel Petrovich, getting up from his chair. 'But after the amiable readiness you have shown I have no right to be offended with you . . . And so, everything is arranged . . . By the way, do you have pistols?'

'Where would I have got pistols, Pavel Petrovich? I am not a warrior.'

'In that case I offer you mine. You can be assured that I haven't fired them for five years.'

'That's very comforting information.'

Pavel Petrovich got his cane . . .

'Now, my dear sir, it only remains for me to thank you and to restore you to your studies. I have the honour to take my leave of you.'

'I look forward, my dear sir, to our next meeting,' said Bazarov, seeing his guest to the door.

Pavel Petrovich went out, and Bazarov stood a while in front of the door and suddenly exclaimed, 'Hell and damnation, how noble and how silly! What a comedy we've been playing! Like performing dogs dancing on their back legs. But it was impossible to say no. He'd have been quite likely to hit me, and then . . .' (Bazarov went pale at the very thought. All of his pride reared up, as it were.) 'Then I'd have had to strangle him like a kitten.' He went back to his microscope, but his heart was beating hard, and the calm one needs for observation had gone. 'He saw us today,' he thought, 'but was he really standing up for his brother? And what's so special about a kiss? There's something else here. Bah! Is he in love himself? Of course he's in love. That's clear as daylight. Just think, what a mess! . . . A nasty business!' he pronounced finally. 'A nasty business, whichever way you look at it. First, I've got to offer him my head, and in any case I've got to leave. Then there's Arkady . . . and that wet Nikolay Petrovich. A nasty, nasty business.'

The day went by especially quietly and sluggishly. Fenechka might not have existed on this earth: she sat in her little room like a mouse in its hole. Nikolay Petrovich had a worried look. He'd been informed rust had appeared on his wheat for which he had had special hopes. Pavel Petrovich brought everyone down with his frigid politeness, even Prokofyich. Bazarov half started a letter to his father but tore it up and threw it under the table. 'If I die,' he thought, 'they'll hear about it. But I won't die. No, I'm going to be hanging around this world of ours a long time yet.' He told Pyotr to come and see him the next day at crack of dawn on an important matter. Pyotr imagined he wanted to take him with him to St Petersburg. Bazarov went to bed late and was tormented all night by disordered dreams . . . Odintsova was spinning round in front of him, she was his mother, she was followed round by a kitten with black whiskers, and that kitten was Fenechka. And Pavel Petrovich came to him in the shape of a great forest which he still had to fight. Pyotr woke him at four. He dressed right away and went out with him.

It was a lovely fresh morning. The pale, clear azure of the sky was dappled with little fleecy clouds. A light dew had fallen on the leaves and grass and shone silver on the spider webs. The moist, dark earth seemed to hold the rosy traces of sunrise. The whole sky rang with the song of larks. Bazarov went as far as the wood, sat down at its edge and only then disclosed to Pyotr the service he required of him. The well-trained servant was mortally scared, but Bazarov calmed him with the assurance that he had nothing to do but to stand at a distance and watch, and that he wasn't exposed to any responsibility. 'And then,' he added, 'just think what an important role you'll have!' Pyotr made a gesture with his hands, lowered his eyes and leant against a birch tree, looking green.

The road from Marino skirted the little wood. It was covered with light dust, untouched by wheels or human feet since the previous day. Bazarov involuntarily looked down the road, picked a blade of grass and chewed it and kept repeating to himself, 'How silly this is!' The morning chill made him shiver a couple of times . . . Pyotr gave him a despairing look, but Bazarov only grinned; he wasn't afraid.

The clattering of horse's hooves came down the road . . . A muzhik appeared from the trees. He was driving two hobbled horses along in front of him and, as he went past Bazarov, he gave him a strange sort of look and didn't remove his cap, which clearly bothered Pyotr as an unfavourable omen. 'He too has got up early,' thought Bazarov, 'and he at least is working, but what are we doing?'

'I think they're coming,' Pyotr whispered suddenly.

Bazarov raised his head and saw Pavel Petrovich. Wearing a light checked jacket and trousers that were white as snow, he was walking quickly down the road. Under his arm he carried a case wrapped in green cloth.

'Excuse me, I think I have kept you waiting,' he said, bowing first to Bazarov and then to Pyotr, whom at that moment he treated with something like respect, as a second. 'I didn't want to wake my valet.'

'It doesn't matter,' Bazarov replied. 'We've only just got here ourselves.'

'Ah, so much the better!' Pavel Petrovich looked around. 'I can't see anyone, no one is going to interfere . . . Can we begin?'

'Let's.'

'I imagine you don't require any further explanation.'

'No, I don't.'

'Would you be so good as to load?' asked Pavel Petrovich, taking the pistols out of the case.

'No. You load, and I'll start measuring out the paces. I have longer legs,' Bazarov added with an ironic smile. 'One, two, three . . .'

'Yevgeny Vasilyich,' Pyotr stammered awkwardly (he was shaking as if he had a fever), 'with your permission, I'll move off.'

'Four . . . five . . . You do that, my friend, you move off. You can even go behind a tree and block your ears, only don't shut your eyes, and if anyone falls, run and pick them up. Six . . . seven . . . eight.' Bazarov stopped. 'Is that enough?' he said, turning to Pavel Petrovich. 'Or shall I add a couple of paces?'

'As you please,' he said, putting in a second bullet.

'So, we'll add two more paces.' Bazarov marked a line on the ground with the toe of his boot. 'Here's the barrier. By the way how many paces should each of us go back from the barrier? That too is an important question. There was no discussion of that yesterday.'

'Ten, I think,' Pavel Petrovich replied, offering both pistols to Bazarov. 'Be so kind as to choose.'

'That I will. But you must agree, Pavel Petrovich, that our duel is comically out of the ordinary. Just look at our second's face.'

'You're always wanting to make jokes,' Pavel Petrovich answered. 'I don't deny the peculiarity of our duel but I consider it my duty to warn you that I intend to fight seriously. À bon entendeur salut!'[2]

'Oh, I am in no doubt that we have made up our minds to eliminate each other. But why not have a laugh and combine utile dulci?[3] There – you said something to me in French and I respond to you in Latin.'

'I am going to fight seriously,' Pavel Petrovich repeated and went off to his place.

Bazarov on his side counted off ten paces from the barrier and stopped.

'Are you ready?' Pavel Petrovich asked.

'Yes, quite ready.'

'We can engage.'

Bazarov quietly moved forward, while Pavel Petrovich walked towards him, putting his left hand into his pocket and gradually raising the barrel of his pistol . . . 'He's aiming right at my nose,' Bazarov thought, 'and he's trying so hard, with his eyes all screwed up, the old devil! But it's a disagreeable sensation. I am going to look at his watch chain . . .' Something whizzed sharply right by Bazarov's ear and at that moment there came the sound of a shot. 'I heard it, so I must be all right' was the thought that quickly flashed through his head. He took one more step and, without aiming, pressed the trigger.

Pavel Petrovich flinched slightly and grabbed at his thigh with his hand. A stream of blood went down his white trousers.

Bazarov threw the pistol aside and went towards his opponent.

'Are you wounded?' he said.

'You had the right to call me to the barrier,' said Pavel Petrovich, 'and this is trivial. By the rules each of us has one more shot.'

'Well, forgive me, that can wait till another time,' Bazarov answered and put his arms round Pavel Petrovich, who was beginning to go pale. 'Now I am no longer a duellist but a doctor and first of all I must inspect your wound. Pyotr! Come here, Pyotr! Where are you hiding?'

'That's all nonsense . . . I don't need anyone's help,' Pavel Petrovich said very slowly, 'and . . . we must . . . again . . .' He tried to pull at his moustache, but his arm was too weak; he rolled up his eyes and lost consciousness.

'Here's something new! Fainting! What next!' Bazarov couldn't help exclaiming as he lowered Pavel Petrovich on to the grass. 'Let's see what the problem is.' He took out a handkerchief, wiped the blood and felt round the wound . . . 'The bone isn't broken,' he muttered through his teeth, 'the bullet has gone right through, not very deep, it's grazed one muscle, *vastus externus*. He'll be dancing in three weeks! . . . But fainting! I've had enough of these high-strung types! Look at what delicate skin he has.'

'Is he dead?' Bazarov heard Pyotr's tremulous voice babbling behind him. He looked round.

'Go and get some water, my friend, be quick, and he'll out-live us both.' But the latest model of servant didn't appear to understand his words and didn't move. Pavel Petrovich slowly opened his eyes. 'He's going!' Pyotr whispered, and began crossing himself.

'You're right . . . What a stupid face!' said the wounded gen-tleman with a forced smile.

'Damn you, go and get some water!' cried Bazarov.

'I don't need any . . . It was just a momentary *vertige*[4] . . . Help me up . . . like that . . . We just need something to tie up this scratch, and I'll walk home, or if not they can send the droshky for me. If you agree, we won't resume our duel. You have behaved nobly . . . today, today I mean.'

'There's no reason to go over the past,' Bazarov retorted, 'and we needn't worry ourselves about the future either, because I mean to go off at once. Come, I'll now bandage your leg. Your wound isn't dangerous, but it's still better to stop the bleeding. But first we have to bring this creature back to his senses.'

Bazarov shook Pyotr by the collar and sent him off to fetch the droshky.

'Take care you don't scare my brother,' said Pavel Petrovich to him. 'And don't even think of reporting this to him.'

Pyotr hurried off, and while he was running to fetch the dro-shky the two opponents sat on the ground without speaking. Pavel Petrovich tried not to look at Bazarov. In spite of everything he didn't want to make his peace with him. He was ashamed of his arrogance, of his failure, he was ashamed of the whole thing he had started, although he also felt the outcome couldn't have been more favourable. 'At least he won't be hanging about here,' he consoled himself, 'and many thanks for that.' The silence con-tinued, heavy and awkward. Both men felt uncomfortable. Each knew the other understood him. That kind of knowledge is agree-able for friends, and for enemies very disagreeable, especially when they can't either have it out or separate.

'Have I made the bandage on your leg too tight?' Bazarov asked at last.

'No, it's all right, fine,' Pavel Petrovich answered and added after a short pause, 'We won't be able to keep this from my brother, we'll have to tell him we fought over politics.'

'Excellent,' said Bazarov. 'You can tell him I was rude about all Anglophiles.'

'That's very good. What do you suppose that man thinks of us now?' Pavel Petrovich went on, pointing to that muzhik who had driven his hobbled horses past Bazarov a few minutes before the duel and who was now coming back along the road. He stepped deferentially aside and took off his cap at the sight of 'gentlemen'.

'Who knows!' answered Bazarov. 'It's most likely he doesn't think anything. The Russian muzhik is the mysterious stranger whom Mrs Radcliffe[5] used to go on about. Who can understand him? He can't himself.'

'Oh, now you're starting that!' Pavel Petrovich began, then exclaimed suddenly, 'Look what your idiot Pyotr has gone and done! My brother is hurrying here!'

Bazarov turned and saw Nikolay Petrovich sitting in the droshky, white-faced. He jumped down before it had stopped and rushed to his brother.

'What's going on?' he said in an anxious voice. 'Yevgeny Vasilyich, please, what is all this?'

'Nothing at all,' answered Pavel Petrovich. 'There was no point in alarming you. Mr Bazarov and I had a small quarrel, and I have paid a bit for it.'

'What was it all about, for God's sake?'

'What can I tell you? Mr Bazarov said something disrespectful about Sir Robert Peel.[6] I hasten to add that in all of this only I am to blame and Mr Bazarov behaved very well. I called him out.'

'But, my goodness, you're bleeding!'

'Do you think I have water in my veins? But this bloodletting will even do me good. Won't it, doctor? Help me get into the droshky and don't give in to depression. Tomorrow I'll be recovered. That's it, excellent. Coachman, get going.'

Nikolay Petrovich followed the droshky; Bazarov would have stayed behind . . .

'I must ask you to look after my brother,' Nikolay Petrovich said to him, 'until we get another doctor here from the town.'

Bazarov nodded without saying anything.

An hour later Pavel Petrovich was already lying in his bed, with a proper bandage round his leg. The whole house was in a state of alarm. Fenechka felt unwell. Nikolay Petrovich quietly wrung his hands while Pavel Petrovich laughed and joked, especially with Bazarov. He was wearing a fine batiste nightshirt and an elegant morning jacket and fez. He wouldn't let them lower the window-blind and made amusing complaints about not being allowed to take food.

However, by nightfall he had a fever. His head began to ache. The doctor from the town came. (Nikolay Petrovich hadn't listened to his brother, and this was what Bazarov himself wanted too; he had spent the whole day sitting in his room, looking all jaundiced and angry, and he only came out for the briefest visits to the patient; a couple of times he happened to meet Fenechka, but she recoiled from him in horror.) The new doctor prescribed cooling drinks but in other respects confirmed Bazarov's assurances that no danger need be envisaged. Nikolay Petrovich said to him that his brother had wounded himself through carelessness, to which the doctor replied 'Hm!', but having then been given twenty-five silver roubles in his hand, he pronounced, 'You don't say! That does indeed often happen.'

No one in the house went to bed or undressed. Nikolay Petrovich now and then tiptoed in and out of his brother's room. Pavel Petrovich dozed, groaned slightly, said to him in French, 'Couchez-vous'[7] – and asked for a drink. Nikolay Petrovich once made Fenechka bring him a glass of lemonade; Pavel Petrovich stared at her and drank the glass to the last drop. By morning the fever had risen a little, and he showed some signs of delirium. At first Pavel Petrovich uttered incoherent words, then he suddenly opened his eyes and, seeing his brother by his bed solicitously bending over him, said:

'Nikolay, doesn't Fenechka have something in common with Nelly?'

'What Nelly, Pasha?'[8]

'How can you ask that? Princess R. . . . Especially in the upper part of the face. *C'est de la même famille.*'⁹

Nikolay Petrovich said nothing in reply but in his heart he was astonished at the tenacity of a man's old feelings.

'So that's come up now,' he thought.

'Oh, how I love that simple creature!' Pavel Petrovich moaned, wearily putting his arms behind his head. 'I will not allow any insolent fellow to dare to touch . . .' he babbled a few moments later.

Nikolay Petrovich only gave a sigh. He didn't suspect to whom these words referred.

Bazarov came to see Pavel Petrovich the following day about eight o'clock. He had already packed and released all his frogs, insects and birds.

'Have you come to say goodbye to me?' said Nikolay Petrovich, rising to greet him.

'I have.'

'I understand you and wholly approve. My poor brother of course is to blame. And he's been punished for it. He told me himself that he put you into a situation where it was impossible for you to act otherwise. I don't believe you could have avoided this duel which . . . which to some extent can be explained by the constant antagonism of your respective points of view.' (Nikolay Petrovich was getting lost in his words.) 'My brother is a man of the old school, fiery-tempered and set in his ways . . . Thank God, too, that it's ended like this. I have taken all necessary measures against publicity . . .'

'I'll leave you my address in case you need it, should the story come out,' Bazarov remarked coolly.

'I hope no story comes out, Yevgeny Vasilyich . . . I'm very sorry that your stay in my house has had such a . . . such an end. I feel the worse that Arkady . . .'

'I'll surely be seeing him,' Bazarov retorted: all kinds of 'explanation' and 'clarification' always provoked in him a feeling of impatience. 'In case I don't, please greet him for me and give him my regrets.'

'And allow me . . .' Nikolay Petrovich answered, with a bow.

But Bazarov didn't wait for the end of his sentence and went out.

When he heard of Bazarov's coming departure, Pavel Petrovich said that he wanted to see him and shook hands. But on this occasion too Bazarov appeared cold as ice. He realized that Pavel Petrovich wanted to appear a little magnanimous. He didn't manage to say goodbye to Fenechka: he just caught her eye through a window. He thought her face looked sad. 'That'll surely pass!' he said to himself. 'She'll somehow get over it!' But Pyotr was so moved that he cried on his shoulder till Bazarov put him off with the chilly question 'Do your eyes run?' And Dunyasha was obliged to dash off to the wood in order to hide her emotion. The perpetrator of all this grief got into the carriage and lit up a cigar, and when after a couple of miles at a turn in the road the extended line of the Kirsanovs' manor buildings with the new mansion appeared to him for the last time, he just spat and, muttering 'Bloody gents!', he wrapped himself deeper in his overcoat.

Pavel Petrovich soon felt better, but he had to stay in bed for about a week. He bore his 'captivity', as he called it, patiently, only he took a great deal of pains over his toilet and kept telling them to fumigate the room with eau de Cologne. Nikolay Petrovich read the newspapers to him, Fenechka waited on him as before, brought him broth, lemonade, soft-boiled eggs, tea. But she was overcome by secret terror every time she entered his room. Pavel Petrovich's surprising action had scared everyone in the house and her most of all; only Prokofyich was unperturbed and explained that in his day gentlemen were always fighting, 'only it was noble gentlemen fighting each other, but rubbish like that they'd have had flogged in the stables for impertinence'.

Fenechka had almost no reproaches of conscience but she was troubled at times by the thought of the real reason for the quarrel. And Pavel Petrovich looked at her so strangely . . . so that even when she had her back to him she felt his eyes on her. She had become thinner from the constant inner anxiety and, as usually happens, had become even prettier.

One day – it was in the morning – Pavel Petrovich felt better and moved from his bed to a sofa while Nikolay Petrovich, having inquired after his health, went off to the threshing barn. Fenechka brought a cup of tea, put it down on a table and was about to go. Pavel Petrovich detained her.

'Why are you in such a hurry, Fedosya Nikolayevna?' he began. 'Have you things to do?'

'No . . . yes . . . I have to pour out the tea in there.'

'Dunyasha will do that without you. Sit a bit with the patient. Incidentally, I must talk to you.'

Fenechka sat down on the edge of a chair without speaking.

'Listen,' said Pavel Petrovich and tugged at his moustache. 'I have long been meaning to ask you – you're frightened of me, aren't you?'

'I, frightened of you?'

'Yes, you. You never look at me, as if you had something on your conscience.'

Fenechka went red but she did glance at Pavel Petrovich. He had a strange look, she felt, and her heart began to beat gently.

'You don't have anything on your conscience, do you?'

'Why should I?' she whispered.

'There are plenty of reasons. But whom could you have wronged? Myself? Unlikely. Others here in the house? Also improbable. Then my brother? But you do love him, don't you?'

'Yes, I do.'

'With all your heart and all your soul?'

'I love Nikolay Petrovich with all my heart.'

'Truthfully? Look at me, Fenechka.' (He called her that for the first time . . .) 'You know that lying is a grave sin.'

'I am not lying, Pavel Petrovich. Stop loving Nikolay Petrovich – after that I might as well die!'

'And you wouldn't give him up for anyone else?'

'For whom could I?'

'It could be anyone! Say the gentleman who's just left here.'

Fenechka got up.

'My God, Pavel Petrovich, why are you tormenting me? What have I done to you? How can you say such a thing? . . .'

'Fenechka,' said Pavel Petrovich sadly, 'but I saw . . .'

'What did you see?'

'I saw you there in the arbour.'

Fenechka blushed to her ears and the roots of her hair.

'But did I do wrong there?' she said with some difficulty.

Pavel Petrovich rose.

'Did you really do nothing wrong? Nothing? Nothing at all?'

'Nikolay Petrovich is the only one in the world that I love, and I will love him always!' Fenechka pronounced with a sudden surge of strength while sobs were still choking her throat. 'But as for what you saw, I'll say at the Last Judgement that I bear no blame for that, and it would be better for me to die here and now if people had any suspicions about me there, that I could cause my benefactor, Nikolay Petrovich . . .'

But here her voice failed her and at the same time she felt that Pavel Petrovich had taken hold of her hand and squeezed it . . . She looked at him and froze. He had become even paler than before, his eyes shone, and, most surprising of all, a single tear rolled down his cheek.

'Fenechka!' he said in a kind of odd whisper. 'You must love my brother, love him! He is such a kind, good man. Don't betray him for anyone in the world, don't listen to the fine words of others! Think, what can be more terrible than to love and not to be loved! Don't abandon my poor Nikolay!'

So great was Fenechka's astonishment that her eyes dried and her terror passed. But what did she feel when Pavel Petrovich, Pavel Petrovich himself, took her hand to his lips and pressed it there, without kissing it and only occasionally giving a convulsive sigh . . .

'Lord above!' she thought. 'Is he having a fit? . . .' But at that moment his whole ruined life was quivering within him. The stairs creaked, and there was the sound of hurried footsteps . . . He pushed her away from him, and his head fell back on the pillow. The door opened – and Nikolay Petrovich appeared, all cheerful, fresh and rosy. Mitya, in just a shirt, as fresh and rosy as his father, was jumping up and down on his chest, grabbing the big buttons of his country coat between his bare toes.

Fenechka rushed to Nikolay Petrovich and, putting her arms

round father and son, laid her head on his shoulder. Nikolay Petrovich was astonished. Shy and modest Fenechka never showed him signs of affection in the presence of a third person.

'What's the matter with you?' he said and with a look at his brother he handed Mitya to her. 'Are you feeling worse?' he asked, going up to Pavel Petrovich.

He pressed his face into a batiste handkerchief.

'No . . . it's . . . nothing's the matter . . . On the contrary I'm much better.'

'You were too hasty in moving to the sofa. Where are you off to?' Nikolay Petrovich added, turning to Fenechka, but she had already slammed the door behind her. 'I was bringing in my big boy to show him to you – he was missing his uncle. Why did she take him away? But what's the matter with you? Did something happen in here between you?'

'Brother!' Pavel Petrovich said solemnly.

Nikolay Petrovich shivered. He felt scared, he didn't understand why.

'Brother,' Pavel Petrovich repeated, 'give me your word you'll meet one request of mine.'

'What? Tell me.'

'It's very important. In my view the whole happiness of your life depends on it. All this time I've been reflecting a lot on what I now want to say to you . . . Brother, do your duty, your duty as an honest and noble man, put an end to the seducer's role, to the poor example you set, you who are the best of men!'

'Paul, what do you mean?'

'Marry Fenechka . . . She loves you, she's the mother of your son.'

Nikolay Petrovich stepped back a pace and raised his hands.

'Are you saying this, Pavel? You whom I always thought the most inflexible opponent of marriages like that? You are saying this! But don't you know that it is solely out of respect for you that I haven't done what you have justly called my duty!'

'In this case your respect for me was pointless,' Pavel Petrovich retorted with a melancholy smile. 'I am beginning to think that Bazarov was right when he accused me of aristocratism. No, dear Brother, that's enough of putting on airs and thinking about the wider world: we are now old and meek. It's time for us to put all vanity aside. Precisely as you say, we'll start doing our duty. And, mark you, we'll get happiness into the bargain.'

Nikolay Petrovich rushed to embrace his brother.

'You have finally opened my eyes!' he exclaimed. 'I always maintained you were the kindest and cleverest man in the world, and I was right. And now I see that you are as wise as you are big-hearted.'

'Shush, shush.' Pavel Petrovich interrupted him. 'Don't hurt the leg of your wise brother, who at the age of nearly fifty has gone and fought a duel, like a subaltern. And so, that's decided. Fenechka will be my . . . *belle-sœur*.'[10]

'My dear Pavel! But what will Arkady say?'

'Arkady? He'll be in ecstasy, I should think! Marriage is not one of his principles, but his sense of equality will be flattered. And indeed how can class matter *au dix-neuvième siècle*?'[11]

'Oh Pavel, Pavel! Let me kiss you again. Don't worry, I'll be careful.'

The brothers embraced.

'What do you think, why not declare your intentions to her here and now?' asked Pavel Petrovich.

'Why such a hurry?' Nikolay Petrovich answered. 'Did you have words?'

'Words? *Quelle idée!*'[12]

'Very well, then. First recover your health; this matter isn't going to run away from us, we must think it through, and consider . . .'

'But you've made up your mind, haven't you?'

'Of course I have and I thank you from my heart. Now I'll leave you, you must rest. Upsets are bad for you . . . But we'll talk more. Go to sleep, my dear, and get well, with God's help!'

'Why is he thanking me?' thought Pavel Petrovich when he was alone. 'As if it didn't depend on him! And as soon as he marries I'll go off somewhere far away, Dresden or Florence, and live there till I drop dead.'

Pavel Petrovich moistened his forehead with eau de Cologne and closed his eyes. Lit by the bright light of day, his handsome, wasted head lay on the white pillow like the head of a dead man . . . And he was indeed a dead man.

XXV

At Nikolskoye Katya and Arkady were sitting on a turf seat in the garden, in the shade of a tall ash. On the ground by them lay Fifi, her long body forming the elegant curve sportsmen call a 'hare's lie'. Neither of them spoke. He held in his hands a half-open book while she took from a basket the remaining crumbs of white bread and threw them to a small family of sparrows which with their usual mixture of timorousness and cheek hopped and chirruped right by their feet. A slight breeze stirring in the leaves of the ash gently shifted pale golden patches of light back and forth over the dark path and Fifi's yellow back. Arkady and Katya were in full shade; only occasionally a bright streak of light played in her hair. Both were silent, but their very silence and the way they sat next to one another spoke of their trust and intimacy. Neither appeared to be thinking of their neighbour, but each was secretly glad of the closeness. And their expressions had changed since we saw them last: Arkady seemed calmer, Katya livelier and bolder.

'Don't you find,' Arkady began, 'that the ash tree – *yasen'* – is very well named in Russian: there is no tree with its light, clear – *yasny* – transparency in the air?'

Katya raised her eyes and said 'yes' – and Arkady thought, 'Well, she doesn't criticize me for fine phrases.'

'I don't like Heine,'[1] said Katya looking at the book in Arkady's hands, 'when he's laughing or when he's weeping. I do like him when he is pensive or melancholy.'

'But I like him when he's laughing,' said Arkady.

'Those are still the old traces of your satirical way of thinking . . .' ('Old traces!' thought Arkady. 'If Bazarov heard that.') 'Wait a little and we'll change you.'

'Who will change me? You?'

'Who will? My sister, and Porfyry Platonych, with whom you no longer quarrel, and my aunt, whom you took to church the day before yesterday.'

'I could hardly refuse! As for Anna Sergeyevna you'll remember that she herself agreed with Yevgeny about many things.'

'My sister was then under his influence, like you.'

'Like me! Have you noticed that I'm already liberated from his influence?'

Katya said nothing.

Arkady went on. 'I know you never liked him.'

'I can't judge him.'

'You know, Katerina Sergeyevna, every time I hear that reply, I don't believe it . . . There is nobody whom none of us can judge! It's just an excuse.'

'Well, then I'll tell you that he . . . it's not that I don't like him, but I feel he's alien to me, and I to him . . . and you're alien to him.'

'Why's that?'

'How can I say it . . . he's a predator and you and I are domestic animals.'

'I'm one too?'

Katya nodded.

Arkady scratched behind his ear.

'Listen, Katerina Sergeyevna, that's really offensive.'

'Would you like to be a predator?'

'Not a predator, but strong, energetic.'

'That can't be had by wishing . . . Your friend doesn't wish that, but he is that.'

'Hm! So you think he had a big influence on Anna Sergeyevna?'

'Yes. But no one can have the upper hand over her for long,' Katya added in a low voice.

'Why do you think that?'

'She's very proud . . . I didn't mean that . . . she very much values her independence.'

'Who doesn't?' Arkady asked, while the thought 'Why does she?' went through his mind. The same thought went through

Katya's. Young people who meet often and become intimate constantly have the very same thoughts.

Arkady smiled and, moving a little closer to Katya, whispered:

'Admit you're a bit scared of her.'

'Scared of whom?'

'Of *her*,' Arkady repeated, with emphasis.

'And what about you?' Katya asked in her turn.

'I am too. Note that I said I am too.'

Katya wagged her finger at him.

'I am surprised about that,' she began, 'my sister has never been so fond of you as right now, much more than when you came here first.'

'Oh really!'

'Didn't you notice that? Aren't you pleased?'

Arkady thought a moment.

'How could I have earned Anna Sergeyevna's goodwill? Maybe because I brought her your mother's letters?'

'Yes, that, and there are other reasons, which I won't say.'

'Why?'

'I won't say.'

'Oh, I do know – you're very stubborn.'

'I am.'

'And observant.'

Katya looked sideways at Arkady.

'Does that perhaps annoy you? What are you thinking about?'

'I'm wondering where you got these powers of observation, which you really do have. You're so apprehensive and mistrustful, you keep at a distance from everyone . . .'

'I've lived a lot by myself: willy-nilly one starts to reflect on things. But do I really keep at a distance from everyone?'

Arkady gave Katya a grateful look.

'That's all very well,' he went on, 'but people in your position, I mean to say with your fortune, seldom have that gift: it's as hard for the truth to get through to them as to the Tsar.'

'But I'm not rich.'

Arkady was taken aback and didn't immediately understand Katya. 'So in fact the estate is all her sister's!' was the thought that then came into his head: he didn't find it unpleasant.

'How well you said that!' he pronounced.

'What do you mean?'

'You said that so well – simply, without being ashamed and without dramatizing. By the way, I imagine that the feelings of someone who knows and says that they are poor do have something special, a particular kind of vanity.'

'I never experienced anything of that kind, thanks to my sister. I mentioned my lack of fortune simply because the subject came up.'

'Very well. But do admit you have a bit of that vanity I was just talking about.'

'Give me an example.'

'For example – you must excuse my question – you wouldn't marry a rich man, would you?'

'If I loved him very much . . . No, I suppose even then I wouldn't.'

'Ah, you see!' Arkady exclaimed and after a pause went on: 'But why wouldn't you marry him?'

'Because the old song says like should go with like.'

'Maybe you want to dominate or . . .'

'No, no. Why do you say that? On the contrary I am ready to submit, only inequality is hard to bear. To have self-respect and to submit – that I do understand; that's happiness. But a subordinate existence . . . no, I've had enough of that.'

'Enough of that,' Arkady repeated after Katya. 'Yes, yes,' he went on, 'you're not Anna Sergeyevna's sister for nothing. You're as independent-minded as she is. But you're more reserved. I am sure you would never be the first to declare your feelings, however strong or sacred they might be . . .'

'How else could I act?' asked Katya.

'You're just as clever, you have just as strong a character as she has, if not stronger . . .'

'Please don't compare me with my sister,' Katya quickly interrupted. 'It puts me too much at a disadvantage. You seem to have forgotten that my sister is both a beauty and very clever,

and . . . you especially, Arkady Nikolayevich, shouldn't be saying such things, and with such a serious expression.'

'What does that mean – "you especially" – and what makes
you think I am joking?'

'Of course you're joking.'

'Do you think so? But what if I'm convinced of what I'm saying? If I find that I haven't yet expressed myself strongly enough?'

'I don't understand you.'

'Don't you? Well now I see – I really overestimated your
powers of observation.'

'In what way?'

Arkady made no answer, and Katya looked in the basket for
a few more crumbs and began to throw them to the sparrows,
but she moved her hand too brusquely, and they flew away
before they could peck at the bread.

'Katerina Sergeyevna!' Arkady said suddenly. 'You probably
don't care, but you must know that I wouldn't exchange you
for your sister – or for anyone else in the world.'

He got up and quickly went away as if he was frightened of
the words that had burst from his lips.

And Katya let both hands and her basket drop on to her
knees and, bowing her head, looked after Arkady for a long
time. Slowly a crimson colour lightly flushed her cheeks, but
her lips didn't smile, and her dark eyes showed bewilderment
and another feeling too, which didn't yet have a name.

'Are you alone?' She heard Anna Sergeyevna's voice close by.
'I thought you went into the garden with Arkady.'

Katya slowly raised her eyes to her sister. Elegantly, even
exquisitely dressed, she was standing on the path and tickling
Fifi's ears with the tip of her open parasol. 'I'm by myself,'
Katya said slowly.

'I can see that,' the other said laughing. 'So he must have
gone to his room.'

'Yes, he has.'

'Were you reading together?'

'Yes.'

Anna Sergeyevna took hold of Katya's chin and raised her
face.

'I hope you haven't quarrelled.'

'No, we haven't,' said Katya and gently moved her sister's hand away.

'What a solemn answer! I thought I would find him here and suggest he came for a walk with me. He is always asking me. Your boots have come from the town. Go and try them on – I noticed yesterday your old ones are quite worn. In general you don't bother enough about that kind of thing, and you have such pretty feet. And your hands are nice . . . only they're rather large. So you must make the most of your feet. But you aren't a flirt, my dear.'

Anna Sergeyena walked on down the path, her beautiful dress gently rustling. Katya got up from the bench and also went off, taking Heine – but it wasn't to try on the boots.

'Pretty feet,' she thought, slowly and lightly climbing the stone steps of the terrace baking in the sun. 'Pretty feet you say . . . Well, he'll be at those feet.'

But she immediately felt ashamed of herself and quickly ran upstairs.

Arkady walked down the corridor towards his room. The butler found him and reported that Mr Bazarov was sitting in there.

'Yevgeny!' Arkady stammered, almost scared. 'Has he been here long?'

'The gentleman came only this minute and asked not to be announced to Anna Sergeyevna but told me to take him straight to you.'

'Has there been an accident at home?' Arkady wondered. He hurriedly ran up the stairs and threw open his door. Bazarov's expression reassured him, though a more experienced eye would have detected signs of inner agitation in the features of his unexpected guest – they showed their usual energy but were drawn. A dusty overcoat over his shoulders and a cap on his head, he was sitting on the window-sill. He didn't get up even when Arkady rushed to embrace him with noisy greetings.

'What a surprise! What has brought you here?' he repeated, walking round the room like a man who fancies himself pleased and wants to show it. 'Is everything all right at home, is every-one well?'

'Everything's all right at your home but not everyone is well,' said Bazarov. 'Stop chattering and tell them to bring me some kvass,[2] sit down and listen to what I'm going to tell you, briefly but, I hope, forcefully.'

Arkady fell silent, and Bazarov told him about his duel with Pavel Petrovich. Arkady was quite astonished, even upset, but he didn't feel he should show that; he only asked if the wound was really not serious and, having got the reply that the wound was a most interesting one, only not in a medical sense, he gave a forced smile. But at heart he felt wretched and somehow ashamed. Bazarov seemed to understand this.

'Yes, my friend,' he said, 'that's what comes of living with feudal barons. You become one yourself and take your part in knightly tournaments. So I set off for "the home of my fathers",' Bazarov concluded. 'And on the way I called in here . . . to report all this, I might have said, if I hadn't thought it stupid to tell a pointless lie. No, I called in here – devil knows why. You see, a man must sometimes grip himself by the hair and pull himself out, like a radish from its bed in the soil. The other day I did that myself . . . But I wanted to take a look once more at what I had left, at the bed where I lay.'

'I hope those words don't refer to me,' Arkady exclaimed with feeling, 'I hope you aren't thinking of parting from *me*.'

Bazarov gave him a fixed, almost piercing stare.

'Would that really so upset you? It seems to me you've already parted from me. You're so very fresh and clean . . . your affair with Anna Sergeyevna must be going really well.'

'What affair with Anna Sergeyevna?'

'Wasn't it for her you came here from the town, my little fledgling? By the way, how are the Sunday schools coming on? Aren't you in love with her? Or do you feel it's time to be coy?'

'Yevgeny, you know I've always been open with you. I can assure you, I swear to God that you are mistaken.'

'Hm! That's a new word,' Bazarov said in a low voice. 'But you needn't get all hot under the collar. I really don't care. A romantic would say, "I feel our ways are beginning to part," but I simply say we've had enough of each other.'

'Yevgeny . . .'

'My friend, that's not a disaster. If that were all one has enough of in this world! But I wonder, shouldn't we say goodbye now? Since I've come here I feel really soiled, as if I'd been reading too much of Gogol's letters to the Kaluga governor's wife.[3] By the way I haven't yet told them to unharness the horses.'

'I'm sorry, you really can't!'

'Why not?'

'I'm no longer speaking of myself, but it would be extraordinarily rude to Anna Sergeyevna, who will certainly want to see you.'

'Well, there you're wrong.'

'On the contrary, I'm certain I'm right,' Arkady countered. 'And why are you pretending? If it comes to that, haven't you come here for her?'

'That's perhaps fairly said, but you're still wrong.'

But Arkady was right. Anna Sergeyevna did want to see Bazarov and sent a message by the butler for him to come to her. Bazarov changed his clothes before he went in to her: he turned out to have packed his new clothes since they were there to hand.

Anna Sergeyevna received him not in the room where he had so unexpectedly declared his love for her but in the drawing room. She amiably extended to him the tips of her fingers, but her face involuntarily showed strain.

'Anna Sergeyevna,' Bazarov said hurriedly, 'first I must give you some reassurance. Before you is a mortal who long ago came to his senses and hopes that others too have forgotten his folly. I am going away for a long time, and you must agree that, though I'm no soft creature, it would be depressing for me to take away with me the thought that you remember me with disgust.'

Anna Sergeyevna sighed deeply like someone who has just climbed a high mountain, and her face came to life with a smile. She gave her hand to Bazarov a second time and responded to his handshake.

'Let bygones be bygones,' she said, 'especially since, in all conscience, I too was to blame, if not by flirting then in another way. In a word – let's be friends as before. That was a dream, wasn't it? And who remembers dreams?'

'Who does remember them? Besides love . . . is just a feeling one assumes.'

'Really? I very much like hearing that.'

Those were Anna Sergeyevna's words, and those were Bazarov's; both thought they spoke the truth. Did their words hold the truth, the whole truth? They didn't know it themselves, much less does the author. But their conversation went as if they completely believed one another.

Anna Sergeyevna asked Bazarov among other things what he had done at the Kirsanovs'. He almost told her about his duel with Pavel Petrovich but he restrained himself as he thought she might suppose he was showing off and answered her that he had been working the whole time.

'At first,' said Anna Sergeyevna, 'I became depressed, God knows why. I even planned to go abroad, imagine that! . . . Then the mood passed. Your friend Arkady Nikolayevich came, and I again got into my routine, into my true role.'

'What role is that, if I may ask?'

'That of aunt, teacher, mother, whatever you want to call it. Oh, you must know that at first I didn't properly understand your close friendship with Arkady Nikolaich, I found him rather insignificant. But now I've got to know him better I'm sure he's intelligent . . . But, most importantly, he's young, young . . . not like you and me, Yevgeny Vasilyich.'

'Is he still so shy in your presence?' asked Bazarov.

'But surely he wasn't . . .' Anna Sergeyevna began and after a moment's thought went on, 'Now he has become more confident, he talks to me. Before he used to avoid me. But I didn't seek his company. He and Katya are great friends.'

Bazarov felt annoyed. 'Women can't help pretending!' he thought.

'You say he avoided you,' he stated with a cold smile, 'but I don't suppose it was any secret to you that he was in love with you.'

'What? He was too?' Anna Sergeyevna burst out.

'He was too,' Bazarov repeated, making a humble bow. 'Did you really not know that, and have I told you something that is news to you?'

Anna Sergeyevna lowered her eyes.

'You are wrong, Yevgeny Vasilyich.'

'I don't think so. But perhaps I shouldn't have mentioned that.' 'And don't go on pretending,' he added to himself.

'Why not mention it? But I suppose that here too you are attaching too much significance to a momentary impression. I am beginning to suspect that you're inclined to exaggeration.'

'We'd better not talk about that, Anna Sergeyevna.'

'Why not?' she retorted but she herself led the conversation on to another subject. She still felt awkward with Bazarov although she had both told him and also assured herself that all was forgotten. As she exchanged the simplest remarks or even joked with him, she felt a tremor of fear. In the same way people on a steamship at sea talk and laugh light-heartedly exactly as on dry land, but if there is the slightest halt, the slightest sign of something untoward, at once every face shows an expression of special alarm – evidence of their constant awareness of constant danger.

The conversation between Anna Sergeyevna and Bazarov continued for not much longer. She began to think her own thoughts, to answer distractedly and eventually proposed to him they went to the saloon, where they found the princess and Katya. 'But where's Arkady Nikolaich?' asked the hostess and, learning that he hadn't shown himself now for more than an hour, she sent for him. He wasn't found quickly: he had gone off to the bottom of the garden and was sitting there, cupping his chin on his folded hands and lost in his thoughts. Those thoughts were deep and important ones but they weren't sad. He knew that Anna Sergeyevna was sitting alone with Bazarov and he felt no jealousy as he used to. On the contrary his face was quietly radiant; he seemed to be wondering at something and to be happy and to be making some decision.

XXVI

The late Odintsov didn't like innovations but he tolerated 'a certain play of refined taste' and consequently had erected in his garden, between the hothouse and the pond, a building like a Greek portico constructed of Russian brick. In the blind rear wall of this portico or gallery were made six niches for statues which Odintsov intended to order from abroad. These statues were going to represent Solitude, Silence, Meditation, Melancholy, Modesty and Sensibility. One of them, the goddess of Silence, with her finger to her lips, had been brought and set up, but the very same day the farm boys had knocked off her nose, and, though a local plasterer had undertaken to make her a nose 'twice as good as the old one', nevertheless Odintsov had ordered her to be removed, and she found herself in a corner of the threshing barn, where she stood for many long years, exciting the superstitious terror of the peasant women. The front part of the portico was overgrown with thick shrubs: only the capitals of the columns could be seen above the dense foliage. Inside the portico itself it was cool even at midday. Anna Sergeyevna didn't like to visit this place ever since she had seen a grass snake there, but Katya often came to sit on a big stone bench which had been set up below one of the niches. Surrounded by freshness and shade, she used to read or work or surrender herself to that sensation of complete quiet which probably is familiar to everyone and the charm of which lies in the barely conscious, mute observation of the broad current of life, ceaselessly flowing around us and within ourselves.

The day after Bazarov's arrival Katya was sitting on her favourite bench, and next to her again sat Arkady. He had prevailed on her to go with him to the 'portico'.

There was still about an hour before luncheon; the heat of the day had already succeeded the dew of morning. Arkady's face had kept its expression of the previous day; Katya looked anxious. Immediately after tea her sister had called her into her study and, after a caress, which always scared Katya, had advised her to be more careful in her behaviour with Arkady and particularly to avoid conversations with him alone, which had apparently been remarked by their aunt and the whole household. Moreover, the previous evening Anna Sergeyevna had been in a bad mood, and Katya herself had felt awkward as if she were acknowledging guilt. Acceding to Arkady's request, she told herself it was for the last time.

'Katerina Sergeyevna,' he began with a kind of shy forwardness, 'ever since I had the happiness of living in the same house as you, I have talked to you about many things, but now there is one, for me very important . . . question, which I haven't yet touched on. Yesterday you remarked that I had been changed here,' he added, both catching and avoiding the questioning look which Katya turned on him. 'Indeed I have changed in many respects, and you know that better than anyone else – you, to whom in fact I owe that change.'

'I do? . . . To me? . . .' said Katya.

'I am no longer the arrogant boy who came here,' Arkady went on. 'After all, I am now twenty-three. I still want to be of service, I want to devote all my strength to the truth. But I won't be looking for my ideals where I once did. They now present themselves to me . . . somewhere much nearer by. Up till now I haven't understood myself, I've given myself tasks which are beyond me . . . My eyes have recently been opened thanks to a certain feeling . . . I'm not expressing myself very clearly but I hope you will understand me . . .'

Katya made no answer but stopped looking at Arkady.

'I suppose,' he began again in a more agitated voice, while above him a chaffinch sang its carefree song in the leaves of a birch tree. 'I suppose that it's the duty of every honest man to be completely open with those . . . with those . . . with those people who . . . in a word with people close to him, and therefore I . . . I intend . . .'

But here Arkady's oratory let him down, he became confused, stumbled in his words and had to be silent for a moment. Katya still didn't raise her eyes. She seemed not to understand where he was leading with all this, and to be waiting for something.

'I can tell I'll surprise you,' Arkady began plucking up his courage again, 'especially as this feeling relates in a way . . . in a way, I say – to you. Yesterday I remember you reproached me for lack of seriousness,' Arkady went on with the look of a man who has gone into a swamp and feels that with every step he is sinking deeper and deeper and still hurries on, in the hope of extricating himself sooner. 'This reproach is often directed at . . . falls . . . upon young men, even when they no longer deserve it. And if I had more self-confidence . . .' ('Well, help me, help me!' Arkady thought desperately, but Katya still didn't turn her head.) 'If I could hope . . .'

'If I could be sure of what you're saying' – at that moment they heard the clear voice of Anna Sergeyevna.

Arkady at once fell silent, and Katya went pale. A path ran past the shrubs which screened the portico. Anna Sergeyevna was walking down it, accompanied by Bazarov. Katya and Arkady couldn't see them, but they could hear every word, the rustle of her dress, their very breathing. Anna Sergeyevna and Bazarov took a few steps and stopped right in front of the portico, as if deliberately.

'You see,' Anna Sergeyevna went on, 'you and I have made a mistake. We're neither of us in our first youth, especially me. We have lived, we are tired. We are both – why pretend otherwise – intelligent people. At first we interested one another, curiosity was aroused . . . but then . . .'

'But then I lost my appeal,' Bazarov continued.

'You know that wasn't the reason for our disagreement. But whatever it was we didn't need one another, that's what was important. We had too much . . . how to say it . . . in common. We didn't understand that at once. On the contrary, Arkady . . .'

'Do you need him?' asked Bazarov.

'Stop it, Yevgeny Vasilyich. You say that he's not indifferent to me, and I myself have always felt he likes me. I know I could be his aunt, but I don't want to conceal from you that I've begun to think about him more often. This fresh, young feeling has some charm . . .'

'The word *fascination* is more generally used in such

circumstances,' Bazarov interrupted – one could hear the seeth-
ing bile in his calm but hollow tone. 'Arkady was being a bit
secretive with me yesterday evening and didn't talk either about
you or your sister . . . That's an important symptom.'

'He's just like a brother with Katya,' said Anna Sergeyevna,
'and I like that in him although perhaps I shouldn't allow such
intimacy between them.'

'Is that the . . . sister speaking in you?' Bazarov said, drawing
out the words.

'Of course . . . But why are we standing here? Aren't we having a strange conversation? And could I have expected that I'd
be talking to you like this? You know that I'm frightened of you
. . . and at the same time I trust you because you're really very
kind.'

'First, I'm not kind at all, and secondly, I've lost any importance for you, and you tell me I'm kind . . . It's exactly like laying a wreath of flowers at a dead man's head.'

'Yevgeny Vasilyich, we don't have the power . . .' Anna
Sergeyevna began, but the wind started up, rustled the leaves
and carried away her words.

'Now you are free,' Bazarov said after a short pause.

Nothing more could be heard, the footsteps moved on . . .
everything became quiet.

Arkady turned to Katya. She was sitting in the same position, only she had lowered her head further.

'Katerina Sergeyevna,' he said in a trembling voice, clenching his hands, 'I love you, for always, irrevocably, and I love
no one but you. I wanted to tell you that, to learn what you
thought and to ask for your hand, because I too am not rich
and I feel I am ready for every sacrifice . . . Why don't you
answer? Don't you believe me? Do you think I'm speaking
frivolously? But look back on these last days! Haven't you
realized long ago that everything else – understand that –
absolutely everything else has vanished without a trace? Look
at me, say one word to me . . . I love . . . I love you . . . believe
me!'

Katya gave Arkady a meaningful look, with radiant eyes,
and after a long pause for thought she said:

'Yes.'

Arkady jumped up from the bench.

'Yes! You said yes, Katerina Sergeyevna! What does that word mean? That I love you, that you believe me . . . Or . . . or . . . I daren't finish . . .'

'Yes,' Katya said again, and this time he understood her. He took her big, beautiful hands and, breathless from joy, he pressed them to his heart. He was barely able to stand and only repeated 'Katya, Katya . . .' while she started crying in an innocent way, quietly laughing herself at her tears. He who hasn't seen such tears in the eyes of a beloved hasn't yet experienced the full degree of happiness a man can have on this earth, overcome by gratitude and shame.

The following day, early in the morning, Anna Sergeyevna had Bazarov called to her study and with a forced laugh handed him a folded sheet of writing paper. It was a letter from Arkady: in it he asked for her sister's hand.

Bazarov quickly skimmed the letter and made an effort not to reveal the feeling of malice which suddenly surged in his breast.

'So that's it,' he said, 'and I think only yesterday you were supposing that his love for Katerina Sergeyevna was the love of a brother. What do you intend to do now?'

'What is *your* advice to me?' asked Anna Sergeyevna, continuing to laugh.

'Well, I think,' said Bazarov, also laughing, although he didn't feel at all cheerful and, like her, didn't feel like laughing at all, 'I think one should give the young people a blessing. It's a good match in every respect. Kirsanov is not badly off, he's his father's only son, and the father's a good fellow, he won't object.'

Anna Sergeyevna walked up and down the room. She went red, then pale in turn.

'Do you think so?' she said. 'All right. I don't see any obstacles . . . I am happy for Katya . . . and for Arkady Nikolaich. Of course I'll wait for his father's response. I'll send Arkady himself to him. And so it turns out I was right yesterday when I said to you we're both old people now . . . Why didn't I see this? That astonishes me!'

Anna Sergeyevna again started laughing and at once turned away.

'The young people of today have become seriously crafty,' said Bazarov and also laughed. 'Goodbye,' he said after a short silence. 'I hope you close this affair in the most agreeable way, and I will rejoice from afar.'

Anna Sergeyevna quickly turned to him.

'Are you really leaving? Why *now* don't you stay? Do stay . . . it's fun talking to you . . . like walking on the edge of a precipice. At first one's nervous but then courage takes over from somewhere. Do stay.'

'Thank you for the offer, Anna Sergeyevna, and for your flattering opinion of my conversational talents. But I find even now I've spent too long in a world alien to me. Flying fish can stay a while in the air but they soon have to flop down into the water. Let me splash back into my element.'

Anna Sergeyevna looked at Bazarov. A bitter smile played over his pale features. 'This man loved me!' she thought – and she felt sorry for him and held out her hand to him in sympathy.

But he understood her.

'No!' he said and took a step backwards. 'I'm a poor man but I've never yet taken charity. Goodbye and good luck.'

'I am sure that this isn't the last time we shall meet,' Anna Sergeyevna said, making an involuntary movement.

'Anything can happen!' Bazarov answered. He bowed and went out.

'So did you have the idea of building yourself a nest?' he said that same day to Arkady, as he squatted down to pack his trunk. 'Why not? It's a good thing. Only you shouldn't have pretended. I was expecting you to go in a completely different direction. Or maybe it surprised you yourself.'

'I certainly wasn't expecting this when I left you,' said Arkady. 'But you too shouldn't pretend and say "it's a good thing", as if I didn't know your view of marriage.'

'Oh, my good friend!' said Bazarov. 'What a way of speaking! You see what I am doing – there's some empty space left in my trunk, and I pack hay in there. So it is in our trunk of

life: whatever we pack it with, don't leave any empty space.
Please don't take offence. You probably don't remember what
was always my view of Katerina Sergeyevna. Some young
ladies have the reputation of being intelligent because they sigh
intelligently, but yours will stand up for herself, and in doing
so she'll take you in hand too – and that's how it should be.'
He slammed shut the lid of the trunk and got up from the floor.
'And now in saying goodbye I'm going to say it again . . .
because there's no point in deceiving ourselves: we're saying
goodbye for good, and you sense that yourself . . . you have
acted intelligently, you're not made for this hard, bitter, solitary life of ours. You don't have audacity or anger in you – you
have the courage and the fervour of youth, but they're not up
to our task. You aristocratic lot can't get beyond noble resignation or noble ardour – that's just nonsense. You don't fight,
for example – and you think yourselves fine fellows – but we
do want to fight. We will too! The dust we make will blind
you, our dirt will soil you – we've grown up and you haven't,
you're wrapped up in yourself without realizing it, you enjoy
criticizing yourself – but we find that boring. Give us some
others! We need others to bring down! You're a nice fellow,
but you're still a soft little gentleman's son – *e volatu*,[1] as my
good father says.'

'Are you saying goodbye to me for good, Yevgeny?' Arkady
said sadly. 'And have you no other words for me?'

Bazarov scratched the back of his head.

'Yes, Arkady, I do have other words, but I'm not going to say
them because that's romanticism – that means becoming all
sugary. Get married quickly, get your nest going, have lots of
children. They'll be clever just because they'll be born at the
right time, not like you and me. Aha! I see the horses are ready.
It's time. I've said goodbye to everybody . . . So . . . what now?
Give me a hug.'

Arkady threw his arms round his old teacher and friend, and
the tears gushed from his eyes.

'That's youth!' Bazarov said quietly. 'I rely on Katerina
Sergeyevna. You just see how quickly she'll calm you down!'

'Goodbye, my friend!' he said to Arkady as he got into the

carriage, and added, pointing to a pair of jackdaws sitting side by side on the stable roof: 'Look at them! Learn!'

'What does that mean?'

'What? Are you so bad at natural history or have you forgotten that the jackdaw is the most worthy family bird? A model for you! . . . Goodbye, signor!'

The carriage rolled away with a jingle of harness.

Bazarov spoke the truth. Talking to Katya that evening, Arkady completely forgot about his teacher. He was already beginning to submit to her, and Katya sensed that and was not surprised. The next day he was due to go to Marino to see Nikolay Petrovich. Anna Sergeyevna didn't want to constrain the young couple and only for form's sake didn't leave them too long alone. She kindly kept the princess away from them – the news of the coming marriage had sent her into a tearful rage. At first Anna Sergeyevna was afraid that the sight of their happiness might be somewhat depressing for her. But quite the opposite happened – it not only didn't depress her, it engaged her and eventually moved her. That made her both happy and sad. 'Bazarov was obviously right,' she thought, 'curiosity, just curiosity, and love of a quiet life, and egoism . . .'

'Children!' she said loudly. 'So, is love just a feeling one assumes?'

But neither Katya nor Arkady understood her. They felt shy of her; they couldn't get the conversation they had accidentally overheard out of their heads. However, Anna Sergeyevna soon set their minds at rest. And it wasn't difficult for her – her own was at rest too.

XXVII

The old Bazarovs rejoiced all the more at their son's sudden arrival because they hadn't expected it. Arina Vlasyevna got into such a state and scurried about the house so much that Vasily Ivanovich compared her to a 'little partridge': the cut tail of her short blouse indeed added something birdlike to her appearance. But he himself just mumbled and chewed the side of his pipe's amber mouthpiece and turned his head, gripping his neck between his fingers, as if he were testing whether it was properly screwed on. Then he suddenly opened his wide mouth and let out a soundless laugh.

'Old man, I've come to stay with you for a whole six weeks,' Bazarov said to him. 'I want to work, so please don't get in my way.'

'You'll forget what I look like, that's how much I'll be in your way,' answered Vasily Ivanovich.

He kept his promise. Having installed his son in his study as before, he virtually hid from him and kept his wife from making any excessive declarations of affection. 'Mother,' he said to her, 'on Yenyusha's first visit we got on his nerves a bit. Now we must be wiser.' Arina Vlasyevna agreed with her husband but she didn't gain much from this because she only saw her son at table and was completely scared of talking to him. 'Yenyushenka!' she would say – and he would hardly have time to turn round before she was fiddling with the strings of her bag and mumbling, 'Nothing, it's nothing, I was just . . .' Then she would turn to Vasily Ivanovich and say to him, resting her cheek on her hand, 'How can we find out, dear, what Yenyusha would like for dinner today, cabbage soup or borshch?' 'Why don't you ask him yourself?' 'But I'll get on his nerves!' However, it was Bazarov himself who stopped shutting himself away: the work fever had left him and was replaced by a dull boredom and a vague feeling of anxiety. A strange fatigue was apparent in all his movements; his way of walking had been firm, fast and assured, and now even that changed. He stopped going for solitary walks and looked for company. He drank tea in the drawing room, strolled round the vegetable garden with Vasily Ivanovich and smoked a silent pipe with him; once too he inquired after Father Aleksey. At first Vasily Ivanovich was happy at this change, but his happiness didn't last long. 'Yenyusha is breaking my heart,' he quietly complained to his wife. 'It wouldn't matter if he were dissatisfied or angry, but he's distressed, he's wretched, that's what's so terrible. He doesn't speak – if only he would shout at us both. He's getting thin, and the colour of his skin is so bad.' 'Lord, lord!' the old woman whispered. 'I'd like to put a holy amulet round his neck, only he wouldn't let me.' Vasily Ivanovich tried several times very cautiously to ask Bazarov about his work, about his health, about Arkady . . . But Bazarov gave him a brusque and reluctant answer, and once, noticing that his father was gradually leading the conversation up to something, said to him crossly, 'Why do you always tiptoe around me? That habit's worse than your old one.' 'There, there, I didn't mean anything!' poor Vasily Ivanovich hastily answered. His political hints were just as fruitless. He once started talking about progress in connection with the imminent liberation of the serfs and hoped to engage his son's sympathy. But Bazarov said, showing no interest, 'Yesterday I was walking by the fence, and the local peasant boys, instead of some old song, were bawling out, "The time of truth is coming when hearts can feel it's love . . ."[1] That's progress for you.'

Sometimes Bazarov would go out to the village and start up a conversation with a muzhik, sarcastic as usual. 'Well, mate,' he would say to him, 'give me your views on life. They tell us that in you lie Russia's strength and the future. A new age in history is beginning with you, and you'll be giving us a true language and our laws.' The muzhik would either not answer or utter something like the following: 'Well we can . . . because we also, that is . . .that's our boundary, like.' Bazarov interrupted him: 'Explain to me the world of your *mir*, your commune – and is it the same *mir* which rests on three fishes?'[2]

'It's the earth, sir, that rests on three fishes,' was the muzhik's soothing reply, given in a genial patriarchal singsong, 'but set up against our *mir* you know we've got the master's will – because you are our fathers. And the stricter the master's demands, the dearer they are to his muzhik.'

Once, after hearing a speech like that, Bazarov scornfully shrugged his shoulders, and the muzhik went on his way home.

'What was he going on about?' he was asked by another muzhik, middle-aged and sombre-visaged, who had witnessed his conversation with Bazarov in the distance from the door of his hut. 'Was it the rent we haven't paid?'

'What rent, my friend!' the first muzhik replied and his voice now had no trace of the patriarchal singsong. On the contrary it had in it something rough and grim. 'He was just blathering something or other, he was itching to talk. Of course, he's a master, what can he understand?'

'Nothing!' replied the other muzhik. They shook out their caps and straightened their belts, and both began discussing their own affairs and needs. Alas! The Bazarov who had scornfully shrugged his shoulders, who knew how to talk to the muzhiks (as he had boasted during his quarrel with Pavel Petrovich), that self-confident Bazarov didn't even suspect that in their eyes he remained some kind of buffoon . . .

However, he finally found himself an occupation. Vasily Ivanovich was binding up a muzhik's injured leg, but the old man's hands shook, and he couldn't cope with the bandages. His son helped him and from then on began to take a part in his practice, at the same time continuing to mock both the methods he himself counselled and his father, who immediately applied them. But Bazarov's mocking remarks didn't upset Vasily Ivanovich at all; they even reassured him. Holding together his greasy dressing-gown over his stomach with his fingers and smoking his pipe, he listened to Bazarov with delight, and the more edge there was in his sallies the more genially his delighted father laughed, showing every one of his black teeth. He even repeated his sallies, which were often crude and absurd, and, for example, for several days he kept on repeating 'that comes last at number nine' quite irrelevantly, just because his son had used that expression on learning he was going to morning service. 'Thank God! He's stopped being depressed!' he whispered to his wife. 'He really worked me over today. Wonderful!' Moreover the thought that he had such an assistant made him ecstatic and filled him with pride. 'Yes, yes, my dear,' he would say to some peasant woman in a man's coat and horned headdress as he gave her a bottle of Goulard water[3] or a pot of henbane ointment, 'you must thank God every minute that I have my son staying with me. You're being given the most scientific and up-to-date treatment, do you realize that? The Emperor of the French, Napoleon[4] himself, doesn't have a better doctor.' And the woman, who had come to complain she'd been taken by the 'cramps' (though she couldn't have explained the meaning of these words), only bowed and reached into her bodice, where she had four eggs wrapped in the corner of a towel.

Bazarov once pulled a tooth for a visiting cloth pedlar, and, although the tooth could be classed as ordinary, Vasily Ivanovich kept it as a rarity and, showing it to Father Aleksey, kept repeating:

'Look at those roots! Yevgeny's so strong! The pedlar jumped right into the air . . . I think that oak there would have come out! . . .'

'Most commendable!' Father Aleksey said finally, not knowing what to answer and how to get away from the old man's raptures.

One day a muzhik from the neighbouring village brought Vasily Ivanovich his brother, who had typhus. The poor man lay face down on a bundle of straw and was dying; dark blotches covered his body, and he had long lost consciousness. Vasily Ivanovich expressed his regret that no one had sought medical help earlier and stated that there was no hope. And in fact the muzhik didn't get his brother home: he died in the cart.

Three days later Bazarov came into his father's room and asked if he had any lunar caustic.[5]

'Yes, I do. Why do you need it?'

'I need . . . to cauterize a cut.'

'On whom?'

'On myself.'

'What do you mean, on yourself? Why? What is this cut? Where is it?'

'Here on my finger. Today I went over to the village, you know – the one they brought the muzhik with typhus from. For some reason they were going to do an autopsy, and it's a long time since I had any practice in that.'

'So then what?'

'So I asked the district doctor – and, well, I cut myself.'

Vasily Ivanovich went all pale and without a word rushed to his study. He came back at once with a piece of lunar caustic in his hand. Bazarov was going to take it and go out.

'For God's sake,' said Vasily Ivanovich, 'let me do this myself.'

Bazarov smiled ironically.

'You are a glutton for practice!'

'Please don't make jokes. Show me your finger. The cut isn't big. Is that painful?'

'Press harder, don't be frightened.'

Vasily Ivanovich stopped.

'What do you think, Yevgeny, wouldn't it be better to cauterize it with iron?'

'We should have done that before. But now, in real terms, even the lunar caustic is no use. If I've got infected, it's too late now.'

'How . . . too late?' – Vasily Ivanovich could hardly bring out the words.

'It surely is that. It's been a bit more than four hours since then.'

Vasily Ivanovich cauterized the cut a little more.

'Didn't the district doctor have any lunar caustic?'

'No, he didn't.'

'My God, how can that be! A doctor – and he doesn't have such an essential thing.'

'You should have seen his lancets,' said Bazarov and went out. Till that evening and in the course of the next day Vasily Ivanovich picked on every excuse to go into his son's room, and, though he not only didn't mention his cut but even made an effort to speak about wholly extraneous subjects, he nonetheless looked so fixedly into his eyes and observed him so nervously that Bazarov lost patience and threatened to leave. Vasily Ivanovich gave him his word not to worry, especially since Arina Vlasyevna, from whom of course he concealed everything, was beginning to nag him why he wasn't sleeping and what was the matter with him. He held out for two whole days although he very much didn't like his son's look – he watched him furtively all the time . . . but on the third day at dinner he couldn't contain himself any more. Bazarov was sitting with his head slumped and hadn't touched a single dish.

'Why aren't you eating, Yevgeny?' he asked, putting on an unconcerned expression. 'I think they've cooked the food nicely.'

'I'm not hungry, so I don't eat.'

'Don't you have any appetite? What about your head?' he added in a timid voice. 'Does it ache?'

'Yes, it does. Why shouldn't it ache?'

Arina Vlasyevna sat up and listened alertly.

'Don't get angry, Yevgeny, please,' Vasily Ivanovich went on. 'But won't you let me take your pulse?'

Bazarov raised himself a bit.

'Without taking it I can tell you I have a fever.'

'And have you been shivering?'

'Yes, I have. I'll go and lie down, and send me in some lime tea. I must have caught a chill.'

'So that's why I heard you coughing last night,' said Arina Vlasyevna.

'I caught a chill,' Bazarov repeated and went out.

Arina Vlasyevna busied herself with making the lime tea while Vasily Ivanovich went into the next room and silently tore his hair.

Bazarov didn't get up that day and spent the whole night in a heavy semi-conscious slumber. At one in the morning he opened his eyes with an effort, and in the light of the icon lamp he saw his father's pale face above him. He asked him to go. Vasily Ivanovich obeyed but very soon came back on tiptoe and kept his eyes on his son, half screened by the doors of a cupboard. Arina Vlasyevna too didn't go to bed; from time to time she opened the study door a crack and came to listen 'how Yenyusha is breathing' and to look at Vasily Ivanovich. She could only see his hunched and motionless back, but even that gave her some comfort. In the morning Bazarov tried to get up. His head turned and he had a nose-bleed and he went back to bed again. Vasily Ivanovich ministered to him, and Arina

Vlasyevna came into his room and asked him how he felt. 'Better,' he replied and turned to the wall. Vasily Ivanovich gestured to his wife to leave, with both hands. She bit her lip so as not to cry and went out.

It was as if everything in the house had gone dark. Everyone's face looked drawn, and a strange quiet reigned: they took away a noisy cock from the yard to the village, who for a long time just couldn't understand why they were doing this to him. Bazarov continued to lie with his head to the wall. Vasily Ivanovich tried to put various questions to him, but they tired Bazarov, and the old man sat still in his chair, just cracking his knuckles from time to time. He went into the garden for a few minutes and stood there like a statue, as if he'd been struck by some inexplicable shock (an expression of shock never left his face). Then he returned to his son and tried to avoid his wife's questions. Finally she grabbed his hand and asked him feverishly, almost threateningly, 'What's the matter with him?' He pulled his thoughts together and made himself give her a smile in reply, but to his own horror, instead of a smile somehow there came out a laugh. In the morning he had sent for the doctor. He thought he should warn his son of this so he didn't become angry.

Bazarov suddenly turned round on the couch, gave his father a fixed, blank stare and asked for a drink.

Vasily Ivanovich gave him some water and in doing so felt his forehead. He was on fire.

'Dad,' Bazarov began in a slow, hoarse voice, 'my case is no good. I'm infected, and in a few days' time you'll be burying me.'

Vasily Ivanovich stumbled as if someone had hit him on the legs.

'Yevgeny!' he stammered. 'Why are you saying that? . . . For God's sake! You've got a chill . . .'

'Stop it,' Bazarov interrupted him. 'A doctor can't talk like that. All the signs of infection are there, you know that.'

'Where are the signs . . . of infection, Yevgeny? . . . For goodness' sake!'

'And what's this?' said Bazarov, and, pulling up the sleeve of his shirt, he showed his father the ominous red patches that had come up.

Vasily Ivanovich shivered and went cold from terror.

'Let's assume,' he said eventually, 'let's assume then . . . if . . . even if . . . this sort of . . . infection . . .'

'Pyaemia,' his son said quietly.

'Yes . . . a kind of epidemic . . .'

'*Pyaemia*, blood-poisoning,' Bazarov repeated sternly and clearly. 'Or have you forgotten your lecture notes?'

'Well yes, yes, as you like . . . But we'll still get you better!'

'Not a hope! But that's not the point. I wasn't expecting to die so soon. To tell the truth, this piece of luck is most unpleasant. You and Mother must both take advantage of the strength of your religion: there's an opportunity to put it to the test.' He drank a bit more water. 'But I want to ask you something . . . while I'm still in control of my head. You know, tomorrow or the day after my brain will be handing in its resignation. Even now I'm not altogether sure if I'm expressing myself clearly. While I was lying there, I kept on thinking that red dogs were running round me while you were pointing me like a blackcock. It was as if I was drunk. Do you understand me all right?'

'Really, Yevgeny, you're talking quite properly.'

'So much the better. You told me you'd sent for the doctor . . . That was to keep yourself happy . . . now do the same for me. Send a special messenger . . .'

'To Arkady Nikolaich,' the old man interrupted.

'What Arkady Nikolaich?' said Bazarov hesitantly. 'Ah yes! The fledgling! No, don't bother him: he's now gone and joined the jackdaws. Don't look surprised, I'm not raving yet. Send a special messenger to Anna Sergeyevna Odintsova. There's a landowner near here of that name . . . Do you know of her?' (Vasily Ivanovich nodded.) 'Say Yevgeny Bazarov sends his respects and wants her to know he is dying. Will you do that?'

'I will . . . Only can it really be possible that you will die, you, Yevgeny . . . Think about it yourself! After this where can there be any justice?'

'That I don't know. Just send the messenger.'

'I'll send him this very minute and I'll write the letter myself.'

'No, why do that? Say he sends his respects, nothing more is needed. And now I'll go back to my dogs. Odd! I want to fix my thoughts on death, but nothing comes of it. I see some sort of blur . . . and that's all.'

He turned again heavily to the wall. Vasily Ivanovich went out of the study and, going to his wife's bedroom, slumped down on his knees before the icons.

'Pray, Arina, pray!' he cried. 'Our son is dying.'

The doctor, the same district doctor who didn't have any lunar caustic, came and, after examining the patient, counselled a policy of waiting it out. At this point he said a few words on the possibility of recovery.

'And have you had occasion,' Bazarov asked, 'to see people in my position who have *not* been despatched to the Elysian Fields?'[6] He suddenly gripped the leg of a heavy table standing by the couch and moved it from its place.

'Strength, strength!' he said. 'It's all there still, but I have to die! That old peasant at least had time to lose the desire for life, but I . . . Yes, you go and try to say no to death. Death says no to you, and that's it! Who's crying there?' he said after a pause. 'Mother? Poor thing! Who will she feed now with her amazing borshch? Vasily Ivanovich, I think you're snivelling too. Well, if Christianity doesn't help, be a philosopher, a Stoic[7] or something. Didn't you boast you were a philosopher?'

'I'm no philosopher!' cried Vasily Ivanovich, and the tears dripped down his cheeks.

With every hour Bazarov became worse. The disease took a rapid course, as is often the case with surgical infections. He hadn't yet lost his memory and understood what was said to him; he was still fighting. 'I don't want to become delirious,' he whispered clenching his fists, 'that's so absurd!' And then he said, 'So take ten from eight, what's left?' Vasily Ivanovich went about like a madman, proposing one treatment after another, but did nothing but cover up his son's legs. 'Wrap him in cold sheets . . . an emetic . . . mustard plasters on the stomach . . .

blood-letting,' he kept saying with an effort. The doctor, whom he had begged to stay, said yes to his proposals and made the patient drink lemonade; for himself he asked for a nice little pipe, then for something 'warming and restorative', namely vodka. Arina Vlasyevna sat on a small, low bench by the door and only from time to time went away to pray; some days before a toilet mirror had slipped from her hands and broken, and she always considered that a bad omen. Even Anfisushka couldn't say anything to her. Timofeich had set off for Odintsova's.

Bazarov had a bad night . . . He was tormented by a high fever. The morning brought some relief. He asked Arina Vlasyevna to comb his hair; he kissed her hand and drank a couple of mouthfuls of tea. Vasily Ivanovich's spirits were raised a bit.

'Thank God!' he kept repeating. 'The crisis has come . . . the crisis has passed.'

'Fancy that!' said Bazarov. 'All that in a word! He's found one, he says "crisis" and he's comforted. It's amazing how man still believes in words. For example, if you call him a fool and don't beat him, he'll be wretched. Call him a genius and don't give him any money – he'll be quite satisfied.'

This little speech of Bazarov's, reminiscent of his earlier 'sallies', stirred Vasily Ivanovich's emotions.

'Bravo! Brilliantly said, brilliant!' he exclaimed, pretending to clap his hands.

Bazarov smiled sadly.

'So what do you think?' he said. 'Has the crisis passed or come?'

'You're better, that's what I see and that's what makes me happy,' Vasily Ivanovich answered.

'Excellent. To be happy is never a bad thing. And that message to her, you remember, did you send it?'

'I did, of course.'

The change for the better didn't last long. The attacks of the illness began again. Vasily Ivanovich sat by Bazarov and seemed in special torment. Several times he tried to speak – and couldn't.

'Yevgeny!' he eventually uttered. 'My son, my darling, my beloved son!'

This unusual appeal had an effect on Bazarov . . . He turned his head a little and, with an obvious effort to break out of the unconsciousness that lay heavy on him, pronounced the words:

'What, Father?'

'Yevgeny,' Vasily Ivanovich continued and fell on his knees in front of Bazarov although his son didn't open his eyes and couldn't see him. 'Yevgeny, you are better now. God willing, you will recover. But take advantage of this moment, give comfort to your mother and to me and do your duty as a Christian![8] It's terrible for me to say this to you, it's terrible. But even more terrible . . . it's for eternity, Yevgeny . . . think, how terrible . . .'

The old man's voice broke, and now there passed over his son's face a strange look, although he continued to lie with his eyes closed.

'I don't refuse, if it can give you comfort,' he said finally. 'But I don't think there's any need yet for hurry. You yourself say I'm better.'

'Yes, you are better, Yevgeny, you are. But who knows, it's all in God's will, and, having done your duty . . .'

'No, I'll wait,' Bazarov interrupted him. 'I agree with you that the crisis has come. But even if you and I are wrong, it doesn't matter – they can give communion to the unconscious.'

'Please, Yevgeny . . .'

'I'll wait. And now I want to sleep. Don't bother me.'

And he laid his head where it had been before.

The old man got up, sat in his chair and, putting his chin in his hands, began to chew his fingers . . .

He suddenly heard the rumble of a sprung carriage, the rumble which sounds so very clear in the depths of the countryside. The wheels rolled nearer and nearer, and now he could hear the horses snorting . . . Vasily Ivanovich jumped up and rushed to the window. A two-seated carriage harnessed to four horses was entering the yard of his little house. Without considering what this might mean, overcome by a surge of

mindless joy, he ran out on to the porch . . . A liveried footman opened the doors of the carriage. A lady in a black veil
and cloak got out.

'I am Odintsova,' she said. 'Is Yevgeny Vasilyich still alive?
Are you his father? I've brought a doctor with me.'

'Our benefactor!' cried Vasily Ivanovich and, seizing her
hand, pressed it convulsively to his lips. Meanwhile the doctor
Anna Sergeyevna had brought, a small man with spectacles and
a German cast of face, unhurriedly got out of the carriage. 'He's
still alive, my Yevgeny's still alive and now he'll be saved! Wife!
Wife! An angel from heaven has come to us . . .'

'Lord above, what is it?' the old woman stammered, running
out of the drawing room and, without understanding anything,
there in the hall she fell at Anna Sergeyevna's feet and began to
kiss her dress like a madwoman.

'Don't! Don't!' Anna Sergeyevna repeated, but Arina
Vlasyevna didn't listen to her while Vasily Ivanovich just went
on saying, 'An angel! An angel!'

'*Wo ist der Kranke?*[9] Und ver is the patsient?' the doctor said
finally, not without some signs of annoyance.

Vasily Ivanovich collected himself.

'In here, in here, please follow me, *wertester Herr College*,'[10]
he added, from distant memory.

'Ach!' said the German with a sour smile.

Vasily Ivanovich took him into the study.

'It's the doctor from Anna Sergeyevna Odintsova,' he said,
bending right down to his son's ear, 'and she herself is here.'

Bazarov suddenly opened his eyes.

'What did you say?'

'I am saying that Anna Sergeyevna Odintsova is here and has
brought this gentleman to see you, who is a doctor.'

Bazarov looked around him.

'She's here . . . I want to see her.'

'You will, Yevgeny. But first the doctor and I must have a
chat. Since Sidor Sidorych has gone' (that was the name of the
district doctor) 'I'll tell him the whole history of your illness,
and we'll have a little consultation!'

Bazarov looked at the German.

'Well be quick about your chat, and don't do it in Latin. I do understand the meaning of *iam moritur*.'[11]

'*Der Herr scheint des Deutschen mächtig zu sein*,'[12] the new alumnus of Aesculapius[13] began, turning to Vasily Ivanovich.

'*Ikh . . . gabe. . .*[14] We had better speak Russian,' the old man said.

'Aha! Zo zat is how it is . . . Be zo gut . . .'

And the consultation began.

Half an hour later Anna Sergeyevna came into the study accompanied by Vasily Ivanovich. The doctor had already managed to whisper to her that one shouldn't even think of the patient's recovery.

She looked at Bazarov . . . and stopped at the door, she was so shocked by his inflamed and the same time ghastly face and the lacklustre eyes staring at her. She simply felt chill, agonizing fear. Momentarily the thought flashed through her mind that she wouldn't have felt that if she had really loved him.

'Thank you,' he said with an effort. 'I didn't expect this. It's kind of you. Now we are meeting once more, as you promised.'

'Anna Sergeyevna was so kind,' Vasily Ivanovich began.

'Father, leave us. Anna Sergeyevna, you won't mind . . . I think that now . . .' He pointed to his wasted prostrate body.

Vasily Ivanovich went out.

'Thank you,' he said again. 'A tsar's kindness. They say tsars too visit the dying.'

'Yevgeny Vasilyich, I hope . . .'

'Oh, Anna Sergeyevna, let's speak the truth. I am finished. I've fallen under the wheels. And in the end there was no point in thinking about the future. Death is something ancient, but it comes fresh to each of us. Up till now I haven't been scared . . . but then will come unconsciousness and *phut*!' (He made a feeble gesture with his hand.) 'So what shall I say to you . . . I loved you! That didn't make any sense then, and now even less. Love is just a form, but my own form is already disintegrating. Let me say rather – how wonderful you are! And now you're standing here, so beautiful . . .'

Anna Sergeyevna shivered involuntarily.

'It doesn't matter, don't be alarmed . . . sit down there . . .
Don't come near me: my illness is infectious.'

Anna Sergeyevna quickly walked across the room and sat
down in a chair next to the couch on which Bazarov lay.

'You are so generous!' he whispered. 'Oh, so near and so
young, fresh, pure . . . in this foul room! . . . Well, goodbye!
Live a long life – that's best of all – and take advantage of it
while there's time. Look at this hideous sight: a worm that's
half crushed but still wriggling. And I also used to think I'll
achieve a great deal, I won't die, not me! I have a task ahead
and I'm a giant! And now the giant's whole task is how to die a
decent death, although no one else cares about that . . . No
matter: I'm not going to start wagging my tail.'

Bazarov fell silent and began to feel for his glass with his
hand. Anna Sergeyevna gave it to him so he could drink, without taking off her glove and breathing nervously.

'You will forget me,' he began again, 'a dead man is no friend
for the living. My father will say to you, what a man Russia is
losing . . . That's nonsense but don't disillusion the old man.
Anything to keep a child happy . . . you know. And be kind to
my mother. You won't find people like them in your big world
even with a torch by daylight . . . Russia needs me . . . No, she
clearly doesn't. And who is needed? A cobbler is needed, a
tailor is needed, a butcher . . . he sells meat . . . a butcher . . .
Wait, I'm getting confused . . . There's forest . . .'

Bazarov put his hand on his forehead.

Anna Sergeyevna leant over him.

'Yevgeny Vasilyich, I am here . . .'

He quickly removed his hand and raised himself.

'Goodbye,' he said in a sudden surge of energy, and his eyes
flashed one last time. 'Goodbye . . . Listen . . . I didn't kiss you
then . . . Blow on the dying lamp and let it go out . . .'

Anna Sergeyevna put her lips to his forehead.

'That's enough!' he said and fell back on the pillow. 'Now
. . . the dark . . .'

Anna Sergeyevna quietly went out.

'What happened?' Vasily Ivanovich whispered to her.

'He's gone to sleep,' she answered barely audibly.

Bazarov was never to wake again. Towards evening he went into complete unconsciousness and died the next day. Father Aleksey performed the last rites over him. When he was given extreme unction, when the holy chrism touched his breast one of his eyes opened and it seemed as if for a moment, at the sight of the priest in his robes and the smoking censer and the candles before the icons, something like a look of horror passed over his deathly pale features. When he had finally given his last sigh, and the whole household raised its lament, Vasily Ivanovich was seized by sudden fury. 'I said I would cry out in defiance,' he shouted hoarsely, his face twisted and aflame, shaking his fist in the air as if threatening someone, 'and I will cry out, I will cry out!' But Arina Vlasyevna in tears put her arms round his neck and they both fell prostrate to the ground. 'So side by side,' Anfisushka recounted later in the servants' room, 'they laid down their heads like lambs at noon . . .'

But the heat of noon passes, and evening and nightfall, and there comes the return to the quiet refuge where there is sweet sleep for the tormented and the weary . . .

XXVIII

Six months passed. Midwinter had come – cloudless frosts, harsh and still, thick, crunchy snow, pink hoar-frost on the trees, a pale emerald sky, caps of smoke on the chimneys, puffs of steam coming out of doors opened for a moment, people's fresh faces looking as if they'd been nipped and the measured trot of horses, chilled to the bone. The January day was already drawing to a close. The cold of evening held the windless air in a tighter grip, and a blood-red sunset faded quickly. Lights were being lit in the windows of the Marino house, and Prokofyich, in black tail coat and white gloves, was laying seven covers on the table with special ceremony. A week before, two weddings had taken place in the little parish church, quietly and with almost no witnesses – those of Katya and Arkady, and of

Nikolay Petrovich and Fenechka. Today Nikolay Petrovich was giving a farewell dinner for his brother, who was leaving for Moscow on business. Anna Sergeyevna had gone there immediately after the wedding, having generously provided for the young couple.

They all came to the table at exactly three o'clock. A place had also been laid there for Mitya, who had already acquired a nursemaid in a brocade *kokoshnik*.[1] Pavel Petrovich took his seat between Katya and Fenechka. The 'bridegrooms' were placed on either side of their wives. Our friends have changed recently: they have all gained in looks and in maturity. Only Pavel Petrovich has become thinner; that incidentally has given his expressive features even more of the elegant look of a *grand seigneur*[2] . . . Fenechka too has changed. In a new silk dress, with a broad velvet snood over her hair and a gold chain round her neck, she sits calmly, with a sense of respect towards herself and towards all around her, and with a smile on her lips as if she would say, 'I'm sorry, it's not my doing.' And she wasn't the only one smiling – the others also all smiled apologetically. Everyone felt a little awkward, a little sad but, if truth be told, in a very good mood. Everyone looked after their neighbours with comic attentiveness as if they had all agreed to play out some artless comedy. Katya said less than anyone. She looked trustingly around her, and it was obvious that she had already completely won the heart of Nikolay Petrovich. Before the end of the meal he rose and, taking a glass in his hand, turned to Pavel Petrovich.

'You are leaving us . . . you are leaving us, dear Brother,' he began, 'however, not for long; but still I can't tell you what I . . . what we . . . how much I . . . how much we . . . The problem is, we don't know how to make speeches! Arkady, you speak.'

'No, Papa, I haven't prepared anything.'

'And you think I'm well prepared! Brother, let me simply embrace you and give you our best wishes – and come back to us very soon!'

Pavel Petrovich exchanged kisses with everyone, naturally including Mitya. He also kissed Fenechka's hand – which she didn't yet know how to offer properly – and, drinking from his refilled glass, with a deep sigh he uttered the words, 'Be happy, my friends! *Farewell!*'[3] This little English flourish went unnoticed; but all were touched.

'To Bazarov's memory,' Katya whispered in her husband's ear and clinked glasses with him. In response Arkady pressed her hand hard but he wasn't brave enough to propose that toast.

This surely would seem to be the end. But perhaps some of our readers would like to know what each of the characters I have portrayed is doing now, at this moment.[4] I am ready to satisfy their curiosity.

Anna Sergeyevna has recently married, out of principle rather than love, one of our future Russian statesmen, a very clever man, a legal brain, with a powerful practical sense, a firm will and a remarkable gift for words – a man still young, amiable and cold as ice. They live together very harmoniously and one day perhaps they will find happiness together. . . perhaps even love. Princess Kh–aya is dead, forgotten the day she died. The Kirsanovs, father and son, have settled in Marino. Their business is beginning to improve. Arkady has become a keen landlord and the 'farm' is already bringing in a significant income. Nikolay Petrovich has been made an arbitrator[5] and is working extremely hard. He never stops travelling round his district and makes long speeches (his view is that we must get the muzhiks to 'hear the voice of reason', namely, reduce them to a state of exhaustion by the frequent repetition of the same words). And yet, to tell the truth, he isn't altogether to the taste either of the educated gentry, with their fashionable or glum talk of *mancipation* (pronounced with a nasal French *an*), or their uneducated fellows who roundly swear at *thut muncipation*. Both sides find him too soft. Yekaterina Sergeyevna has had a son, Kolya, and Mitya is now a splendid little boy running about and chattering away. Fenechka – now Fedosya Nikolayevna – adores her 'daughter-in-law' only less than her husband and Mitya, and when Katya sits down at the piano, she will happily stay with her all day. A word now about Pyotr. He has become quite rigid with stupidity and self-importance and is so refined he pronounces all his *e*'s as *u*'s,[6] but he too has married and got a sizeable dowry with his bride, the daughter of the town market gardener, who had turned down two decent suitors just because they didn't have watches: whereas Pyotr didn't just have a watch, he had patent leather boots.

On the Brühl Terrace[7] in Dresden, between two and four o'clock, at the most fashionable time for the promenade, you can meet a man of about fifty, now gone completely grey and limping as if he has gout, but still handsome, elegantly dressed and with that special mark given to a man only by a long sojourn in the highest society. It is Pavel Petrovich. From Moscow he went abroad for his health and took up residence in Dresden, where he associates mainly with the English and with visiting Russians. With the English he behaves simply, almost modestly, but not without dignity. They find him a little dull but admire him as 'a perfect gentleman'.[8] With Russians he is more open, he gives vent to his bile and mocks himself and them but he does it all very endearingly, with easy good manners. He holds Slavophile[9] opinions: that is well known to be thought *très distingué*[10] in the highest circles. He reads nothing Russian but has on his writing table a silver ashtray in the shape of a muzhik's bast shoe.[11] Our Russian tourists pay great court to him. Matvey Ilyich Kolyazin, finding himself 'temporarily in opposition',[12] has paid him a state visit on his way to take the waters in Bohemia.[13] And the local inhabitants, of whom incidentally Pavel Petrovich doesn't see much, almost worship him. No one can get a ticket for the Court choir, for the theatre and so forth as easily and speedily as *der Herr Baron von Kirsanoff*. He still does some good, to the extent he is able to; he still causes a bit of a sensation in society – he really had been a lion once; but life is hard for him . . . harder than he himself suspects . . . One only needs to look at him in the Russian church leaning against a wall to one side. For a long time he stands motionless, lost in thought, and bites his lips with a bitter expression, then he suddenly remembers where he is and almost imperceptibly begins to cross himself . . .

Kukshina too has gone abroad. She is now in Heidelberg, no

longer studying the natural sciences but architecture, a subject in which she claims to have discovered new laws. She still makes friends with students, especially with young Russian physicists and chemists. Heidelberg is full of them. They first amaze the naive German professors with their sober view of life, and go on to amaze those same professors with their total inertia and absolute sloth. Sitnikov is in St Petersburg. There he goes around with two or three chemists of that sort, unable to distinguish oxygen from nitrogen but full of rebellion and self-esteem. He also keeps company with the great Yelisevich[14] – since he himself aspires to greatness. In all this he professes to be continuing Bazarov's 'work'. There's a rumour he was recently beaten up, but he's got his own back – with an obscure little piece printed in an obscure little journal: in it he hints that his assailant is a coward. He calls that irony. His father is still ordering him about, and his wife thinks him an idiot . . . and a man of letters.

There is a small village graveyard in a remote corner of Russia. Like almost all of our graveyards it has a sad look. The ditches round it are long overgrown. The grey wooden crosses are leaning and rotting under their gables, which once had a coat of paint. The stone slabs have all shifted as if being pushed up from beneath. Two or three wretched trees barely give meagre shade. Sheep wander freely over the graves . . . But among them is one grave untouched by man, untrodden by beast: only birds rest there and sing at daybreak. It is surrounded by iron railings and two young fir trees are planted at either end. Yevgeny Bazarov is buried in that grave. Two old people often come to it from a little village near by – a husband and wife, now infirm. Supporting each other and with heavy steps, they go up to the railings, fall down on their knees and weep long and bitterly, and long and fixedly they look at the mute stone, under which their son lies. They exchange a few words, they wipe the dust from the stone and adjust a fir branch, and they say another prayer, unable to leave this place, where they feel nearer to their son and their memories of him . . . Are their prayers and tears really in vain? Has love, holy, devoted love, really lost its power over all? No, no! The grave may hold

a passionate, sinful, rebellious heart, but the flowers growing
on it gaze serenely at us with their innocent eyes. They do not
only speak to us of everlasting peace, of that great peace of
'indifferent' nature. They also speak of eternal reconciliation
and of life without end[15] . . .

Notes

Dedication

1. *BELINSKY*: V. G. Belinsky (1811–48), the leading Russian literary critic of the first half of the nineteenth century. His radical, Westernizing views were extremely influential and remained so after his death. He had given a very positive review to Turgenev's first book, *Sketches from a Hunter's Album*, and had become a close personal friend. The text was also originally preceded by an epigraph, which Turgenev subsequently dropped:

   '*Young man to middle-aged man*: You had substance but no strength.
   Middle-aged man: And you have strength without substance.
   (*From a modern conversation.*)'

Chapter I

1. *20 May 1859*: Among other things Turgenev's novel is placed very exactly in recent time, almost two years before the momentous Emancipation of the Serfs in February 1861.
2. *souls*: Estates before Emancipation in 1861 were traditionally measured in the numbers of 'souls' of (male) serfs owned.
3. *War of 1812*: 'The Patriotic War' against Napoleon after his invasion of Russia.
4. *Agathe*: Young girls of good family would speak as much (often bad) French as Russian and would be known by French versions of their name.
5. *dacha*: Suburban villa, usually of wood and for summer use.
6. *1848*: That year saw revolution in many European countries, including the German states, the Austrian Empire and France.
7. *tarantas . . . trio of carriage horses*: A four-wheeled Russian carriage

without springs. This *tarantas* uses a traditional arrangement of carriage or sleigh horses harnessed as a *troika* or trio.

Chapter II

1. *Vasilyev*: The usual Russian combination of Christian name and father's or patronymic, the latter often abbreviated as here from Vasilyevich to the more plebeian Vasilyev.
2. *shaft-horse*: The control horse of the *troika*, harnessed between the shafts.

Chapter III

1. *quit-rent*: Under the quit-rent system peasants farmed a land-owner's land in return for an annual rent in money or kind.
2. *bailiff*: A bailiff or steward, often a liberated serf, would run an estate for a landowner.
3. *house serfs*: Serfs attached to household duties as opposed to out-door or agricultural ones.
4. *Il est libre, en effet*: He is indeed free (French).
5. *townsman*: Or *meshchanin*, one of the historic and legally defined 'classes' in Russian society at the level below merchants.
6. *roubles*: 250 roubles, presumably the more valuable silver rather than paper currency, would be approximately £750 or US $1,500 in modern terms. But it is probably more useful to give a few examples of contemporary value. The poll tax a peasant paid in 1861 was one silver rouble p.a.; the *obrok* or quit-rent paid by peasants to landowners (outside the wealthier black-earth areas) was 10.5 silver roubles per male p.a. And a 'bucket' (*vedro*, a measure of something like 2½ gallons) of vodka was supposed by law to cost three roubles.
7. *Catherine the Great*: The Empress Catherine II reigned 1762–96.
8. *Pushkin . . . Eugene Onegin*: A. S. Pushkin's famous novel in verse (1825–31). The quotation is from the second stanza of chapter VII.

Chapter IV

1. *new silver*: This is meaningful if one knows that Russian silver, though polished, is traditionally not cleaned of its dark oxidiza-tion.
2. *shake hands*: In English, thus, in the original.
3. *s'est dégourdi*: Has lost his rough edges (French).

4. *Gambs*: For two generations the Alsatian Gambs (more properly Hambs) firm had been the most fashionable cabinet-makers in St Petersburg, supplying furniture to among others the imperial family and Pushkin.

5. *Galignani*: *Galignani's Messenger*, a liberal English-language daily newspaper published in Paris.

Chapter V

1. *settled boundaries*: Part of the preliminary reorganization of land leading up to Emancipation.

2. *Vous avez changé tout cela*: You have changed all that (French).

3. *God . . . rank*: A slightly misquoted line from *Woe from Wit*, A. S. Griboyedov's comedy of 1824 (Act II, Scene 5).

4. *Hegelists*: The idealism of the German philosopher Friedrich Hegel (1770–1831) was very popular with the Russian intelligentsia of the 1830s and 1840s, Turgenev's own generation.

5. *Aesop*: Sixth-century BC Greek author of fables, here meaning 'a character'.

Chapter VI

1. *Liebig*: Justus Liebig (1803–73), German chemist.

Chapter VII

1. *Corps des Pages*: Founded in 1697 and housed in the Vorontsov Palace in St Petersburg, the Corps of Pages was socially the most exclusive of Russian military schools. Its cadets acted as pages at court ceremonies.

2. *Baden*: Baden-Baden, the famous spa in the German Black Forest, frequented by many fashionable Russians including Turgenev himself, who settled there for a while.

3. *Marino . . . in honour of his wife*: I.e. Marino after Mariya.

4. *Wellington . . . Louis-Philippe*: The Duke of Wellington (1769–1852), victor over Napoleon at the Battle of Waterloo and British Tory politician; Louis-Philippe (1773–1850), King of the French (1830–48).

5. *their estate isn't divided*: Normally, after a death an estate or inheritance would be divided up among the heirs.

6. *Galignani*: See chapter IV, note 5.

Chapter VIII

1. *Mais je puis te donner de l'argent*: But I can give you money (French).
2. *polite form of address*: I.e. she called them 'you' rather than 'thou'.
3. *St Nicholas the Thaumaturge*: Or 'Wonderworker', fourth-century Bishop of Myra, a major saint of the Orthodox Church and also the original Santa Claus.
4. *Yermolov*: A. P. Yermolov (1772–1861), a famous Russian general, who fought against the French in 1812 and in the wars in the Caucasus.
5. *Streltsy*: Historical novel set in the reign of Peter the Great (1832) by the popular novelist K. P. Masalsky.
6. *fireplace*: The point being that a fireplace was a Western import, Russian houses traditionally having stoves.

Chapter IX

1. *bad luck*: I.e. by praising them, as he's done to the baby.
2. *Bene*: Good (Italian).
3. *Schubert's Erwartung*: 'Expectation', a song of 1815, D 159, by the Austrian composer Franz Schubert (1797–1828).
4. *pater familias*: Father or head of a family (Latin).

Chapter X

1. *Stoff und Kraft*: *Kraft und Stoff* (*Force and Matter*), a controversial materialist book by the German physician Ludwig Büchner (1824–99) was published in 1855 and translated into Russian in 1860.
2. *'The Gypsies'*: A long dramatic poem of 1825.
3. *inspection of the province*: Senior civil servants carried out regular inspections of the local administration (the theme of Gogol's famous play *The Government Inspector* of 1836).
4. *Privy Councillor*: No. 3 in the (civilian) Table of Ranks.
5. *general aide-de-camp*: A military rank attached to the Tsar's person.
6. *bien public*: Public good (French).
7. *liberation*: I.e. the coming Emancipation of the Serfs.
8. *un barbouilleur*: Scribbler (French).
9. *Moscow . . . was burnt down by a penny candle*: Referring to the fire that destroyed much of Moscow during Napoleon's invasion of 1812.

10. *Raphael*: Raffaello Sanzio (1483–1520), one of the most celebrated artists of the Italian Renaissance, famous for the perfection of his paintings.

11. *A Maiden at the Fountain*: An actual ultra-realistic painting of 1859 by Novikovich.

12. *peasant commune*: Or *mir*, the primitive Russian peasant commune, organized on the basis of collective responsibilities, thought by some to contain the essence of agrarian socialism.

13. *vieilli*: Antiquated (French).

14. *bon soir*: Good evening (French).

Chapter XI

1. *Pardon, monsieur*: Sorry, sir (French).

Chapter XII

1. *marshal of nobility*: Elected every three years by the *dvoryanstvo* or nobility of a province to represent their interests.

2. *l'énergie . . . d'état*: Energy is the first quality of a statesman (French).

3. *Guizot*: François Guizot (1787–1874), conservative French politician and historian.

4. *Alexander I*: Nicholas I's initially liberal but in the end reactionary elder brother who ruled Russia as Tsar 1801–25.

5. *Madame Svechina*: Sofiya Petrovna Svechina (1782–1859), mystical writer and fashionable salonnière.

6. *Condillac*: Étienne Bonnot de Condillac (1715–80), French philosopher of the Enlightenment.

7. *is quite a favourite*: In English in the original text.

8. *il a fait son temps*: It has had its day (French).

9. *Bourdaloue*: Louis Bourdaloue (1632–1704), influential French divine and preacher.

10. *Slavophile's*: The Slavophile movement, in politics, literature, art and philosophy, was opposed to Westernization and Western ideas and stressed Russian tradition and national peculiarity. Slavophiles would indicate their persuasion in their dress and home as well.

11. *with the corners turned down*: As etiquette decreed, indicating the visiting card had been left personally.

12. *émancipée*: Emancipated (French).

13. *state liquor business*: The government monopoly in the sale of spirits was leased out to individuals – a famously corrupt business.

Chapter XIII

1. *Entrez*: Enter (French).
2. *Moskovskiye vedomosti*: *The Moscow Gazette*, a semi-official journal published from 1756 to 1917. Kislyakov is a fictitious name.
3. *George Sand*: Pen name of Aurore Dupin (1804–76), free-living feminist and prolific novelist. Her work had been very popular with intellectual Russia in the 1840s.
4. *Emerson*: Ralph Waldo Emerson (1803–82), American philosopher.
5. *Yelisevich*: A fictitious name for a radical journalist.
6. *Pathfinder*: *The Pathfinder* is one of a series of novels known as the 'Leatherstocking Tales' by James Fenimore Cooper (1789–1851) recounting the adventures of Natty 'Hawkeye' Bumppo (who is the 'pathfinder').
7. *Bunsen*: Robert Bunsen (1811–99), German chemist and Professor of Chemistry at Heidelberg 1852–89.
8. *mon amie*: My friend (French).
9. *Proudhon*: Pierre Joseph Proudhon (1809–65), French journalist, economist and social thinker, an opponent of the emancipation of women.
10. *Macaulay*: Thomas Babington Macaulay (1800–1859), British historian and liberal politician.
11. *Slavophile*: See chapter XII, note 10.
12. *Domostroy*: Sixteenth-century manual for the conducting of life; it was supposed to advocate wife-beating.
13. *Michelet's De l'Amour*: Jules Michelet (1798–1874), French journalist and historian. His *De l'Amour* was published in 1859.
14. *Et toc . . . tin-tin-tin*: Refrain from 'The drunkard and his wife' by the French song-writer Pierre-Jean de Béranger (1780–1857).
15. *Seymour Schiff's romance 'Drowsy Granada slumbers'*: Seymour Schiff, popular composer and pianist. The closing lines of the romance 'Night in Granada', for which he wrote the music, are misquoted.

Chapter XIV

1. *en vrai chevalier français*: Like a true French knight (French).
2. *Enchanté*: Enchanted (French).
3. *crinoline*: A stiffened petticoat or structure of metal hoops to support the voluminous skirts of the period. Not to wear one

would be the sign of an emancipated woman and could be viewed as 'shocking'.

4. *said 'si j'aurais'. . . certainly*: The mistakes are that he says 'if I would have' instead of 'if I had' and 'absolutely' instead of 'certainly'.

Chapter XV

1. *good Russian*: The point being that many aristocratic Russian women, educated by foreign governesses, spoke poor Russian.
2. *Optime*: Very good (Latin).

Chapter XVI

1. *Alexandrine*: The name given to the architectural style of a simplified neoclassicism associated with the reign of Alexander I (1801–25).
2. *Speransky*: Count Mikhail Speransky (1772–1839), statesman during the reigns of Alexander I and Nicholas I, sometimes known as the father of Russian liberalism.
3. *Saxon Switzerland*: A hilly and scenic area of Saxony in southwestern Germany on the Elbe, beloved of artists.
4. *sinful*: Because sugar used to be clarified with blood.
5. *préférence*: A whist-like card game.
6. *Fantasy in C-Minor*: The Fantasy in C-Minor, K. 475, of 1785 by Wolfgang Amadeus Mozart (1756–91).

Chapter XVII

1. *Toggenburg . . . Minnesingers . . . troubadours*: Toggenburg, the knightly hero of *Ritter Toggenburg* (1797), Schiller's ballad of chivalrous love; Minnesingers and troubadours were the German and Provençal medieval poets and minstrels of courtly love.
2. *Notions générales de Chimie*: This work, *General Principles of Chemistry,* by two professors of chemistry at the École Polytechnique, had been published in Paris in 1853.

Chapter XVIII

1. *Ganot's Traité élémentaire de physique expérimentale*: Adolphe Ganot's *Treatise of Experimental Physics* had been published in Paris in 1851, and a Russian translation appeared in 1862.

Chapter XIX

1. *crossed herself*: In thanks for the departure of the, to her, unwelcome guests.

Chapter XX

1. *homme fait*: A real man (French).
2. *Hufeland*: Christoph-Wilhelm Hufeland (1762–1836), German scientist known for his *The Art of Prolonging Human Life (Macrobiotics)*, published in 1796 – i.e. long out of date.
3. *summer now*: I.e. the bathhouse wasn't being used.
4. *Suum cuique*: To each his own (Latin).
5. *quit-rent*: See chapter III, note 1.
6. *Friend of Health*: *Drug zdraviya*, a medical periodical published in St Petersburg 1833–69.
7. *Schönlein and Rademacher*: J. L. Schönlein (1793–1864) and J. G. Rademacher (1772–1849), German medical scholars.
8. *Hoffman . . . humoral pathologist . . . Brown . . . "Vitalism"*: Friedrich Hoffman (1660–1742), German medical scholar; humoral pathology refers all disease to the state of the cardinal humours, the four chief fluids of the body; John Brown (1735–88), Scottish doctor and founder of the Brunonian system; Vitalism was a biological theory which proclaimed the presence in all organisms of a governing life-force.
9. *voilà tout*: That's all (French).
10. *Prince Wittgenstein and of Zhukovsky*: Prince Peter Wittgenstein (1768–1842), Russian field-marshal and commander in the 1812 war against Napoleon; V. A. Zhukovsky (1783–1852), poet and tutor of Alexander II as a boy.
11. *men of 14 December from the Army of the South*: An allusion to the Decembrist rising against Tsar Nicholas I of 14 December 1825 and the part played in it by the 'Southern Society', leading members of which served in the Army of the South.
12. *Paracelsus*: T. B. Paracelsus (1493–1541), famous Swiss doctor.
13. *In herbis, verbis et lapidibus*: With herbs, words and minerals (Latin).
14. *ad patres*: To his fathers (Latin).
15. *Napoleon III . . . Italian question*: The Italian independence movement, the Risorgimento, and the involvement in it of Napoleon III, Emperor of the French, were major European issues of the day.
16. *preserves*: The sweet course of an old-fashioned Russian dinner would consist of home-made fruit conserves and jams.

17. *Horace*: Quintus Horatius Flaccus (65–8 BC), Latin lyric poet.
18. *Morpheus*: The Roman god of dreams.
19. *holy idiots*: The mentally deficient were thought to be blessed by God and often lived off charity.
20. *Maundy Thursday salt*: Salt specially prepared on the Thursday before Easter was regarded as a universal panacea.
21. *Alexis, or The Cottage in the Wood*: A popular sentimental novel (1788) by the French writer F. G. Ducray-Dumesnil (1761–1819), which was very successful in its Russian translation.
22. *bows to the ground*: The traditional greeting of serf to master.

Chapter XXI

1. *Cincinnatus*: Lucius Quinctius Cincinnatus, Roman patrician, according to tradition called from the plough on his farm in 458 BC and appointed dictator against the Aequi enemy.
2. *Jean-Jacques Rousseau*: Swiss Enlightenment philosopher (1712–78), who among other things advocated the benefits of the simple life.
3. *en amateur*: As an amateur (French).
4. *homo novus*: A new man (Latin).
5. *kissed him on the shoulder*: A traditional salutation of respect from an inferior.
6. *amice*: My friend (Latin).
7. *Robert le Diable*: An opera of 1831 by the German composer Jakob Meyerbeer (1791–1864).
8. *Suvorov*: Prince Alexander Suvorov (1729–1800), great Russian commander against the Turks and against Napoleon – famous for his crossing of the Alps in 1799.
9. *Castor and Pollux*: Classical Greek twin demigods and heroes.
10. *Dioscuri*: 'Sons of Zeus', another name for Castor and Pollux as sons of the king of the gods.
11. *Vladimir*: The military order of St Vladimir, founded by Catherine II in 1792, which conferred hereditary nobility on the recipient.
12. *handshake*: The traditionally devout would kiss a priest's hand while he would bless them.
13. *silver*: Silver money was worth more than paper banknotes.

Chapter XXII

1. *poor Nikolay Petrovich was having a hard time*: Nikolay Petrovich's problems with running his estate echo Turgenev's own difficulties with his peasants at Spasskoye.

2. *desyatina*: An old unit of land measurement equivalent to 2.7 acres.

3. *Council of Trustees*: Founded by Catherine II to safeguard the interests of orphans. In the course of time it became responsible among other things for the provision of credit and mortgage facilities.

4. *Du calme, du calme*: Calm, calm (French).

5. *Sunday schools*: Schools for adult literacy were developed from 1859 onwards.

Chapter XXIII

1. *Baltic barons*: The noble landowners of the Baltic provinces, mostly of German origin.

Chapter XXIV

1. *comme il faut*: Gentlemanly style (French).

2. *À bon entendeur salut*: He that hath ears, let him hear (French).

3. *utile dulci*: The useful with the pleasant (Latin).

4. *vertige*: Giddiness (French).

5. *Mrs Radcliffe*: Ann Radcliffe (1764–1823), successful English writer of 'Gothic' novels, the most famous being *The Mysteries of Udolpho* (1794).

6. *Sir Robert Peel*: (1788–1850), British Conservative politician and prime minister.

7. *Couchez-vous*: Go to bed (French).

8. *Pasha*: Affectionate diminutive of Pavel.

9. *C'est de la même famille*: It's the same type (French).

10. *belle-sœur*: Sister-in-law (French).

11. *au dix-neuvième siècle*: In the nineteenth century (French).

12. *Quelle idée*: What an idea (French).

Chapter XXV

1. *Heine*: Heinrich Heine (1797–1856), German Romantic lyric poet, many of whose poems were set to music.

2. *kvass*: A lightly fermented home-made drink made with rye flour.

3. *Kaluga governor's wife*: The reference here is to the writer Nikolay Gogol's letter to A. O. Rosset-Smirnova of 6 June 1846 originally excised by the censor from his selected correspondence. First published in 1860 under the title 'What is a governor's wife?', it was criticized by liberals as reactionary and sententious.

Chapter XXVI

1. *e volatu*: A mangled version of the French *et voilà tout*, 'and that's all'.

Chapter XXVII

1. *The time . . . love*: I.e. a trashy romance.
2. *mir which rests on three fishes*: There is a play on words here between *mir*, commune, and *mir*, world or earth. Also in early Russian mythology the earth rested on three fishes.
3. *Goulard water*: A lead-acetate-based lotion named after the French physician Thomas Goulard (1720–90)
4. *Napoleon*: He means Napoleon III, then on the French throne (1852–70).
5. *lunar caustic*: *Lapis infernalis*, 'the stone of hell' – silver nitrate, used by doctors to cauterize wounds.
6. *Elysian Fields*: In Greek mythology the paradise of the blessed.
7. *Stoic*: A follower of the Stoa, a Greek philosophical school characterized by the austerity of its ethics
8. *duty as a Christian*: I.e. receive the last rites of the Church.
9. *Wo ist der Kranke*: Where is the sick man (German)?
10. *wertester Herr College*: Respected colleague – in the Russian a bit garbled from the German.
11. *iam moritur*: Now he's dying (Latin). Latin had been the international language of medicine.
12. *Der Herr scheint des Deutschen mächtig zu sein*: The gentleman clearly understands German (German).
13. *Aesculapius*: The Greek god of medicine.
14. *Ikh . . . gabe*: *Ich habe*, I have (German), garbled.

Chapter XXVIII

1. *kokoshnik*: The traditional Russian headdress, which now survived chiefly at court and as part of a nursemaid's costume.
2. *grand seigneur*: Great nobleman (French).
3. *Farewell*: In English in the original.
4. *at this moment*: I.e. after Emancipation in February 1861.
5. *arbitrator*: A newly created official who after Emancipation regulated relations between landowners and former serfs.
6. *e's as u's*: The examples of Pyotr's 'refinement' given by Turgenev are *tyupyur'* and *obyuspyuchyun*, for *teper'* (now) and *obespechen* (guaranteed).

7. *Brühl Terrace*: The terrace on the River Elbe, named after Count
    Brühl, minister of Augustus the Strong of Saxony.
8. *a perfect gentleman*: In English in the original.
9. *Slavophile*: See chapter XII, note 10.
10. *très distingué*: Very distinguished (French).
11. *bast shoe*: Traditional peasant shoe made of bast, strips of the
    inner bark of lime trees; leather would either have been unavail-
    able or too expensive.
12. *temporarily in opposition*: To the Tsar's reforms.
13. *the waters in Bohemia*: Carlsbad and the other Bohemian spas
    were the height of fashion with the Russian upper classes.
14. *Yelisevich*: A fictitious name.
15. *eternal reconciliation . . . life without end*: These words echo the
    language of the Russian Orthodox service for the dead.